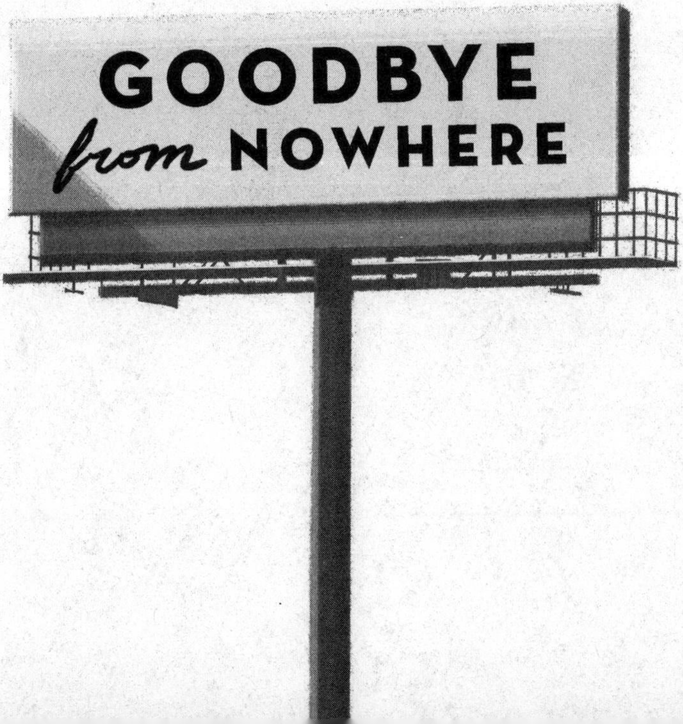
GOODBYE
from NOWHERE

ALSO BY SARA ZARR

GOODBYE *from* NOWHERE

SARA ZARR

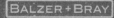

BALZER + BRAY
An Imprint of HarperCollinsPublishers

Balzer + Bray is an imprint of HarperCollins Publishers.

Goodbye from Nowhere
Copyright © 2020 by Sara Zarr
HarperCollins Children's Books, a division of HarperCollins
Publishers, 195 Broadway, New York, NY 10007.
www.epicreads.com

ISBN 978-0-06-243468-5

Typography by Brad Mead
20 21 22 23 24   PC/LSCH   10 9 8 7 6 5 4 3 2 1

First Edition

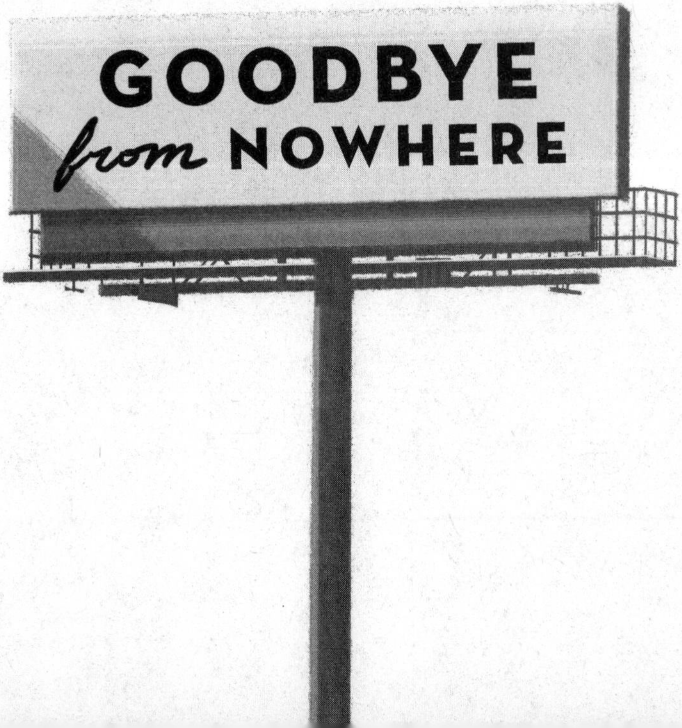
GOODBYE
from NOWHERE

Part I

THANKSGIVING

1

KYLE ADJUSTED the rearview mirror and watched the freeway unspool behind him for a few seconds, keeping a safe distance from the other cars, driving at the speed of traffic. He loved being in motion. A glance at Nadia, shotgun, then back at the road.

"I'm excited for you to meet my family," he said.

"Do you think they'll like me?" Nadia asked.

He laughed. That open smile, how good she was at listening, how smart she was, her sweet voice . . . no way every last member of the Baker family would not love her.

"Yeah. They'll like you."

He rested his hand on her leg. The hand-on-the-leg-while-driving thing was one of the many unexpectedly comforting aspects of being in an actual relationship. He remembered making this same trip to his grandparents' house as a kid for summers and holidays, wedged in the back seat of the car—Taylor on one side and Megan on the other—with a clear view of everything that went on between their mom and dad. Her hand on his leg, his hand on hers. The little touches on the arms and shoulders. How his mom sometimes got in a yoga pose in the passenger seat to relieve her back, one bare foot pressing against the outside of his dad's thigh while he drove. They were barely two separate bodies.

"I like you too, by the way," Kyle added.

"That's one thing I'm not worried about, babe."

"What *are* you worried about?"

"I'm not *worried* worried. Just . . . there's going to be a lot of them and only one of me." She tapped his fingers with hers. "What if I don't like *them*? And then I'm stuck there, six hours from home."

"Seven with traffic. At least."

"My point."

"Okay, my grandpa can sometimes come off like he thinks no one but him knows anything. And Aunt Brenda gets really extra after a few drinks, and you've met my dad—"

"Aw, I like your dad."

"He's hardly ever around enough for you to know if you like him."

"He's nice, though."

"Yeah, he's nice." *Nice and busy. Nice and stressed. Nice and quiet.* "Anyway, worst case scenario, everyone drives you crazy, and you just hang with me and Emily."

"She's the one I'm most worried about."

"Why?"

Nadia laughed. "Really?"

Emily was Kyle's closest cousin, only a few months apart in age, so they'd always defaulted to each other at every holiday, every cousin camp at the farm, every Baker family get-together. And ever since they had both gotten phones around ninth grade, they texted all the time.

"You'll love Emily. She's the coolest."

"Cool and pretty."

"I guess." Kyle had to take his hand off her leg to get across two lanes of traffic to their exit. They were going to stop in San Jose for ramen before driving the last couple hours up to the farm.

Nadia stayed quiet.

"She'll like you," he assured her. "You'll like her. It'll be great. She's not how you probably think. She's not like a popular mean girl or something."

"I've seen pictures."

"She's kind of a nerd, though. I don't even think she has that many friends."

"It's okay, Kyle," Nadia said. "You don't have to make her sound like a loser so I can feel better." She gripped his thigh. "I'm excited to eat. Thanks for making the reservation."

It had been literally the first time he'd ever made a restaurant reservation, and he felt super grown-up about it. And about driving to a family thing in his own car—his provisional license restrictions lifted a few weeks ago—with his own girlfriend and no parents or sisters, and as he circled the streets around the restaurant, he saw it would also be the first time he'd use a valet, because a parking spot was not in the plan. He even had some cash in his pocket to take care of it. From his dad, but still.

He helped Nadia out of the car while the valet got behind the wheel. "Milady," Kyle said as she took his extended hand.

She gave him a quick kiss and his head spun slightly and he imagined them together for a long time. Driving to the farm every Thanksgiving. Reminiscing about this one: the ramen place, the first time Nadia met his whole family. Becoming a real couple, like Aunt Brenda and Uncle Dale, like Aunt Jenny and Uncle Mike. Like his mom and dad.

"I have to pee so bad," Nadia said.

"We're almost there."

"You've been saying that for half an hour."

Kyle could tell she wasn't mad, though. They'd been getting along so good. Cooper had acted like this trip was the worst idea ever. "Six hours in the car, dude, each way. Plus all the time with your family? Who does that unless you're, like, engaged?" Kyle brushed him off but had also worried, a little, ever since that conversation. Like Nadia would turn into a different person or something. She didn't, though. She was just herself.

"You can't tell in the dark, but it's really pretty up here. You'll see tomorrow."

When you lived in or near the cities, it was easy forget California was mostly agricultural land. Up where Kyle's grandparents lived, the sprawl of Silicon Valley and San Francisco gave way to fields and hills and vineyards, grazing cows and horses, trees and the bald patches where fires had burned. Before you knew it, you were in the country.

They drove for a while, quiet and holding hands. Then he pointed out the first sign to Nadia.

Nowhere Farm
Pears, Apples, Grapes, Olives, and More

Hanging under that was the part of the sign that changed a few times a year:

U-Pick CLOSED for Season
THANK YOU!!!

Nadia took her foot off the dashboard. "Nowhere Farm. That's them? I love that."

"I guess when my grandparents bought it, right after they got married, my grandma's mom freaked out on her, told she was going to ruin her life, moving to the middle of nowhere with a nobody like my grandpa." They'd grown apples, grapes—wine and table—some olives, and also silage crops they could sell to ranchers to feed livestock. Now they only did a little of the farming themselves, leasing out various parts of the farm to other people who actually did the work and got most of the profits, but no one could say they'd even come close to ruining their lives.

"Harsh. So naming it Nowhere was kind of a screw-you to her mother?"

"Pretty much."

"It's hardly nowhere, though," Nadia said. "People come here for expensive vacations and stuff. It's definitely a somewhere."

"Irony."

They got to the second sign: **Nowhere Farm 1 Mi**. He turned down the long drive, his excitement building. He pointed ahead. "Up there is the swing set my dad and Uncle Mike built after Megan was born." Megan, Kyle's sister and the oldest of all the cousins, wasn't even coming this year because she wasn't speaking to their parents. Again.

Nadia clutched her stomach. "I'm nervous, Kyle. And I *super* have to pee. Like right away."

"Good news, the house has bathrooms."

It had gotten pretty dark out, but the lights in the huge kitchen were on and the front and back patio lights were also on, giving the whole place a kind of warm glow that made Kyle happy and proud to show Nadia. Yeah, Megan was always in some fight with their parents, and there was friction between various other family and in-laws, but that's everyone's family, basically.

And there was Emily, getting up from a patio chair, a blanket wrapped around her shoulders. They hadn't seen each other since summer, and he couldn't help the exhilarated surge in his chest at the sight of her.

She walked over, grinning, while Kyle parked behind his mom's car.

"That's Emily," he said to Nadia.

"Yeah, I recognized her."

As soon as his car was stopped, Nadia bolted out. "Hey, Emily! Nice to meet you! I have to pee! Sorry!"

"I'll take you in," Emily said.

Nadia glanced back at Kyle as Emily led her into the house. He couldn't quite read her face in the low light. He watched through the windshield as they disappeared for a second, then reappeared in the kitchen window, and Kyle saw his grandmother try to hug Nadia, but Emily was already pushing her into the little half bath off the kitchen.

Emily, he saw, waited for her. She was too good a person to leave Nadia to come out of the bathroom to meet a bunch of strangers by herself.

Kyle got out and unloaded their bags, the night around him a contended sigh.

"Don't worry," Aunt Brenda said, with her arm around Nadia. "We don't expect you to remember all our names. Not on your first visit."

"Kyle's actually been quizzing me for a week. He drew me a family tree."

They were all in the kitchen, and it was too many people for the space. Kyle hugged everyone. He wanted to get to talk to Emily without abandoning Nadia, and the day of driving was catching up with him. But Aunt Brenda tended to prolong things when her switch was flipped to on, as it clearly was now.

"Is the tree he drew you annotated, though?" Brenda asked. "With who is the favorite aunt, for example?"

"Bren," Kyle's dad said, "don't drag her into it."

"She should have all the facts, is all. Kyle's never brought a girl here. I want her to know *everything* so she can feel like one of us."

"She" is standing right here, Kyle wanted to say, but Uncle Mike had already taken over, freeing Nadia from Brenda's arm and pointing around the room.

"I think Brenda will be satisfied if I just give you a quick refresher on who's who, then we'll let you unpack." He pointed to each: "Aunt Jenny goes with me, and Martie is our kid. She's turning fifteen in March, and you'll probably be invited to her quinceañera. Eliseo, aka Grandpa Navarro, aka Jenny's dad, aka my father-in-law. With me so far?"

Grandpa Navarro had been a worker on the farm when he first came up from Oaxaca, then a foreman, and eventually Grandpa Baker's right-hand man. Then his daughter, Jenny, fell in love with Uncle Mike when they were teenagers, and later on they had Martie.

"Yep," said Nadia. "All on the tree. Hola," she said to Grandpa Navarro. "Mucho gusto."

Grandpa Navarro laughed, lifted his Dodgers cap to scratch his still-full head of still-black hair. He squinted at her. "High school Spanish?"

Nadia blushed and said yes. "My dad's grandmother was Peruvian, but I grew up with only English."

Kyle picked up the intros: Uncle Dale and Alex—Emily's dad and little sister—were standing next to Aunt Brenda. Nadia already knew Kyle's parents and his sister Taylor, a freshman at USC. That left Grandma and Grandpa Baker, the ones who had started everything.

"And Great-Aunt Gina isn't here," Alex said.

"Getting a new hip, right?" Nadia asked.

Kyle saw his grandparents exchange a look. They loved Nadia already, just for remembering that one detail.

But then it got quiet, and the Bakers were never that quiet, not when they were in a group, and Kyle hoped they wouldn't be acting formal around Nadia the whole weekend. She touched her wrist to Kyle's; he grabbed her pinkie. Martie jumped in. "I like your sweater," she told Nadia.

Kyle felt Nadia relax a little next to him.

Grandma Baker said, "Okay, show's over. Everybody get out of my kitchen. Except you." She grabbed Grandpa Baker's shirttail as he pretended to try to get away. "I need you and one of my sons to go get the turkey from the garage. It's a thirty pounder." Then she crooked her finger at Kyle and Nadia. "Nadia, since Gina's not here, you can have the room she usually stays in all to yourself. I thought you'd prefer that to sharing with Emily and Alex. Unless you think you'll mind being so close to the noise in the kitchen?"

"No, that's perfect," Nadia said. "Thank you."

"You're welcome, honey. It'll be nice to have your own space to retreat to every once in a while. All these lunatics you don't even know."

"Thank you," Nadia repeated.

Kyle led her down the little hall off the kitchen to the only bedroom on the main floor, always reserved for Great-Aunt Gina so she didn't have to climb stairs. "Your grandma's a saint," Nadia whispered. "I am not used to sharing."

"What if you could share with me?" He put her bags on the bed and pulled her to him, leaning his back against the closed door. She fit perfectly with his body. Her hips on his hips, her toes overlapping his, her head in the crook of his neck. Like they were made for each other. He lifted her hair, whispered in her ear. "I want to share everything with you."

"Me too," she murmured.

She kissed his jaw and crept her hands under his shirt,

feeling his belly, his chest, gliding a finger over the scar from his shoulder surgery last season. Kyle gripped her waist and pulled her closer, even closer, touching the skin at the small of her back, gently pinching flesh, aching for every millimeter of her to be a part of him. He'd never felt that with a girl, not emotionally, not beyond the imme-diate urge to get off. With Nadia it wasn't just that he wanted her. With Nadia he wanted to become something new and better, more him than he was without her.

Her fingers went to the button on his jeans and she kissed him deeply, laughed through her nose, at how wild it was to be fooling around in his grandparents' house.

There was a giant thud right outside the door, and she pulled back her hand like she'd been caught about to steal something. Kyle caught her eyes—brown and bright and joyful.

"Goddamnit, Jeff!" Jeff was Kyle's dad, and that was Grandpa yelling at him. "I told you I didn't have a grip on it!"

"I think my dad dropped the turkey," Kyle whispered.

Nadia stood a few feet away from him, her hand pressed to her heart. "That scared me!"

They heard scrambling in the hall. "Slippery son of a bitch," Grandpa said.

"Dad, let go," Kyle's dad said. "I've got it. This is not a two-person job. I've *got* it!"

"You don't have to be so precious," Grandma called. "It's wrapped in three layers of plastic. Just kick it down the hall!"

Nadia slapped her hand over her mouth and bent forward, trying to suppress laughter.

Grandma continued: "I only sent you both to get it so you'd talk to each other."

"Very subtle, Mom," Kyle's dad said, his voice fading a little.

"Come back," Kyle said, reaching for Nadia.

"I can't. I can't." She fanned her face. "Unless that door has a lock, I'm not touching you again the rest of this trip."

Kyle turned and checked the door. No lock. "There are other rooms."

"Come back tonight," she said. "When everyone's asleep." She hugged him from behind. "Now let me get settled. I know you want to go see Emily."

2

KYLE TOOK his stuff up to his usual room before finding Emily, in need of some alone time after being with Nadia. His fingertips were still alive with the warmth of her skin.

Maybe he was in love. How did people know? If they were in love or not?

He threw his duffel bag on the twin bed. This had been Uncle Mike's room he was a kid. The bed against the wall and under a window, a small closet, a chest of drawers. Kyle knew from seeing the old pictures in one of his grandma's photo albums that Uncle Mike used to have the walls plastered with band posters. Van Halen and Mötley Crüe when he was younger and just going along with whatever Kyle's dad thought was cool, because Kyle's dad was the big brother. Then Uncle Mike got into his own thing. General Public and the English Beat and the Pretenders and Echo and the Bunnymen. Kyle's dad and Uncle Mike had basically stopped talking for two years back then. Over rock versus New Wave.

Now the walls were bare except for some framed photos of Kyle and his cousins, and a random painting of flowers.

He got out his phone and texted Emily.

looking right now at that pic of you and me and the pumpkin

They were maybe three or four years old, sitting on the ground in Grandma's kitchen garden, Kyle in a striped T-shirt and Emily wearing only a pair of shorts. Both of them hugging this giant pumpkin.

Aw. Where are you??

Upstairs, unpacked. Meet on swings?

She sent back a thumbs-up and a zany face.

There was a bite in the air special to this place that they didn't get down in Southern California. Kyle huffed out breaths to see if it would form visible condensation. Not quite. Not that he could see in the dark, anyway.

Emily waved from where she sat on one of the swings,

her feet dragging through the pine straw. Everything since he and Nadia got there had been kind of a blur, with Kyle tuned in to Nadia and her nervousness during the introductions and then to her body, alone in her room. He'd barely said hi to any of his family, because their attention had been on Nadia too. He felt like it had gone well, but most of the Bakers were pretty good at being nice and friendly no matter what they really thought. It wasn't like they were going to boo Nadia off the stage, even if they hated her.

But who could hate Nadia?

"Hurry up," Emily called. "Why so slow?"

"I'm thinking."

"What are you thinking?"

Finally he got close enough to really see her. She had on gray jeans and a maroon Stanford hoodie, hood up. Her mom—Aunt Brenda—was a professor in the theater department there, and Emily and Uncle Dale had a whole wardrobe of Stanford sweatshirts and T-shirts and hats.

Her longish blondish hair stuck out from the hood in a stringy mess, like always. Kyle had gone his whole life hearing his grandma tell Emily to brush her hair, and Emily ignoring her. "It's swimmer's hair," she always said. Kyle knew she was proud of it, the same way he was proud of the farmer's tan he got from putting in time on the baseball field.

He sat on the swing next to her. "I'm thinking about Nadia."

"Is she okay?" Emily asked. "It's a lot of Bakers at once for a newbie."

"Yeah, she's fine. She knew I wanted to come talk to you."

"That's nice. She probably also wanted to be alone."

"Probably." He wrapped his jacket cuffs around his hands and then grasped the swing's chains. He didn't like the metallic smell they left on his skin. "Do you think everyone likes her?" he asked. "They were nice, but I was thinking about how easy it is to be nice."

"We only talked to her for five minutes, so nice is probably all you're going to get at first." She dug her toes into the ground. "I hope she likes old musicals, though. We need to discuss our film fest."

"Wait, though." He looked at her in the faint glow given off by the solar path lights lining the driveway. Full cheeks, no makeup. Still the girl who hugged the pumpkin. "What do *you* think of Nadia?"

"Literally just met her, but I know what *you* think of her and everything you've told me. You care about her, and I can tell she cares about you. What Grandma or Uncle Mike or whoever thinks of her can't change that, right? So why worry about it?"

Why worry about it.

"Maybe it's one of those things that's different for you," Kyle said. "You know."

Emily gazed at him and kept quiet long enough for him to feel uncomfortable, like he'd said something wrong. Not that she was mad at him, because that wasn't Emily. More as if she could see through his skull into his brain, and found his thoughts basic and naive.

"Never mind, I guess?" he said with a laugh.

"I mean, just because I'm not into the romance or crush thing doesn't mean I can't understand caring what people think. Wanting them to like or care about something you like or care about. That's just human. But maybe it is different when you throw romance into the mix."

Two summers ago, Taylor and Martie had been talking about boys they liked at school and Emily had called them boring and walked off into the olive grove. Kyle, also bored by the conversation, followed Emily. She told him with a shrug, "I don't care about that stuff. I never have."

He'd asked her straight up if she liked girls. "If you do, you know it makes no difference to me." He wanted to say it wouldn't make any difference to anyone, but Grandpa was kind of weird about it all and the most likely to think something was wrong with one of them if they'd been gay. Grandpa always said it was just his generation and his religion, but Grandma was in the same generation and the same religion, and she was totally accepting of everyone.

"No," Emily had said. "I don't get crushes. Not on boys, not on girls. But it's kind of personal and I don't want it to be, like, a topic of family conversation, so."

Now she said, "I just think if you and Nadia are happy with each other, that's what counts."

"Look at my parents, though," Kyle said. "Most of the family never really loved my mom, and you can feel it, right? They're nice and everything and she's family, but there's a little distance, I guess, or a difference when it comes to her. She can feel it and it's hard for her to be here sometimes."

"I can see that. It's not like you and Nadia are getting married, though."

He sighed. The word "married" didn't really feel right, but he'd definitely been thinking about forever, or at least a long long time, on the drive up. "Back to the film fest," he said.

"I feel like Alex is ready for *West Side Story*."

"Are you sure? She's so . . . in her feelings." Kyle could barely watch it himself without having a breakdown. "What about *Meet Me in St. Louis*? That's more holiday-ish."

She made a face. "Too corny."

"Literally every old movie we like is corny. Corny is like the definition of old musicals."

"I have a bad reaction to that one for some reason. I think's it's Judy Garland's bangs. How about *South Pacific*?"

"I hate that one," Kyle said. "Grandpa would like it, though."

"He always falls asleep fifteen minutes in. We could pretend we're going to watch that and then when he's out, switch to something else."

"When are they going to make a *Hamilton* movie?"

"Not soon enough." Emily jumped off her swing. "Here comes your sister."

Taylor was walking fast up the drive, pumping her arms. Either she was doing some cardio or she was mad about something.

"What's wrong?" Kyle asked.

"Nothing, but are you guys ever coming back to the house? Aunt Brenda is trying to get Nadia on her charades team. It's a lot. She needs you."

"What time is it?" He'd left his phone in his room.

Taylor held up hers so he could see.

"Oh, shit."

"I'm saying." Taylor looked at Emily. "You guys were talking about Nadia, I bet."

"No," Kyle said. Taylor *always* had opinions about the girls Kyle liked, which was *always* annoying, but this time it was more than that. He felt protective of Nadia and needed Taylor to stay out of it. "We were talking about what movies we're going to watch."

"Of course you were. The Kyle and Emily National Boredom Fest. I forgot."

"No one is forcing you to come," Kyle said.

"There's nothing else to do!"

"Then stop complaining."

"Maybe you could pick something from the twenty-first century once in a while?"

"Guys," Emily said, and pointed toward the house. "There's a girl down there who needs to be saved from charades with my mom."

3

KYLE WOKE up in his own bed the next morning. Well, Uncle Mike's old bed. Which was not the plan. He was supposed to have stayed awake and then gone down to Nadia's room, then crept back to his before everyone else woke up. But the family games went late— Nadia crushed charades on a team with Martie and Taylor and Aunt Brenda, and then was on the verge of destroying everyone at Bananagrams before Kyle sensed her pulling back to give Alex a chance to win. After Alex and the grandparents and half the aunts and uncles went to bed, the rest of them stayed up for a round of Cards Against Humanity.

Nadia had been perfect the whole time. When she got up to use the bathroom during the break after Bananagrams, Martie looked at Kyle and said, "She's the literal best," and the rest of them agreed.

It was all exhausting, though, on top of the long drive. He must have totally passed out. When he checked his phone, there were no messages from Nadia or anything, and a small current of anxiety buzzed through him because what if she was mad? What if she'd waited and waited and he'd fallen asleep like an idiot, and now she wasn't talking to him?

No. Nadia didn't play games. She'd told him from the beginning that she'd say what she meant and mean what she said. Kind of like Emily, actually. A lot like Emily.

He messaged Nadia. **u up?**

hahaha NO

It was early, and the house quiet. Maybe they still had some time to be together. He cleaned up a little and went downstairs. The kitchen light was on and there was coffee in the pot, pans of what he knew were pecan rolls under towels. From the corner of his eye he saw movement on the patio off the kitchen. Probably Grandma. He was thinking about going out to say hi to her, and when he looked again he saw it was his mom. She had her back to the sliding glass door, her phone to her ear.

Kyle paused. Did he *want* to talk to his mom? They'd

barely seen each other in the last few months. Kyle spent basically all his free time with Nadia, and his parents had a lot going on with their contracting business.

No, he could talk to his mom anytime and there were only so many chances to get into a warm bed with Nadia—

Too late. His mom turned the second he decided to try to sneak past, and they saw each other. She waved for him to come outside, and she put her phone facedown on the patio table.

"Hey, honey." She gave him a hug and pressed her cold cheek to his. "I feel like we haven't talked since you got here."

"We haven't." Not like they were *that* close to begin with, but they weren't *not* close, and they'd definitely been talking less since Nadia. His mom looked different somehow, in a way he hadn't noticed last night and he couldn't quite define it now.

"I was just checking some work messages before Grandma takes away my phone." Grandma had a thing about phones when the family was all together—she'd be collecting them all after breakfast and wouldn't give them back until after dinner. His mom wrapped her gray cardigan tighter around herself. "I forgot how cold it is here in the mornings."

"Yeah, it's freezing." *And my girlfriend is all warm and*

cozy under the covers, waiting for me. "I'm gonna . . ."

"Kyle, no, sit with me for a minute. I miss you. We can go inside if you want."

"Uh . . ." Mom versus girlfriend. Pay up with some Mom time now, and get to spend more time with Nadia later without feeling guilty. "It's okay, we can stay out." He flipped the hood up on his sweatshirt and shoved his hands in the pockets. His mom pulled patio furniture cushions out of the storage bench and arranged them so they could sit on the chairs, still damp from the fog and cold.

"How was your drive yesterday? You made great time."

"Yeah, it was easy. We left early and everything." School was out all week and technically they could have come a day earlier, like everyone else, but Nadia's family had not been that into the idea of her being gone for Thanksgiving weekend, let alone extra days, and they'd kept her to themselves until he'd picked her up yesterday. "Did you get a haircut?" Kyle asked his mom.

"And color."

"It looks cool." It was sort of edgy, for his mom. Wavy and asymmetrical and darker than it had been, or maybe just less gray.

She ran her fingers through it. "Thanks. I wanted a

change. So. How are you and Nadia doing? With all of this?"

"Fine?"

"Families can be hard on a relationship."

He laughed. "We've barely been here twelve hours."

She lowered her voice. "You know how it is for me. I've always felt a little left out of all of this. And if Nadia needs someone to vent to, or you do, I'm here."

"I think it'll be fine."

"But if you do."

There was something in her eyes, her voice, that seemed way more serious than any of this really was. He glanced toward the house. They needed a new topic before this turned into a sex talk. "Later I want to show Nadia the bunkhouse, which—"

"Kyle, you need to remember that you're the one who can be the bridge for her." She leaned forward, grasped his forearm. "It's important, especially in a big, close family like this. Your dad hasn't been great at that. For me."

He should have gone straight to Nadia's room. His dad was definitely no relationship genius, but whatever issues his mom had with the Bakers she partly brought on herself by always staying at this judgmental distance. Nadia would never be like that.

Then his mom muttered, "Speak of the devil . . ." and Aunt Brenda came out through the sliding door.

"Good morning and happy Thanksgiving, mind if I smoke?"

Kyle's mom sighed. "What if I said yes?"

Brenda nearly fell into a chair with no cushion and lit up. She had major bedhead and makeup smeared around her eyes. "Kyle, why aren't you in bed with your girlfriend?"

"Really, Brenda."

Aunt Brenda laughed. "You know I just say shit like that to watch you turn red, Karen. Just kidding, Kyle. This is a sex-free household."

"Um, okay, so . . ." He stood up, but Brenda grabbed his sweatshirt sleeve and pulled him back down.

"Oh no you're not. I want to talk to you! You're my favorite nephew."

That was his cue to say, "I'm your only nephew," so he did.

Sometimes he could not believe Aunt Brenda was Emily's mom, except they had the exact same nose and also they were both so no-bullshit. Except Aunt Brenda was no-bullshit in a way that could make people uncomfortable or offended. Emily's way of being no-bullshit didn't involve embarrassing people. The real head-scratcher was that Aunt Brenda was his dad's sister. Those two were night and day.

"You know you're the first grandkid to bring a

significant other up here," Brenda said. She pointed with her cigarette to his mom. "I remember meeting your mom for the first time, when she and your dad were in high school. I was just an annoying twelve-year-old."

"*Very* annoying," his mom said, mostly succeeding in making it sound like a joke.

"What was my mom like?" Kyle asked. He'd heard this story before, but not for a while.

"Quiet. Watching. You could see her taking mental notes on us."

"Oh, come on," his mom said. "You were twelve. You do not remember that."

"I do." Brenda inhaled. "I even remember what you were wearing. You were such a basic eighties bitch, with a spiral perm and Reeboks."

"Yeah, yeah, okay." His mom stood up. "I'm going to need more coffee for this."

"But you loved my brother. We could all tell." Brenda craned her neck to watch Kyle's mom go in. "That's all that matters!" she said at a volume that guaranteed anyone still asleep in the house was awake now. Brenda kicked Kyle's shin with her slippered foot. "You love Nadia," she said. "Or at least you like her a whole lot."

"Yeah."

"What's your favorite thing about her? Besides her hot

bod?" She cracked up again. "Sorry. That's inappropriate. You know how Emily is, and I don't get to talk boyfriends or girlfriends with her. And Alex still plays with her stuffed animals, so."

"It's pretty cold out here, and I was supposed to meet up with Nadia." Kyle tried standing again. This time she let him.

"One thing. Tell me one thing you love about Nadia." She leaned forward to stub her cigarette out in a flower-pot. "The rest of us can see what she looks like, so not that. And she's great at games, this we know. Something about her we wouldn't be able to see."

This was the playwright in her. That was always her excuse for being nosy, anyway.

"Okay. She's . . ." What was the word he wanted? Nice? Yeah, she was, but that wasn't it. "I don't know. Like, she sees the best in people. She doesn't have enemies, you know? People she gossips about or whatever. I never really noticed how much people talk shit about other people until I spent more time with her and she didn't."

Brenda gazed at him with eyes almost exactly like his dad's. "That's an amazing quality, Kyle. Emily has that. *No* idea where she got it from. I guess her father is a little like that. It's a wonder we're still married. Anyway, you're lucky, trust me." She looked past him, into the house. "Well, here comes everybody."

Kyle turned. Grandpa was in the kitchen, sliding the pans of pecan rolls into the oven. Alex was in there too, bouncing around. When Kyle checked his phone, there were messages from Nadia.

I hear people. should I come out?

is there a system for who gets to shower first?

also I need to talk to emily or taylor or martie? whoever might have pads or tampons. help.

Uncle Mike's truck rumbled in the distance, which meant Aunt Jenny and Martie were back. They lived nearby, which was why they didn't sleep over at the farm for family stuff. He'd meet them in the driveway and send Martie to Nadia.

it's gonna be Martie. she's here all the time so she'll know. 2 minutes.

The morning was getting away. Kyle wanted to take Nadia up to the bunkhouse, show her where all the cousins used to sleep in the summer. He had something to say to her, and that was where he wanted to do it.

He watched Grandpa and Alex in the kitchen, through the glass door. Grandma came in and Grandpa kissed her on the cheek, got a coffee mug out of the cupboard for her. Alex was talking a mile a minute, from the looks of it. Grandma and Grandpa smiled, nodded, listened.

Kyle tried to imagine his own parents getting that old. His own future kids, if he had any, as old as Alex.

It seemed impossible that he would get to have that someday, and impossible that he wouldn't.

4

THE BUNKHOUSE was falling apart. Cobwebs hung from the corners, and light came in where the tin roof had warped away from the wood of the main structure. The two long walls had bunk beds—four top and bottom bunks along each side, sleeping sixteen. Back in the day when the land was actively farmed, this was where seasonal workers slept. Behind the building there was an outhouse and a hose that served as a shower. Cold water only. There used to be a small fridge and a sink and a two-burner propane stove along the short wall, but the appliances were long gone.

"It didn't always look this bad," Kyle said, holding on to Nadia's hand.

"'Grandma's House: Where Cousins Go to Become Best Friends,'" Nadia read aloud. "Aww."

"Uncle Dale made that a long time ago. Emily's dad." He'd burned the phrase into a piece of wood that hung inside, over the doorway. He had been burning shit into wood a lot that year, before he got into screen printing, and then making weird metal jewelry, and now literally knitting.

"Is it true? Are you all best friends?"

He held Nadia's hand, led her toward the window at the other end of the building where they could see the pear orchard. "I mean, Emily. But I'm the only guy cousin, so there's no cousin version of, like, Cooper or Mateo. I don't know if I'd call those guys my best friends, but you know what I mean."

"Yeah, like people you see every day and hang with. It's weird, though, how sometimes you're closer to the ones you only see sometimes. Like you tell those people more stuff? Because you almost have to keep a certain wall up with the ones you see every day. I don't know . . ." She leaned on the windowsill. "This place is huge. Your grandparents did all this?"

"Not by themselves. Them plus farm workers. The

people who lived in this bunkhouse. Grandpa Navarro did a ton. He oversaw the whole thing." He untwined his fingers from hers. "Do you keep a wall up with me?"

"What? Oh, no, I just mean like . . . the way you can meet some random person at camp for a week and tell your whole life story and all your secrets, things you don't tell your best friends at home because then they'd always be there to remind you."

An uneasy feeling crept over Kyle. What was she saying, exactly? She had secrets she hadn't told him? She was closer to random people at some camp he didn't know about than she was to him? It was a stupid, irrelevant thought. But he still wanted to know.

Nadia moved away from the window, touched the wood frames of the bunks. "Weren't you scared to sleep out here when you were little?"

"Yes." He watched her face. It had always seemed so open, so giving. Maybe he'd misread her eyes or her smile and really they were hiding something. "Are there any secrets you want to tell me?" He hoped he sounded playful and not insecure.

"Everyone's got secrets, babe." She slid her arms around his waist.

"But from me?"

She pulled back slightly. "What's wrong?"

Nothing, nothing, he didn't want anything to be wrong.

"I've got a secret to tell *you*." He took both her hands. Held them to his chest. If this were one of the old musicals from the Kyle-Emily film fest, this is when he'd sing. Spin her around. Lift her off her feet and into his arms. But he didn't have music, and he didn't know how to dance. All he had were words. "Nadia," he said, "I love you."

The bunkhouse spun. He squeezed Nadia's hands, then realized he was doing it too tightly, and let go.

Eons ticked by, during which he reminded himself that she didn't need to say it back. Whether she said it or not, it was still true that he loved her, and he wanted her to know that. He found his breath and said it again. "I love you. I'm not saying it so you'll say it. I just . . . I've never said it before other than to my family and I need to, and I want to, and I mean it."

She smiled, the warm and open smile. "What if I want to say it back?"

He laughed, relieved. "No one is stopping you."

"I love you, Kyle."

They kissed. Long but not hot. Deep but not frantic.

After that, the question pushed its way into his mind: Had she ever said it to anyone before? Other than her family and best friends? He knew she had a thing with this senior last year, Jack Mesrobian, who was at college out of state now. They'd slept together. But had she told him she loved him? Or had Jack said it to her?

It was hard sometimes to accept that she'd existed before he met her.

Nadia sucked in her breath and prodded her belly. "Ugh. Really bad cramps. I'm sorry to not be more romantic right now, but I'm very annoyed that my period is early. Can we go back to the house so I can take something?"

No, he wanted to stay here all day and climb up into a bunk with Nadia and hold her and smell her skin. "Okay. We should probably be offering to help my grandma with dinner stuff about now, anyway."

On the walk back to the house, they held hands and Kyle told her all about the film festival—how he and Emily had found a box of VHS tapes in the attic maybe five years ago and watched them out of boredom and then gotten obsessed with these cheesy old musicals and started their film fest the next year.

"Wait, they still have one of those old videotape players? And it works?"

"Their whole setup in the basement is exactly like it was when my uncle Mike put it together in the eighties. That TV can't do anything but play tapes anymore."

One year, he told her, Grandpa Navarro brought some tapes of these ranchero musicals made in Mexico in the thirties, in Spanish with no subtitles but you could tell what was going on. And then there were a whole bunch of tapes that didn't play anymore except in sixty-second chunks, movies you couldn't find streaming, and it all felt like a lost treasure you couldn't spend.

Kyle talked and talked, practically babbling, not wanting to leave any pause in the conversation where he might ask any of the questions rebounding inside his head, things he knew he shouldn't say. *Did you love Jack? What are your secrets? Will you always love me?*

Thanksgiving was Thanksgiving. There was a metric ton of food, mostly thanks to Aunt Jenny and Grandma, plus a couple of side dishes Uncle Dale wouldn't ever let anyone else do or change: bacon-wrapped green beans and cornbread stuffing. Aunt Brenda and Uncle Mike and Kyle's mom all had a lot of wine, and Taylor kept sneaking some and pouring it in a mug. Grandpas Baker and Navarro told farm stories. Kyle's dad was mostly a silent observer. Martie and Nadia sat next to each other, across from Kyle, talking low all through dessert, and Kyle thought about what she'd said about meeting someone for a minute and telling them everything. On one side of him, Emily dug into a slice of pecan pie, and on the other, Aunt Brenda told a story about Uncle Mike from when they were in high school. "This one senior had a fake ID. He was taking orders for alcohol, basically. Mike asked him to get a small bottle of vodka—"

"Michael James," Grandma Baker said. Grandpa was smiling, though, leaning back in his chair.

"Thanks, Brenda, you squealer."

"It was thirty years ago! Anyway, I guess the guy lost his nerve about buying liquor and shows up at school with four packs of wine coolers in a duffel bag and just hands it to Mike."

Kyle's dad laughed. "I don't think I've heard this one. He brought it to *school*?"

"Yes," Uncle Mike said. "He hands me this bag in the morning and it's all rattling around and I was too scared to try and transfer it to my locker and I carried that bag with me to every class."

"Should you be telling this story in front of the kids?" Grandma asked.

"Yes," Alex said, wide-eyed.

"I was terrified all day that someone would ask me what was in it, or trip over it, or I'd drop it. . . ."

"Like it was the nuclear football," Brenda said.

"I wish Megan was here," Kyle said. This was the kind of story she loved. He said it quiet, to just Emily, but his mom tuned in at the sound of Megan's name, with some kind of Mom Spidey sense.

"Well, she was invited. She's always invited."

Aunt Brenda topped off Kyle's mom's wineglass and

said, "She'll come back around eventually. She has to go through her shit."

"Excuse me," Grandma Baker said.

"Sorry, Mom," Aunt Brenda said. "She has to go through her *stuff*. Just like I had to go through my *stuff* and Mike had to go through his *stuff*." She leaned forward to look at Kyle's dad at the other end of the table. "And God knows Jeff had his *stuff*."

"What stuff, Dad?" Taylor asked.

Martie and Nadia were paying attention now. Everyone was. Because Kyle's dad hardly ever said anything about himself or anything interesting at all, and now looked like he wanted to jump out of his chair and crash through the window to get out.

"No stuff, guys. Normal stuff. I thought we were talking about Megan."

He looked at Kyle's mom, and Kyle noticed that she glanced away. Normally when Aunt Brenda and the rest of the family went off, Kyle's parents were in it together, communicating with looks and little gestures, eyebrows and head tilts. Now Kyle's dad studied his pie. Something was off. Kyle shifted his eyes to Taylor to see if she'd noticed; Aunt Jenny was whispering something to her.

"Anyway, Brenda's right," Kyle's dad said. "She'll be back. Maybe Christmas."

"I didn't mean *that* soon," Aunt Brenda said. "Don't get your hopes up."

"Are you in touch with her, Brenda?" Kyle's mom asked in this *tone*, the one she got when she'd had enough of letting things go and decided to call you out. He bumped Emily's leg with with his, like *Here they go.*

"No, I'm not."

"Oh." She nodded and pushed some bits of piecrust around with her fork. "Because it sounded like you knew what you were talking about. My mistake."

Martie cleared her throat, then said something low to Nadia. Kyle caught Nadia's eye and mouthed, "Sorry," and grimaced. She shrugged and gave him a "no big deal" smile.

"No, Karen, I'm just saying that Megan is kind of a rebel and you're . . ." Aunt Brenda took a sip of wine. "You're not. And maybe I get her in different ways than you do."

"Mom—" Emily said at the same time that Uncle Dale jumped in, cutting her off.

"I think we all agree that whenever or wherever Megan decides to show up, we'll be happy to see her." He raised his glass. "To Megan!"

"Oh, Jesus, honey," Brenda muttered.

"Brenda!" Grandma Baker stood up and went to the kitchen, calling over her shoulder. "Don't say that. I'm going to start the dishes."

"Don't say 'Jesus'? I thought you liked Jesus!"

"Brenda, knock it off, okay?" Kyle's dad stood too. "Yes, you're a rebel, we know. It looks an awful lot like being an asshole. I'm gonna go make sure Mom doesn't do a single dish. Feel free to join me since I don't remember you cooking."

"I set the table."

Kyle's dad shot back, "What a hero!" on his way to the kitchen.

"Cigar time," Grandpa Navarro said, and left. Kyle could see Grandpa Baker simmering. He was a pretty easygoing guy, but when he lost it, he lost it. If they were lucky, he'd go out with Grandpa Navarro to the patio to escape, old-man style.

Aunt Jenny reached across the table to touch Nadia's arm and said, "We're not usually like this."

Grandpa Baker slammed his glass down hard enough that it would have broken if there wasn't a tablecloth on the table. "Oh yes you are. Last year it was the fires and you kids fighting about global warming. The year before that it was the election. Brenda, you're never happy at a family gathering if you haven't directed it to a big dramatic conflict like it's one of your plays. No wonder Megan stopped coming!"

Nadia's chill was faltering, Kyle could tell. She'd stopped looking around at whoever was talking and kept her focus on the salt and pepper shakers between her and Kyle.

"Um, 'us kids' weren't fighting about global warming, Dad," Uncle Mike said. "We were united, because we believe in *science*. You were the one fighting. Ditto the election."

"I never said he'd be a good president."

"But you said he wouldn't be that bad!" Aunt Brenda scooted her chair back. "I'm gonna go smoke with Eliseo."

When Brenda was gone, Kyle's mom said, sort of to her plate, "Actually she has no idea if I'm a rebel or not."

Uncle Dale pushed a pie dish toward Nadia. "Did you try the pear brown butter one? It's my favorite."

"Also, you made it," Emily said.

"I am a fan of my own cooking, it's true."

Nadia dug right into the pie dish with her fork, then looked at Uncle Dale wide-eyed. "Oh my god, that's amazing."

Emily reached her fork over and took some too. Then Taylor.

"Did you have some, Grandpa?" she asked.

"I'm stuffed to the gills."

"Come on." She nudged the dish his way until he took a small bite. "Not bad, Dale," he said.

United by pie.

When they'd scraped the dish clean, Uncle Mike said,

"Maybe you guys should show Nadia the bunkhouse?"

"Oh, Kyle already showed me." Nadia smiled at Kyle, met his eyes. *Showed me. Said he loved me.*

The conversation went on, but Kyle didn't care, didn't hear. He forgot about the bickering. He forgot about the weird moment between his parents. All he could think about was Nadia, and her sitting there the next Thanksgiving and the next and the next. Even feeling his mom watch him stare at Nadia didn't make him look away.

Later, after a long good night with Nadia in her room and leaving after she fell asleep, Kyle was not tired. He went out on the patio to look at stars, but the temperature had dropped significantly since the sun went down. Back inside, he did fifty push-ups in the living room, then stretched out his shoulder.

There was a framed picture from his parents' wedding on the hutch—his mom and dad and the whole wedding party. His mom's permed hair was up in a bun, with a few curls arranged around her face. His dad had a lot of hair and a lot of mustache. Aunt Brenda had been in college in her goth phase, her hair dyed black and teased, wearing about five pounds of eyeliner and black lace gloves that clashed with the pastel dress she had to wear to match the other bridesmaids.

Kyle picked up the photo. He'd seen it a hundred times

before, but now he had a different perspective on it, could actually imagine his mom and dad young and in love and excited to start a new life together. How had his parents *known* things would turn out okay?

He put it down and went to the kitchen to investigate leftovers and was eating stuffing with his fingers when his dad walked in, looking basically nothing like the guy in the photo.

"I was thinking sandwich," he said, "but that looks quicker."

Kyle passed him the container of stuffing and found the mashed potatoes and a foil packet of turkey. They stood there eating for a while, then his dad said, "I hope we didn't scare Nadia."

"Nah. She's fine. I mean, every family has its weirdness."

"That's one word for it." His dad opened a plastic bag of leftover rolls that was sitting on the counter and popped one in the microwave. "You guys really get along, huh?"

"Yeah," Kyle said.

They both stared at the microwave, and Kyle had this impulse to exit to upstairs like he normally would. Avoiding getting stuck in conversations with either of his parents before they got serious was his usual strategy. But he thought about the guy in the wedding photo, his mustache and light blue tux and courage.

"It's more than that, though," Kyle continued. "More than getting along."

His dad took the roll out, stuffed some turkey into it. "I can tell. You two are into each other."

"I mean, she's my girlfriend and stuff." Kyle was *not* about to tell his dad he was in love, and had said the words, and was close as you could get to fully having sex. He didn't need a repeat of the sex talk they'd had a couple of years ago. He didn't need warnings. "Okay, Dad, if you had to give me only *one* piece of relationship advice ever, what would it be?"

His dad stared a moment, then turned his back to fill a glass with water from the tap. When he faced Kyle again, he said, "People change."

Kyle waited. And waited. Then he said, "That's it? That's the advice?"

"Well, let each other change, I guess is a better way of saying it. Look, you're not that much younger now than I was when I met your mom. I had no idea I'd be who I am today or that your mom would be who she is. You don't know who *you'll* be when you're my age. In some ways we're all just older versions of who we were at sixteen or seventeen, but in a lot of ways we're completely different than we were." He smiled, looked at the floor. "We'd be strangers to our sixteen-year-old selves."

"*Strangers?*" Kyle laughed a little, because his dad

sounded sad and he didn't like it, wanted to lighten things up. "Some things don't change, right? Look at Grandma and Grandpa. They've been the same as long as I've been alive. Nothing here at the farm has changed."

"You're wrong." His dad raised his head, still wearing that melancholy smile. "I think it's more subtle at their age, but it's still happening. No one is the same person they were at twenty when they're thirty or forty or fifty. Or seventy or eighty. We're *always* changing, all of us, and it's natural to slide into ruts and into roles. But you gotta be able to stay flexible. You can't hold someone to who they were ten years ago."

"That makes sense, I guess."

"That's the advice. I have more, but you asked for the one thing. That's it."

Kyle thought about it. Brenda's goth hair and his mom's perm, Uncle Mike's million hobbies, how his mom thought she'd be a doctor and now she was a bookkeeper, even how Kyle used to think he wanted to be a pro baseball player and now he knew he didn't care enough or want to work that hard.

"That's pretty good, Dad."

But really Kyle just wanted to know what would be happening in ten *weeks*, never mind ten years. If this feeling between him and Nadia would still be there, still be strong.

When he went up to his room and got in bed, he texted Megan.

happy thanksgiving, dude. you're missing all the fun.

Her reply came right away.

haha, I heard. Taylor's been texting me. you know what's fun for me, Kyle? spending holidays ALONE in my PAJAMAS.

But you didn't get to meet Nadia

T sent me pictures. I'm happy for you.

It was impossible with Megan to tell if she meant that. Over text, anyway.

Sure you don't want to come up for the film fest tomorrow? he asked.

She sent back six eye-roll emojis.

What?

Oh god. Those movies you and Em love. They're so STERILE, they're so . . . ugh. I mean, if you like old movies, watch some Bergman, watch some Kurosawa, get out of your weird prim little bubble and grow up!

On second thought, maybe he was glad Megan wasn't there. He couldn't pause long enough to let her know she'd gotten under his skin.

ooookay just thought I'd ask

After that, he immediately texted Emily. She was a turn-the-phone-all-the-way-off-before-bed person, so he knew he wouldn't be bugging her if she'd gone to sleep.

Are you still up?

Ha was just about to text you, she wrote. **We need to finalize. West Side Story and A Star Is Born (Garland/ Mason)?**

Do we really want two tragedies? he asked. **Also they're both super long.**

It's a theme? And we literally have all day unless you want Catan to go on for twelve hours.

Um not really.

Half the aunts and uncles and also Alex had been on a Settlers of Catan thing for the last few Thanksgivings. Kyle and Emily agreed that it took too long to set up, and also they both needed to constantly be reminded of how to keep track of their crops and their lumber and whatever else, which was annoying for everyone.

Okay so West Side plus what else?

How about no tragedies? Kyle said. He'd never told Emily this, but honestly he couldn't handle *West Side Story*. It was all fine and everything up until the last act, when he had to turn it off before the really sad parts.

Maybe the theme should be absolute happiness? Like Singin' in the Rain and Sound of Music?

Sound of Music has Nazis.

But it ends happy, he said.

Yeah, for the Von Trapps maybe!

They talked until they'd settled on *A Star Is Born*, since a new version was out and it would be fun to compare, and then *The Wizard of Oz*, the theme being Judy Garland. They knew from previous viewings that the *Wizard of Oz* tape had a glitch around when the flying monkeys showed up, but that was too intense for Alex anyway.

It seems like Nadia's not scared by what she witnessed at dinner, Emily said. **Did she say anything?**

Not really. We were laughing about it. Nadia thought his dad's line to Brenda about how being a rebel looked like being an asshole was pretty good.

I'm mad at my mom, though, Emily said. **She can be such a jerk sometimes.**

True.

She just thinks she's being funny and interesting and doesn't realize she isn't until it's too late. If ever haha.

I love her anyway, Kyle said. **Everyone does. I mean, my mom is like the most polite person in the family and no one likes her!**

I like your mom!

I don't mean literally no one likes her. She's just like the least favorite.

Debatable, Emily said. **Grandpa Baker and Great-Aunt Gina are in the running.**

I don't count the old people.

Ohhhhh. Well then, yeah, your mom.

He sent her back a laugh-cry face and said good night.

He opened his window about an inch to let in some air. From his bed, he heard leaves rustle outside, skitter across the concrete patio. Maybe next Thanksgiving he and Nadia would be back. Maybe his grandparents would let them share a room. Maybe they'd have babies and then Taylor would have babies and Martie would have babies, and then those cousins would come here and be complaining to each other about Aunt Megan being a jerk and Emily would defend her and she and Kyle would still be best friends.

Everything exactly like this, always.

5

BY THE time they drove home on Sunday, Kyle and Nadia were talked out and just held hands and stayed mostly quiet. They barely even listened to music. Kyle went over and over the weekend in his head, scanning for anything bad, anything that had gone wrong with him and Nadia. He came up blank. It was all good.

She liked Emily, Emily liked her. She liked the mini film fest and cried at the end of *A Star Is Born*. She liked walking the land with Grandpa Navarro and hearing about the various seasonal things he and the crew did to keep the farm running. She *really* liked Martie, and they ended up going over to Aunt Jenny and Uncle Mike's for dinner on

Saturday so they could hang out mostly with Martie. Nadia wasn't scared off by Aunt Brenda, and when Uncle Mike tried to teach everyone a super-wrong version of the Shiggy, Nadia fixed it and let him post a video with her in it.

Every aunt and every uncle had at some point during the weekend found Kyle to tell him how much they liked Nadia, how they hoped she'd come back.

"So," he said to Nadia now, "it was good, right?"

"Mm-hmm."

He glanced at her. "Are you happy?"

"Yeah, I'm happy. Also so tired. I was really, like, *concentrating* on being likable. It's a lot." She squeezed his hand. "But yes, happy."

"Me too." He adjusted the visor to keep the sun out of his eyes. "I kind of don't want to go back to real life." He had to get back in the gym with the team for baseball conditioning, and his grades had taken a dive lately—partly because classes were hard and partly because all he wanted to do was be with Nadia. But he needed to catch up.

"We can detour to Vegas if you want," she said. She let his hand go and wiggled her fingers. "Put a ring on it."

His heart pounded, but he played along with her light tone. "I'm sure everyone in our families would be very very cool with that."

"Definitely."

On one stretch of highway, the wind blew big tumbleweeds across the lanes. Kyle took Nadia's hand back into his. "I used to be scared of tumbleweeds," he said. "We'd be on a road trip and there'd be a giant one coming toward the car and me and Megan and Taylor would be screaming, 'You're gonna hit it, Dad!'"

Nadia laughed, rubbed her thumb against his palm.

His dad would always say, "Don't worry, it's nothing."

They'd get closer and closer to the tumbleweed and they couldn't swerve and they couldn't brake, not with the other cars around them on the road. And Megan and Taylor would be laughing about it and pretending to be scared, but Kyle really was. Then his dad would drive right through it and it would vanish into a cloud of fibers, no weight, no substance. It would just explode all around them like a special effect in a movie.

It got to where Megan and Taylor would get excited when they saw one coming, the bigger the better. But Kyle never did. Every time they were about to hit one, he thought, *This time it's going to hurt.*

Except right now, with Nadia by his side, he didn't feel that. Right now he felt bigger and more powerful than anything coming at him. And when a huge tumbleweed bounced on a collision course with his car, he stole a glance at Nadia, drove straight through it, and laughed.

Part II
SPRING

1

IT WAS mid-March, and like Martie had promised, Nadia had been invited to her quinceañera. But it overlapped with the start of spring break, which turned out to be a bad time for everyone. Nadia's family had a trip to Chicago planned, and anyway, her parents had other ideas about how much time she should be spending on overnights with Kyle. Taylor was too stressed out by school to go, and Megan was still boycotting the family. Kyle's mom had planned to come, but then she felt like she was getting the flu and didn't want to spread it around. So she said.

She'd been out of it lately—hardly home, working a

lot and forgetting about Kyle's games and other stuff. Not the predictable and reliable Mom she usually was. Pretty much as soon as he got back from the party, Kyle would be taking off for a spring break varsity baseball tournament in Arizona, and he hoped his mom would have his stuff ready.

Anyway, if Nadia was going to be gone, there was no reason to stay home for the weekend when he could be hanging out with Emily and everyone else at the farm. So it was Kyle and his dad alone for the long drive up the coast, his dad listening to a cooking thing on NPR and Kyle texting Nadia.

He took a picture of his dad.

"What?"

"Nothing."

His dad patted the hair around his bald spot and glanced at Kyle. "Are you posting that?"

"Just to Nadia."

"Why?"

"Because I'm bored. And I want her and me to be bored together." He sent off the text.

#dadvibes

She replied with a smile.

"You could ask people's permission before taking pictures of them and sharing it around," his dad said.

"It's just Nadia."

now he's mad. I think he thinks I'm making fun of him

"Maybe I don't want you to send Nadia a picture of me."

well now you are!! Nadia wrote. **btw the hotel we're gonna stay at in Chicago is supposedly haunted.**

"She knows what you look like, Dad."

"Not the point."

he feels violated I guess? u believe in ghosts?

"What *is* the point?"

"Maybe put the phone away for a minute, Kyle. I want to talk to you."

in trouble now haha.

Nadia sent him a string of emojis that Kyle didn't have time to interpret before his dad grabbed his phone and dropped it into the driver's-door cup holder. Kyle stared at his dad and laughed, playful. "I'm sorry, Dad, I'm sorry!"

Kyle wanted his dad to laugh too. He wanted them to crack each other up and find the humor in their own dumb reactions to stuff that wasn't that serious. A quick look at his dad was enough to see that wasn't happening. "I wasn't dunking on you, I swear. I was sending her pictures of the road, other cars, freeway signs, whatever. It wasn't anything."

The muscles in his dad's jaw flexed, like he was clenching his teeth. It didn't look like he'd be giving Kyle's phone back anytime soon. Kyle *thought* they'd been in a good mood. He blew air from between his lips and shook his head. Whatever. He'd just stare out his own window, then. Kyle's mom always said he and his dad were alike that way. Too sensitive, too fast to "go dark," as she put it. "As fast as switching off a light."

"You don't need copper pans, it's the aluminum that actually holds in the heat," the woman on the radio was saying.

"You don't even cook, Dad," Kyle muttered.

They listened to the rest of the tips on buying a sauté pan. The handle should be comfortable. It should be ovenproof. It should have a little hole so you could hang it from a rack. Then his dad turned off the radio and said, "I want to tell you something. That's going on."

Kyle's first thought was: *money*. A couple times every year, there was some big speech about money, the business being unpredictable, them all needing to tighten the belt and be more conscious of the inflows and outflows. His dad would be super serious like this for about ten minutes, and then literally nothing changed and they went on spending exactly as much as always.

"Go ahead," Kyle said, impatient.

"Don't sigh like that. Don't give me attitude."

"I'm not!"

Silence. They went a few more miles. A tumbleweed

skipped across the road, but his dad didn't drive through it. Instead, he slowed down and let it blow past.

Was Kyle supposed to apologize now or something? His dad was being all sensitive and cranky. Maybe they should talk about baseball. Kyle had been moved from outfield to second base and had been playing pretty well there this season. Coach Ito had told him the other day he showed good leadership, but the idea of saying that to his dad right now, like some kind of brag, felt awkward.

He reached for the radio to turn it on again; his dad stopped him, and their hands touched for a second before they both pulled back.

"Mom is seeing someone," his dad said.

"Huh?" Kyle wanted his phone back.

"Mom is seeing someone."

Kyle had no idea what he was talking about. "You mean like a shrink or something?" It wasn't that big a deal. Half the people they knew were in therapy. Mom probably *should* be in therapy, and work out this shit with Megan or whatever else she was going through so she could be more like she used to be. But then his dad's silence worried him. "Or some other kind of doctor?" Kyle asked. "Is she sick? Dad?"

"No," he said quietly.

Then Kyle got it.

Seeing someone. His brain processed the phrase, one you normally didn't hear about married people. A parent. Your parent.

Then his body caught up with his mind, and he felt it in his gut.

"I haven't told your sisters yet. I . . . we . . . haven't told anyone, actually, and I don't even know why I'm telling you now. I didn't plan this."

We haven't told anyone.

"Wait, so . . . Mom knows you know?"

"Yes. But she doesn't know *you* know." He lifted his hands off the wheel and let them fall again. "She's been seeing someone for a couple months. She says."

The world outside the windshield flew by and Kyle wanted to stop it, rewind, make his dad unsay the words.

His brain sorted the pieces of information and tried to make sense of them.

His mother was having an affair. And his father knew and they were still married and living in the same house like everything was fine? And they weren't planning to say anything to anybody. Was he missing something? In what world did any of this make sense?

Not in Kyle's world. Not the one he thought he was living in.

Every muscle in his body wanted to reach over and grab his phone from the driver's-side door and tell Nadia, tell Emily, tell Taylor, tell Megan. **WTF???** he would ask on a group text.

"I don't know what to do, Kyle," his dad went on. "I really don't. We were waiting it out, you know?"

Um, no, I don't know, I have no idea whatsoever.

"We're *still* waiting it out, I guess, and I guess we should separate, but to be honest we can't afford it. I mean, a place for her and a place for me? Rent prices in California, with business how it is? It's such a goddamn expensive industry, Kyle. I always imagined you and the girls taking it over, but I don't want you to. There's so much overhead, and if people don't pay on time or a project goes wrong, you're screwed. Not to mention all the competition now and all the people who watch an hour of HGTV and think they can do everything themselves for five grand."

He'd gone from dropping the bomb of his mom's affair to lecturing Kyle on the cost of running a contracting business?

"We were waiting it out," his dad repeated, sounding bewildered. "And frankly, neither of us thought this would still be going on at this point."

Kyle made his right hand into a fist and gnawed on his knuckle. A thing he used to do when he was stressed out as a kid. But he didn't want to look like a baby right now, so he shoved his hand under his leg and asked, "You're 'waiting out' Mom sleeping with someone else? Like, you discussed it and decided to 'wait it out'? You're just gonna, like, *wait*? For it to not be happening?"

They passed three freeway exits.

"I shouldn't have told you," his dad said at last.

Yeah, no shit. "You did, though."

"I know, I know. Kyle, I'm sorry." His dad reached over and touched Kyle's arm in a way that seemed to try to express some kind of father-son-ness, as if it would make this any better. Kyle recoiled toward the passenger door and brought his hand back to his mouth.

His dad kept talking.

"I don't have answers that are going to make any sense to you. All I can say is life isn't as all-or-nothing as you think. Not after twenty-six years of marriage and fifteen years of our business, and three kids, and two house remodels and one medical scare and"—he gestured to the road they were on, taking them to the big family event— "your aunts and uncles and cousins. A history. A life. You don't just . . ."

His dad was losing it. Kyle had seen his dad angry, seen him depressed, seen him goofy, seen him sad, seen him quiet, seen his eyes go damp, seen him go somewhere deep into himself. But he had never seen him actually truly cry. He didn't even know if he could tell Taylor or Megan this part. Kyle listened to his dad's choppy breathing, pulled at the hair of his knuckles with his teeth.

"Okay." His dad said, exhaling sharply. "Okay. Sorry. Okay."

"It's fine," Kyle said.

Totally fine.

Fine that it turned out his whole world was a tumbleweed, just a mass of dried-up bits that used to be rooted in something but now was fragile, not attached to anything, on the verge of being annihilated if the wind blew it one inch the wrong way.

"Look, we're going to figure this out. Forget I said anything."

"Sure, Dad." Like he could forget. Delete. Backspace.

They drove past more strip malls, gas stations, billboards.

"Seriously, though. This weekend, Martie's birthday. You know, don't say anything. Don't let on."

Kyle nodded. Got it. His dad had pushed past the emotion to some worse place that was all about being practical. Be around the whole family and act like everything is fine. Hang out with his cousins without letting on what was falling apart. Look his grandmother in the eye and be cool.

"The thing is . . . ," his dad continued, "the thing is that the, um, the guy. The other guy? His wife doesn't know. His kid. There's another family on the other side of this, and every town is a small town when it comes to this stuff. Especially considering the business and all, our names out there on the trucks and everything. Anyway, I feel like it's not my place or our place to make that choice for him. The other guy." He glanced at Kyle. "About whether or not to tell."

What was even happening? Was his dad's truck some kind of portal to a parallel universe, where everyone's parents—who previously had been annoying, at most—were actually the worst people on the planet?

"But you're okay making that choice for *me*."

"Well. You're not directly involved."

Kyle wiped the back of his hand on his jeans. "Oh, okay."

"I didn't mean . . . Sorry. That sounded bad. Obviously you're involved now, thanks to me. I . . ." He trailed off. "Christ. Just please don't tell your sisters. Don't tell Nadia."

Nadia. At Thanksgiving, on this road, they had been joking about getting married. At Thanksgiving, on the farm, he'd imaged him and Nadia in a wedding picture like the one of his parents. He'd been so into his big messy-happy family, so into showing it off, like "Someday this could be us."

He had to tell her, right? His dad couldn't control whether or not he said something to his own girlfriend.

"Kyle?"

"I heard you."

"I mean it," his dad said. "This needs to be in the vault."

The vault.

There were a couple things between him and his dad in there. Like when Kyle drove home from Mateo's after drinking and his dad was waiting up and immediately knew and talked to him for over an hour about "Do you want to kill a kid? Is that what you want to do? You want to hit a car and send a baby into the street?" Or "You want a record? You want to not drive again until you're twenty-five? Or never? You want all your college applications rejected?" Then he said he believed in Kyle, believed he was smart and wouldn't make that mistake again. "I'm putting this one in the vault. If you let me down, I can't help you. You'll die alone in prison."

Another thing in there was when Kyle was on a job site with his dad and they found a mistake in how the scaffolding had been set up, the kind of mistake that could have led to the whole thing coming down and injuring or killing workers or people on the street. His dad shut down the site, fired the foreman, and oversaw the fix himself. But before that, he sat in the Baker & Najarian truck with Kyle and said, "That's our name. Ours and Al's. On the trucks. On the site. On the contract. And we could have just lost everything. Don't forget this happened, but never talk about it, Kyle. Put it in the vault."

And Kyle had all kinds of stuff between him and his sisters, pacts they'd made to keep each other out of trouble with their parents. There was also something that had to do with Megan's shitty high school boyfriend, Adam, but Kyle didn't know details and no one ever said his name anymore.

Now this.

Kyle leaned over again to turn the radio back up. The cooking show was over, and now it was a news quiz, with joking and laughing. They listened without cracking a smile. Eventually Kyle's dad said, "Oh," and retrieved Kyle's phone. "Here."

Nadia's texts were there when he unlocked it.

I mean I guess ghosts COULD be a thing, who am I to say?

Hello?

The playful conversation with Nadia was from a different life. He scrolled through it. His cracks, her smileys. His photos, her replies. He had to say something, even though the Kyle in those texts had been left somewhere back behind them on the highway, tumbling into the horizon.

sorry—we're driving into a signal dead zone now

He hit send and turned off the phone.

Then he turned it on again.

Nadia had sent a heart and a waving hand.

See ya, boyfriend who used to tell me everything!

Goodbye, boyfriend's nice family!

He shut it off once and for all and shoved it way down to the bottom of his duffel.

"So," his dad said as they made the turn toward the farm. "Like I said, Mom and I don't know how this is going to play out. It could all be sort of a blip, you know, in the grand scheme of things."

Sure. A blip.

"And if it is that, I don't want everyone to hold it against her down the line. She already feels kind of like an outsider with my family. Anyway, this weekend is about Martie. A celebration. No need to get into anything complicated. Kyle? Hello? Can you acknowledge that you're hearing me?"

"Dad. You've basically said the same thing like a hundred different ways, and I heard all of them. It's in the vault. You don't ever have to say anything about it again."

"I'm sorry," his dad said. "Sorry."

They rounded the turn, and Kyle saw Emily on the swing set at the top of the drive. His throat closed up. How was he going to hang out with her and not tell her what he'd just found out?

"Keep driving," he told his dad.

"You don't want to hop out here and say hi to Em?"

Emily waved at Kyle and slid off the swing.

"Just park first." He waved at her through the window and gestured: *Sorry, no idea what my dad is doing.* She held up her arms: *WTF?*

They kept going, all the way to the big circle of gravel and weeds behind the house that functioned as a parking lot when a bunch of people were there. Grandpa Baker was waiting under the pear tree, his cane in one hand and his big coffee cup in the other, like always, like nothing at all had changed.

2

"**WHAT'S WRONG?**" Emily asked—
literally the first words she spoke to him the moment they
were alone. She'd walked down from the swings, and
Grandma Baker had already put them to work halving
and juicing limes for her famous limeade, half of which
would turn into infamous limeade once Aunt Brenda
added tequila to it.

"Just . . . being in the car with my dad all day."

She handed him another lime half; he pressed it into a
flat disk with the old manual juicer his grandmother had
been using since Kyle's dad was a kid.

"These aren't that juicy," he'd said.

"Yeah, I've seen better." She flexed her fingers to give them a break from slicing. "Are you bummed that Nadia couldn't come up for this?"

Nadia. He had maybe another hour where he could use the trip and being at the farm and family as an excuse for not texting her.

"Pretty much."

He kept pressing limes, pressing limes, pressing limes. Like a machine. Emily's eyes were on him, he felt it. He glanced out the kitchen window. Grandma Baker was playing checkers with Alex on the patio, while Uncle Dale and Kyle's dad were putting up the sun awning. His mom should be there, watching, with her hands wrapped around a cup of coffee, telling Dad to be careful with his knee.

What if he called his mom? Right then. Called her and said, "Dad is out there on the ladder and I think you should be here too. Give everyone the flu, it's fine. Bring Megan. We need to be together."

Then: *oh.* "I think I'm coming down with the flu" sounded like a great way to get out of a family event in order to stay home and do your cheating.

"Did something happen with you and Nadia?" Emily said. "Other than her not getting to come here?"

He shook his head. Saw his dad wobble on the ladder and Uncle Dale steady it, laughing.

"It's not about Nadia."

God, this was so hard and stupid. He couldn't tell Nadia and now he was also going to stand here not telling Emily? His dad should just have left him on the side of the road.

He pressed the last lime and tossed the wrung-out peel into the compost bucket. "Does your family have secrets?" he asked. "I mean your family-family, not like all of us collectively. Like stuff they keep from the rest of the Bakers or even, like, things only you and one of your parents knows but not the other parent, or Alex or whatever?"

She laughed. "Yes. I'm not supposed to tell Grandma that my mom had a dirty play published a couple of years ago. Even though it won an award. I'm not supposed to tell Dad how much Mom really smokes. And I'm pretty sure Grandma and Grandpa aren't supposed to know that Uncle Mike and Grandpa Navarro run a poker game out of Mike and Jenny's house twice a month. But Great-Aunt Gina knows, because she sneaks off to play sometimes when she's visiting."

Kyle *wished* that was the kind of thing he meant, basic "Don't tell Mom" stuff that people seemed to have even when they were adults themselves. "Nothing serious, though?"

"It depends on your definition of serious, I guess." She divided the lime juice between two big pitchers, and they worked on the cleanup together. "So are you going to tell me what's up?"

Kyle leaned on the counter and met Emily's eyes. Her face calmed him, the familiarity of it. There weren't many people he'd known his whole life the way he'd known her. Other than his idiot parents.

"I want to," he said. "It's something I'm not supposed to talk about. Like, my dad told me something and I'm not supposed to tell anyone. But he didn't say that until after he already told me the thing, which I retroactively don't want to know, and now I'm pissed."

"Well that sucks."

"Also, the thing itself that he told me is pretty bad."

"If you want," she'd said, "you can talk to me about it like in a vague way. Without actually telling-telling. If it helps."

He'd nodded. "Yeah, maybe."

"Meet at the bunkhouse later? After the party and the dance?"

Kyle groaned. "God. This family and its dancing."

"Uncle Mike has been working on the playlist for two weeks. He and my mom have been texting about it non-stop."

"Doesn't Martie want to do her own playlist? It's her birthday."

"I'm sure she has her own thing going for when her

friends are here. Uncle Mike's is for the after-party."

It was going to be a long-ass day.

"Where's Martie now?" He wanted to say hi and wish her happy birthday before everything got too chaotic.

"There's a mass, I guess? At their church? With Uncle Mike and Aunt Jenny, and Grandpa Navarro, and Aunt Gina."

The family had this whole Catholic/Protestant thing going on. Or more like the Catholic ones and then the ones who were like "Oh, I'm Protestant" but hardly ever went to church or talked about believing in anything. Grandma and Grandpa Baker grew up going to some church, not Catholic, Kyle didn't know what it was. They were never that serious about church per se, but at the same time they were so traditional. Then Great-Aunt Gina converted to Catholicism and became a nun, and that divided their family when they were young. But everyone who'd been upset about that was dead now.

Grandpa Navarro had always been Catholic, and when Uncle Mike married his daughter and they had Martie, Uncle Mike and Aunt Jenny decided they'd raise her and any other kids they had with some Catholic traditions. There was only Martie, even though Uncle Mike and Aunt Jenny had tried to have more.

"Were we not invited to the mass, or . . . ?" Kyle asked. Emily, living closer to the rest of the family, usually knew more about what was going on.

"I guess it was optional. It's probably mostly Martie's confirmation class and their families. I think they assume we wouldn't want to go and don't want us to feel obligated." She held up her hands. "My fingers are all pruney from lime juice."

Kyle held his up too, and then they pressed their hands together like a super-slow-motion high five. He closed his eyes for a couple of seconds, feeling the contact, the protection of something true.

That night at the dance, Martie and her friends had gotten through their own playlist but kept dancing when Uncle Mike's came on, while the aunts and uncles drank the tequila limeade. The sun had gone down, and the strings of lights lit up the huge patio that was also the dance floor.

Kyle had been hanging back in a shadowy corner, on a folding chair, texting Nadia. He'd been describing everything, staying focused on details like the playlist and outfits and food. Nadia was out too, at some house party, then would be leaving for Chicago in the morning. The response time between his texts and her replies got longer and longer.

Wish you were here, he wrote for probably the third

time in that one conversation. He added a frown face. A cry cat. A broken heart. He knew he looked needy but he didn't care. He *felt* needy. He *was* needy.

He waited, watched Martie and a couple of her friends and Uncle Dale do some choreographed thing, cracking up. He took a picture, sent it to Nadia. Her typing bubbles appeared, disappeared, appeared again. Finally, her reply.

I wish I was there too, but you should try to have some fun anyway!! Don't miss out on your cousin time. We're gonna watch a movie here and I'm putting my phone away so I can get into it. Check back with you when it's done!

Probably because he'd sent her a picture from his party, she sent one back from hers. A selfie of her doing a tongue-out rocker face. She was nestled into the corner of a couch, wearing a peach-colored V-neck. There were other people's elbows and shoulders around her and some people in the background holding red party cups. Kyle zoomed in on the background.

Who all is there?

"Kyle! Get off your phone!" It was Martie, shouting to him from the dance floor.

Babe, Nadia wrote, **I'm going DND. ttyl. Love u.**

One of the guys in the background at her party looked a lot like Jack Mesrobian, her ex. He was turned kind of mostly with his back to the camera, but Kyle recognized the dumb way he always had his sunglasses resting on the back of his neck.

is that jack? he asked.

Someone grabbed his phone out of his hand. Aunt Brenda. She held it over her head and said, "Why aren't you dancing?"

"Come on, Kyle, it's my birthday!" Martie hopped over to the B-52's.

One of her friends grabbed her and they spun away, but Aunt Brenda was not going to give up that easily. She stuck his phone in her back pocket, then took both Kyle's hands and pulled. He was stronger than her, strong enough to resist and probably topple her if he pulled back. That would only make this into a bigger scene than it already was, so he let her drag him into the middle of the patio.

"Everybody had matching towels!" Aunt Brenda shouted in his face, along with the song.

He heard his mom's voice in his head, from when they were driving home after one of the family gatherings: *Brenda just doesn't know when to stop. Not everyone thinks she's fun.*

He wanted his mom to be here, right now. He wanted Nadia, his mom, Megan, Taylor . . . everyone who should be here to *be* here, not off protesting the family or studying for finals or faking flulike symptoms or doing their own thing with Jack Mesrobian lurking around in the background.

Aunt Brenda finally let go of his hands so that she could boogie down low to the ground, as Uncle Mike would say. She got too low and lost her balance. Laughing, drunk, she said, "If you help me up, I'll give you back your phone."

He hoisted her to her feet, but then she said, "Psych!" and went to hide behind Kyle's dad, who was doing an embarrassing white-man two-step and looking a little sloshed on limeade himself. Was Kyle supposed to chase Aunt Brenda around and fight her for the phone? He found Emily's face across the patio; he nodded at her and retreated back into the shadows, then away from the patio completely until he was on the pine-straw path to the old bunkhouse.

The music faded and the stars got brighter, and he found the edge of the olive grove and followed it until he saw the long wooden building with its tin roof, and the two picnic tables where the farm crew used to have their dinners outside. All of it unchanged since Thanksgiving, aside from its being warmer and greener now. He lay down on one of the tables, face up to the moon.

What was his mom doing right now? He pictured her alone at the house, eating one of her big twenty-ingredient salads and binge-watching a show, texting with whoever the guy was. Then he pictured the guy, in his own house with his own wife and own kid, texting her back. Pretending to be looking up scores or something if anyone asked.

Or maybe they were together. Right now.

Together together.

At a hotel? Where had they been meeting up? Kyle's house? He saw them together, blinked it away, then imagined Nadia and Jack at the party—Jack looking at Nadia in that T-shirt and remembering how he'd touched her body before, wanting to do it again, trying it in the dark during the movie, and what if both of them were drinking?

It was so easy to make mistakes; everything suddenly seemed so breakable.

He heard Emily's footsteps in the brush. Thank God.

"I saw my mom trying to Rock Lobster with you."

He blew out a laugh. "Yeah, everyone did."

She sat on the other picnic table, her feet on the bench.

"You should lie down like I'm doing," he said. "There's a really good view of the moon right now." It was three-quarters full, and the night was clear. He could see the valleys and craters and whatever else was up there.

"I have bad memories of ants in my hair at this place. I'll just look up." Crickets chirped, and they listened to that for a few minutes. Then Emily said, "Commence being vague about what your dad told you, if you want."

He spoke slowly. "Okay. So, like. Imagine if . . ." He tried to think of a good metaphor. "Imagine if your mom came to you and she was like, 'Oh, by the way, your dad is a bank robber, but oops I didn't mean to tell you that, don't tell him you know and don't tell anyone else, either, forget I said anything.' What would you do?"

She laughed. "My dad would be the worst bank robber, sorry. Okay. This is like an ethics quiz. My sociology teacher does this sometimes."

"Yeah, think of it like that."

"Is he the kind of bank robber who shoots people during holdups? Does he threaten them with a gun? Or is he more like the kind who has his finger in his pocket and pretends it's a gun and just quietly walks away with a bag of money?"

"Um . . ."

"Just trying to get a sense of who is victimized here. The bank, obviously. Anyone else?"

"Kind of?" If the guy's wife and kid never found out, would it hurt them? Would they only be victims if they knew?

"I guess if my dad was a *violent* criminal, I would have trouble living with him and not saying anything. But if he was, like, a gentleman bank robber and no one got hurt, and the money was helping us survive or he was giving it to the poor, I might be okay with it."

"Really?" Kyle propped himself up on one elbow. "But if he's stealing, even in a nice way, with good intentions, he's still taking something that doesn't belong to him. He's breaking the rules."

"True. But maybe not all rules make sense. Look at capitalism itself, the system we all operate in. One could argue that capitalism has all kinds of victims, and so—"

"Emily," Kyle said, stopping her. "Forget it." It wasn't an ethics exercise, it was his life. If would be better if he forgot it too. He would eat the secret, choke it down, and see if it would stay there.

He could barely see Emily's face in the dark but felt her eyes anyway.

"Okay," she said. "But you know I've trusted you with some stuff, and I want you to know you can trust me, if you ever want to."

They heard voices and laughter coming from the grove. Kyle jumped off the table like he was about to get caught at something, as if his dad was going to appear and be all "What did you say to Emily?"

"It's Martie," Emily said quietly. "And a guy. They haven't seen us yet. Should we scare them?"

Kyle spotted them too, hand in hand and clearly trying to find a good spot to make out.

It would be exactly like him to be on board for the

scare-the-crap-out-of-my-cousin prank, but he was not feeling exactly like himself and called out, "Hey, Martie, it's Kyle and Emily."

It startled them anyway, especially the guy, who sort of scream-yelled before he could stop himself. That made Martie laugh, hand pressed to her chest and doubled over and saying, "Ohmygodyouscaredme!" and then they were all laughing.

"Sorry," Emily said, obviously not that sorry.

"What are you guys *doing*?" Martie said when she'd recovered.

"Just talking," Kyle answered. "What are *you* doing?"

"Showing Julian the bunkhouse. Um, these are my cousins," she said to Julian.

"Hi, yeah," Julian said, "I saw you back at the house."

The two of them looked like such kids to Kyle, even though he was barely two years older. Martie had changed out of her dress into cutoffs and a sweatshirt. Julian had masses of curly hair and a face that looked like it had never had a zit or been shaved.

"Is the party over?" Kyle asked.

"Yeah," Martie said. "It sort of ended when Aunt Brenda hurt her knee doing the safety dance."

"How ironic of her," Emily said.

"That's your mom, right?" Julian asked. "She's cool. She's like . . . the *fun* aunt."

"That's one way to look at it, I guess."

Better your mom be the fun aunt than the cheater aunt, Kyle thought. "We were just about to leave."

"We were?" Emily asked.

"Yeah. I'm pretty tired." That was true.

She shrugged. "Okay."

The thought then crossed Kyle's mind that maybe, as the older cousins, they had some responsibility to keep Martie and Julian from doing anything too stupid. He added, "But we'll see you guys back up there in like ten minutes, right? I'll let your mom and dad know where you are," he said to Martie. "So they don't worry."

She rolled her eyes. "Thanks, Kyle."

Kyle and Emily walked back up the path, listening to their feet in the brush and the crickets and the tree frogs. When the patio came into view, they saw Aunt Brenda with her leg up, icing her knee. Uncle Mike was also there, talking to her. There was no sign of Aunt Jenny or Kyle's dad or anyone else.

"We're leaving early tomorrow," Emily said, pausing just outside the circle of light cast by the house. "My mom needs to be back in time for a performance one of her students is in."

He grabbed her hand. Maybe because he'd had to eat the words he wanted to say, or in sudden need of human touch, or out of the fear of being left alone. He stood there with her hand in his, feeling like, *I'm being weird*, and let it drop.

"Hey, Kyle," Aunt Brenda called, "I have your phone!"

Emily put the hand Kyle had just been holding on his shoulder and faced him. "Even though I have to leave, I'm still here. I'm always here." She took out her phone and shook it. "Okay?"

Kyle nodded, knowing that if he tried to talk, he'd cry.

Later, Nadia texted him.

Hey. Movie done, I'm back home.

Yes that was Jack. Jack still exists in the world and still has some of the same friends I do. As you will recall, I broke up with Jack because our relationship was over. tbh this is even more of a reply than I really owe you for that question, but you're usually not possessive so I don't know what's up.

He started to reply and apologize, but more typing bubbles came up and he waited.

Actually, Kyle, I'm super tired right now and want to just go to bed. I'll try to call you tomorrow between airports and stuff.

All he could do was send a thumbs-up, and as soon as he did he could see it looked sarcastic and petty.

This was all new, a side of her and of himself he hadn't seen, and he didn't know what to say or what to do to make it right. The ground was slipping out from under him.

Mom is seeing someone.

Four words less than a day old.

He pictured his mom and dad driving together, back and forth to the farm for Kyle's whole entire life. Her hand on his thigh, every time, because it belonged there. How she'd always looked at him, and the way they were a team.

That was real. He'd always thought it was so real.

3

KYLE WENT on the Arizona trip with the team. They didn't even make it to the quarterfinals. Coop and Mateo were all depressed about it, but Kyle didn't care. He was just glad that he was able to avoid his mom during the half day between when he got home from the farm and when he got on the team bus to head for the airport.

Now they were hanging out in their motel room with a couple of pizzas, waiting to find out if they were going back home or staying for the rest of the tournament. Coop was on one bed with a pizza box balanced on his stomach,

Mateo on the other, and Kyle was on the floor next to the other pizza, because the rollaway was too uncomfortable to be on while awake.

"That one pitcher," Coop said.

"I know," Mateo said. "Dude was on a tear."

Kyle looked at his phone. He and Nadia had hardly been texting, her in Chicago and him here, and the tension over Jack and everything else still stretched tight. "We're not that good, though," he said. "Even if the pitcher hadn't been so hot."

Mateo didn't say anything, but Coop threw him a glare. "Your attitude sucks. No wonder we lost."

Kyle found a gif from *Damn Yankees* and sent it to Emily.

Baseball and musicals collide. p.s. we lost.

She sent back **there's always next time** plus a "Climb Ev'ry Mountain" clip from *The Sound of Music*.

"Is that Nadia?" Mateo asked.

"It's my cousin."

"The girl?" Coop asked. "The one who came to our game last year?"

"Yeah."

It had been a home game toward the end of the season, and his grandma and grandpa and also Aunt Brenda and Uncle Dale and Emily and Alex all showed up, packed into a minivan. "They all came? Just for this?" Coop had asked, glancing up at the bleachers. "To see you play on our dumb team? I can barely get my own dad to take off work once in a season." Later on, Coop had asked, "Did your cousin say anything about me?"

Kyle had laughed. "No, Coop, she didn't."

"So what's up with you, Baker?" Mateo asked now. "No mojo out there. Not that we had a chance anyway, but you're off."

"Not my week, I guess."

He imagined telling them. *My mom is having an affair.* Mateo he could sort of trust to keep it to himself, but there was no way Coop could keep his mouth shut about something like that. Plus, what if knowing that info made them picture his mom having sex? It definitely would. Kyle had a hard enough time keeping that shit out of his own mind, he didn't need his friends thinking about it.

Coop shoved the pizza box to the side and rolled off the bed to use the bathroom. While he was in there, Mateo asked, "You and Nadia cool?"

"Yeah, man, we're fine. She's just in Chicago with her parents. The team is here. So, you know. We're both busy and stuff right now."

Mateo waited as if he expected Kyle to say more, to relent and be like, *Well, okay, there's more.*

"That's it," Kyle said. "That's all."

Not hungry, he took the last piece of pizza to prove he

was all good, that he came from a big, basically happy family and he had an awesome girlfriend and a healthy appetite. No weakness, no crack in the system. If he could play it like that, maybe it would be true. The "blip," as his dad put it, would unblip, and life would go back to how it was.

And he tried.

One day at a time, he tried. Tried to wait it out. Tried to act normal around his mom, then couldn't, so avoided her. Tried to act normal with Nadia and had the same problem with the same solution: avoidance. It became impossible for him to be around anyone for more than minimal chunks of time, because he was afraid of what would be asked or told once the small talk was over. He skated over just the very top layer of his life, knowing that if he stayed in one place too long, the whole thing would crack beneath him, pull him under.

The only person he could talk to without fear was Emily. She knew something was up, and that he couldn't say what it was. That was enough for her and enough for him and it hadn't changed anything between them. She didn't expect anything from him like Nadia did, like the team did.

After Arizona, he started skipping practice. Missing games. Coach Ito put him on probation. Kyle told Nadia his shoulder was bothering him, even made up some crap about physical therapy, but kept it vague. In fact he mostly used baseball time to drive around.

Driving was his new pastime.

Driving did not require teamwork, talking, being talked to, enduring being cheered up, listening to more lies, pretending to be the same old dumb Kyle he was before. Driving only required gas.

He'd been burning through a tank of it every week, while he drove around during the time he was supposed to be at practice or games. Getting on the 101—south to Ventura one day, north toward Lompoc another. Or inland, AC blasting until he shivered. The best was how when he was driving, it felt like he wasn't in a real place. It wasn't home and wasn't school or Nadia or baseball. It was nowhere.

A couple of weeks after Arizona, Kyle sat in his car in the student lot, in his favorite parking space: under a tree, in the farthest corner. He used to avoid parking near trees, let alone under them, because he didn't want his car covered in bird crap and pollen. Now all he cared about was being hard to find, keeping to the perimeter of the lot, of the halls, of his house—the perimeter of his life where he wouldn't see or be seen head-on. Anyway, if bird crap and pollen and dust got on the car, that meant he could go through the car wash—easing onto the track and shifting into neutral, hands off the wheel as he let the belt chug him forward one inch at a time under the tentacles of the scrubber. He liked the way it made his car a dim cave, a cave inside a cave. And it came out clean. No evidence that anything messy had ever touched it.

He sat there, thinking about going to practice. If he didn't go today, it basically meant he'd be quitting. He *could* play baseball; sure, he *could* go to practice. It wasn't the game itself he didn't like anymore. It was everything else: having to see the team, listen to their stupid talk in the dugout, rib or be ribbed for missed easy catches and awkward strikeouts, hear Coach Ito yell or joke or deploy one of his meaningless phrases about hustle or teamwork—

A knock on his car window made him jump. It was Coop. Kyle turned the key so he could lower his window halfway. "Dude, don't scare me like that."

Coop's face loomed close. Too close. Kyle could see the scraggly blond hairs of the beard that Coop had been trying to make happen for a month.

"Are you coming or not?" Coop asked. "This is it. Shit or get off the pot."

"I don't know," he told Coop.

"What don't you know, Baker? Whether or not you give a crap about literally anything?"

"Ellison is good at second. You don't need me."

"Not the point, dude."

"I'm not feeling too . . ." He couldn't finish.

Coop stared at Kyle, then tried the handle of the locked car door, rattled it a couple times. Like if he tried hard enough, he could reach in and physically drag Kyle out from under this cloud of garbage that had been following him everywhere since the trip up to the farm for Martie's birthday.

Kyle closed his window, and Coop slapped the glass.

"Just get your ass out of the car and show up!" Coop's voice was muffled, but not muffled enough. "You don't have to pretend to like it. Just show up! Drag your ass two hundred yards so Ito doesn't cut you! Think about next year."

Kyle ran his hands around the steering wheel. Pictured himself gliding in slow motion through the car wash.

"You're shit. You know that?" Coop shouted through the window.

Kyle nodded. "Yeah, I know." Absolute shit. The way he'd been ghosting Nadia, ghosting his whole life.

"What did you say?"

He lowered the window half an inch. "I said I know."

Coop put the fingers of both hands through the half inch of open window. Kyle pressed the button to raise it; Coop pulled his fingers out as quickly as he could. Two fingers on one hand got stuck. "Dude!"

Kyle lowered the window enough to release him, started the engine, and backed out carefully while Coop watched, stunned and holding his fingers to his chest. Kyle stayed in reverse, backing all the way across the lot. Coop recovered enough to flip him off.

He meandered from neighborhood to neighborhood in his car. His phone buzzed with texts and calls, all from Nadia, he knew. The situation with her was pretty much like it was with the team: time was up. He'd been given a kind of relationship probation for his avoidance, which Nadia at first thought had to do with Jack being at that party and Kyle being possessive and punishing her somehow. No matter how many times he told her it wasn't that, she didn't believe him.

Why are you breaking up with me? she'd texted a couple of nights ago.

I'm not.

Sure feels like it, Kyle.

It was more like a long, slow process of trying to get her to break up with him because he couldn't do it himself. Because he couldn't bring himself to say what it really was. What if she told someone else at school and word got around? What if his mom's boyfriend was someone connected to school? Or to his parents' company?

Kyle saw every male teacher and wondered, *Is it him?*

Every random dad doing after-school pickups or drop-offs at the traffic circle. Every Baker & Najarian subcontractor or delivery guy. *Him? Him? Him?*

Not only that.

He didn't have the family he'd thought he had at Thanksgiving, the one he'd brought Nadia into, showed her off for. Pictured her being a part of.

It was like he'd already lost her, along with his whole concept of what it meant to be him.

He turned off his phone, drove around a little more, hit the car wash. When he got home, he went in the side door and slipped through the quiet kitchen and straight to his room. Later, he was in there trying to do homework with a movie on when there was a gentle knock on the door. His mom's knock.

This was exactly the situation he didn't want to be in—trapped in a room alone with her. The fact that he'd managed to avoid it for so long kind of made him think she'd been avoiding him too. She hadn't asked about his games or school or Nadia or anything else since he got back from Arizona, and he'd only given her the two-minute summary of the trip before making some excuse to get out of the conversation.

Now, she had on jeans and a light blue tank top that showed off arms she'd obviously been working on in the gym. Normal So-Cal mom clothes, but now Kyle thought about guys . . . men . . . maybe seeing her as attractive. When she sat on the foot of the bed, he scrunched against the wall on the other end with his laptop.

"*West Side Story* again?" she asked. "I thought I heard it through the door."

He should have put on his headphones. Rookie mistake.

She gave him an uneasy smile. "Nadia looks a little like young Natalie Wood. Don't you think?"

Natalie Wood aka Maria was on his screen now, frozen, smiling, feeling pretty. Nadia did have dark hair like that, and expressive eyes. "I don't know," he said, and closed the screen.

"Kyle, so . . ." She tucked a piece of hair behind her ear, and Kyle could see her hand was shaking. "Dad and I were talking last night. And he mentioned that he told you." Her eyes met his for half a second. "About me. Weeks ago."

He pressed his back to the wall, wishing it would absorb him as if he were a ghost in a movie. The Sharks and Jets sang in his head. *Breeze it, buzz it, easy does it.*

"I can't believe you've been carrying this around for weeks," she continued. "And neither of you said a word."

He couldn't look at her. "He told me not to," he muttered. "He said it's in the vault."

"It is. You weren't supposed to know."

"But I do."

"I'm sorry. He promised he wouldn't tell you."

A flare went off in his chest, and he tried giving her a hard stare. "People break promises, I guess, so."

She gave him a hard stare back. Outstaring his mom had never worked, not once in his entire existence. He flinched first, looked away. *Just play it cool, boy.*

"I'm allowed to have a life, Kyle."

What was *that* supposed to mean? "You had one already."

The pause got long, flat. And, in his mind, hissing like a ballgame crowd waiting for something to happen. She lowered her eyes, smoothed out the blanket. Her hands, no longer shaking, looked strong.

"I came in here planning to be in mom mode. I wanted to say something to make it better and reassure you that Dad and I have this under control. That we have a plan, you don't have to worry."

"But?"

"But . . ." She laughed through her nose and looked straight at him. "I don't *know* what I'm doing. Being forty-eight doesn't mean you have it figured out and don't make mistakes. All it does is show you how little you know."

"That's flimsy, Mom." "Flimsy" was one of Coach Ito's

favorite words. Your fielding is flimsy. Your attitude is flimsy. Your excuses are flimsy.

"I didn't want to be a cliché and a liar or to hurt anyone."

"But you are." *All of it.*

"I *know*." She sighed. "I know, Kyle. Right now we're trying to minimize the damage while I figure it out. That's all. I'm trying to not make it worse, and maybe I don't have to lose everything."

Nothing in her voice wavered. She wasn't going to cry like his dad did.

"That's why I'm upset Dad told you, and that's why I'm still hoping to keep your sisters out of it or anyone who might know anyone involved. We really want to contain this. If something gets out and causes trouble for innocent people—"

"Like me?"

She didn't answer.

"Maybe you should contain it by stopping," he said.

"Maybe I should." And the way she said it was like . . . *But I'm not going to.*

Kyle didn't want to look at her face anymore, hear her voice. "Can you, like, get out?"

She met his eyes with the most loving mom face he'd seen in a long time. He couldn't understand it. How she could love him and be doing what she was doing.

"Okay, Kyle."

She left, and Kyle slipped his headphones on and watched Maria dance through her song, a ribbon on top of her head, and it made him think too much about Nadia, so he stopped the movie and went over and over his mom's words. "I'm hoping," she'd said. "We really want," she'd said. She didn't *tell* him not to tell. Okay, his dad had said that, had invoked the vault, but that was weeks ago. Maybe if his mom had said she was going to stop and she was sorry and she was going to be better, or at least seemed like she felt slightly, like, guilty, he'd feel more like keeping her secret. But she didn't, and he was sick of knowing this all by himself.

I want to talk about the thing, he wrote to Emily.

Her face materialized on his laptop screen after he told her it was too complicated for texting. That swimmer's hair was in a bunch of clips all over her head, and she sported a septum ring. "Is that new?" he asked, touching his own nose.

"Yep. My dad is annoyed I didn't tell him ahead of time. And double annoyed because now my mom wants one too."

"It looks cool."

"I agree," she said with a laugh.

"So," he said, trying to think how to ramp up to this.

There wasn't any good way. "The thing my dad told me is that my mom is having an affair."

She scrunched her brows together. "What do you mean?"

"I mean . . . my mom is having an affair?"

"Your mom is having an affair. Is what you mean."

"Yes."

"Like an emotional affair? Or a sex affair?"

She was so matter-of-fact about it, about the word. Given that she was the one who didn't date or hook up, was it ironic that it was easier for her to talk about? Maybe not, maybe it made perfect sense. She'd probably given all this stuff way more thought than he ever had while she was working out her own identity or whatever.

"My dad's exact words were 'Mom is seeing someone.' And I've been dealing with that information for weeks. Not telling anyone. Not Nadia, not you, not my friends. Not Taylor or Megan. Nobody."

"Oh, god, Kyle."

"Just now she came in and talked to me about it, and she was all like . . . this is happening and there's nothing anyone can do about it."

"Wow."

"I mean, those weren't her exact words."

Emily nodded.

"The point is, no remorse or anything. Why should

I keep her dirty secret if she's not even trying to, I don't know, stop? But," Kyle continued, "the affair guy is also married. With a kid. And *they* don't know, and I have no idea who it is, so I'm like not going to go around telling people at school or whatever . . . or anyone. And why would I dump it on Taylor or Megan when they would end up being in the same situation as me? Knowing some garbage they never asked to know." He watched her face. "And neither did you."

She shrugged. "I told you that you could talk to me about it, whatever it was."

"You didn't imagine this, though, I bet."

"Um, no. What is the matter with people? Is sex really worth it?"

He *hated* thinking about the sex part. Maybe before, when it was an abstract idea, he could have handled it. But now that he'd been with Nadia, he knew the great and weird moments, the embarrassing and amazing thing that it could be.

"Sorry," Emily said. "You don't want to talk about that."

"Nope nope nope." Then a thought occurred to him. "Maybe they're in love." Saying it aloud made him uneasy, like he'd jinxed something.

"Maybe *love* is worth it, then?" Emily asked.

"Maybe? But that's not the point. She should love my *dad*."

Emily ran her hand through her hair, scratched at her nose ring.

"What?" Kyle asked.

"I don't know if 'love' and 'should' go together like that."

"Okay, but . . . you know what I mean."

"Yeah, I do," she said. "I can imagine if it was my parents, and like what if I knew something like that *and* I was supposed to keep it from Alex and Grandma and Grandpa and Uncle Mike and Aunt Jenny. I mean, I'd be pissed. Like aside from being sad? I'd be super, super angry."

All Kyle could do was nod. Anger felt like something waiting for him on the sidelines, something he hadn't totally looked at yet, was afraid to.

"So, what now?" Emily asked. "Have they said anything about divorce?"

He explained everything he knew about the money, the business, and not only that but how his parents weren't even sure what they wanted. As if this affair thing was like a losing baseball season, would come to an end and be in the past and they'd rebuild and make a comeback. Only unlike in baseball, this comeback would depend on the whole shitty season being a secret.

And right before he had to go, he told her one more thing he'd hadn't confessed to anyone, even himself, not totally.

"I think me and Nadia . . ." He rubbed his face. Pressed his fingers into his eyes like he could make them stay dry. Chewed on his knuckle. He didn't even have to finish his sentence.

"Oh, no. Kyle."

Emily put her hand up to the camera, and this small gesture let his heart finally crack.

4

KYLE DOUBLED down on his avoidance strategy the whole next week. If he didn't talk to Nadia, the end wasn't final. If he ignored Coach Ito's calls, left his uniform in a heap on his bedroom floor, he wasn't really off the team. If he wasn't at home, there was no home to get wrecked.

He kept burning through tanks of gas and kept texting Emily and she was always there, just like she said she'd be. They would talk about the situation:

My mom moved into Megan's room, now that they're not trying to hide it all from me. No idea what they're going to do when Taylor is home from school in a couple weeks.

Taylor will figure it out!

Or talk about nothing, or randomly send her gifs from musicals, like Donald O'Connor dancing up a wall in *Singin' in the Rain* or Mickey Rooney and Judy Garland doing the conga in *Strike Up the Band.*

Meanwhile, Nadia had been trying to get him alone. She was too good a person to finalize the breakup over text, but he wished she would. He'd managed to slip away from her in the hallways, dodge the whole cafeteria at lunch, lurk in the boys' room until passing period was over, and be late to every class they were in together and the first one out.

If he had any guts, he'd do it himself. Face the reality that he was not in a place where he could be a good boyfriend or any kind of boyfriend, and tell her so.

The problem was, he still loved her.

It felt less painful somehow to try to make her hate him than to actually say goodbye.

One morning he woke up to an all-caps text from her. **WE NEED TO TALK. TODAY, KYLE.**

He cut every class he had with her, and also last period, then drove to one of his favorite car washes in Ventura. It took almost forty-five minutes to get there on the 101, far enough and long enough to feel like he was putting real distance between himself and his life. He listened to the radio a little, then turned it off and sang a few show tunes. "My Favorite Things" from *The Sound of Music* and then "It's the Hard-Knock Life" and basically the rest of *Annie*, but skipping over "Maybe" because it would probably make him cry.

By the time he pulled into the car wash lot, his fuel light was on. Still, he was in an almost decent mood, high on denial and escape, singing, "He's a what? He's a what? He's a music man!" to himself, and then he saw the sign.

CLOSED DUE TO DROUGHT

"Okay," he breathed, the bleak mood creeping back over him.

He checked his phone for the next closest car wash; there was one at a gas station not too far. Perfect. A wash and a fill-up.

When he got there, that car wash was also closed. Kyle went into the station store and asked the guy behind the counter when they'd open it again.

"Never, probably."

"Never?"

"Do you see any rain clouds up there? Take it up with God."

Kyle went back to his car and pulled in front of a gas pump. He cleaned off his windshield with the station's squeegee, which sat in half an inch of dirty water, then inserted his credit card and tried to stave off his gloom with more *Music Man* lyrics. "He sells clarinets to the kids in the town—" The pump interrupted him with three beeps.

PLEASE SEE ATTENDANT blinked across the screen.

He went back into the store. "Can you try running this in here? I'm on number nine."

"'Number nine, number nine,'" the guy said, taking his card. "'You say you want a revolution?'"

"What?"

"Never mind." He punched in some numbers, waited, shook his head. "This is your card, right?"

"Yeah. I mean, it's my dad's." The one Kyle was supposed to use for gas and school supplies and food and clothes. Necessities. A word that Kyle defined a little more loosely than his dad did. "Do you need my ID?"

The cashier held out his hand for it without saying anything. Looked at the driver's license, looked at Kyle, looked at the credit card and then back at the license. He tapped the little picture of Kyle's face. "What happened to you, man?"

"What do you mean?"

"You're all smiling and shit here. Barely looks like you."

Kyle thought he'd been doing a better job than that at

pretending. "It's me." He stared into the cashier's eyes, forced a smile.

He stared back a couple seconds. "Well, Kyle Baker, time to call the old man. Either he cut you off or it's maxed out."

This brought him back to reality. He didn't have any cash or any gas in the tank. He took the card back, his license. "I might sit in your lot for a minute. If that's okay."

"Don't block the pumps."

A bright, dry California day was nice to drive in but not ideal for sitting around in your parked car. The blue of the sky was so sharp it seemed to want to cut open Kyle's brain and expose every thought he'd ever had. Sunglasses helped only slightly.

He started to text Emily about it: the running out of gas, the car wash problem, the sun. She hadn't replied to his last text, though, and he worried he was becoming a pain in the ass with his problems or being on his musical theater bullshit.

Calling his dad for help would mean an awkward conversation about money, not to mention what he was doing in Ventura instead of at baseball. He could call his mom. Different awkwardness, different words. He could and probably should call Nadia, who'd probably be eager to help him out because then he'd be forced to face her.

Megan. He had never been to his sister's apartment, but he knew she lived not too far from where he was right now. They hadn't spoken in at least a month. Still, contacting her seemed like pretty much the only option, unless he was prepared for Nadia. He was not.

Megan answered on the second ring. "*Kyle?* Did someone die?"

"No. Hi."

"Have you heard of texting?"

"I didn't want you to be able to pretend you hadn't seen my texts. I got you now." Kyle watched two little black birds fight over a Flamin' Hot Cheeto in front of the convenience store. "Are you at home right now?"

"No. I'm at Target. In Oxnard." She paused. "I mean, I work here, so I'm at work, but I'm on a break."

"Oh. I thought you worked at that restaurant?"

"I do. Being independent isn't cheap. Hey, my break is over soon, so cut to the chase."

"I'm stranded in Ventura with no money for gas."

"And?"

He rolled his eyes. "Can you . . . help me?"

"I don't have any money for gas, either."

"Do you have a credit card or something?" Kyle asked. "Maybe you could give it to the guy here over the phone and I could fill up. I'd pay you back."

She laughed her famous annoyed laugh, the one he'd

been hearing since Megan turned twelve. "No, Kyle, I do not have a credit card or something. As you may recall."

Right. When Megan had left home, she'd made a show of handing their parents a stack of halved bank cards and store cards and made a big speech about how she wanted to take care of herself, was sick of watching the family and the business get deeper and deeper into debt, didn't want to be a part of it. Kyle felt a pang of guilt now over all the car washes and fill-ups and fast food.

"Listen," she continued, "if you can wait about two hours I can come bring you a few bucks after work to get you home. But why don't you just call Dad? Also, what are you doing in Ventura?"

"Two *hours*?" He switched his phone to his other ear. "His card got declined. I don't want to ask him."

Megan sighed. "Are things that bad? Why doesn't Mom get a freaking *job* instead of giving free labor to Baker and Najarian?"

"She's doing her design consulting . . . and stuff." He'd almost said "on the side."

"I'm sure. Kyle, I really have to go. Do you want to wait, or . . . ?"

He knew at this point that his after/during school wanderings were over—after today, he'd either have to come clean or disappear in ways that didn't cost anything. Might as well see his sister while he had the chance, given that she never came home anymore.

"Yeah, I'll wait."

"Text me where you are. I don't have to work at the restaurant tonight, and I think I have some money left on a gift card to one of those 'casual American dining' places you love so much. We can split a gross dinner. See you later."

"See you," he said. "And . . . thanks."

She'd already hung up.

With time to kill, he couldn't stop himself from texting Emily, even if it did mean he was a pain in the ass.

how DO you feel about schnitzel with noodles? Favorite thing y/n

He didn't even wait for a reply before continuing:

I'm having dinner with Megan later and thinking about telling her about my mom even though I'm not supposed to.

She replied right away to that.

Yes, you should!!! she's your sister!!

Had she been right there at her phone for all his texts but didn't care enough to reply until this one?

But like I wish *I* didn't know. why would I put that on her?

A long pause.

(like I did to you), he added.

More pausing.

Never mind, I'm sorry

He waited and waited for a reply, restrained himself from adding even more. There weren't even typing bubbles. *Come on, Emily!*

His brain took a long soak in a hot bath of anxiety, thinking about Emily being sick of him, Nadia waiting for her chance to tell him off, the team seeing him as a traitor. His mother wanting a life, and Kyle and his dad not being enough of one.

No gas, no money, no team, no girlfriend. No response from Emily to soothe the feeling that he was spinning through space, untethered, yet at the same time completely stuck.

He white-knuckled it until Megan could come save him.

Did you tell her?

Finally. The relief of the text from Emily took about a thousand pounds off his shoulders. She was the one person he could confide in, and he needed that to be all good.

He and Megan had finished their club sandwich and fries, and she'd ordered them a slice of lemon meringue pie before excusing herself to the bathroom. And no, he hadn't said anything about their parents. It wasn't like she could do anything about it, and it would only make her more furious at their mom than she already was. Megan had been mad at her for about five years for no specific reason that Kyle was aware of. His dad had once told him, "Teen girls and their moms. It's just how it is." But Taylor had always gotten along okay with their mom, so that didn't quite explain it.

Still undecided, he replied.

"Who are you texting?" Megan slid back into the booth. "Nadia?"

"Emily."

"Who?"

"Emily Emily. Our cousin?"

"I didn't know you guys were that tight."

He shrugged and put his phone facedown on the table. "If you would ever come back to the farm, you'd know. You'd know a lot of stuff."

"Like, what do you talk about?"

Her big-sister interrogation tone made him want to tell her exactly nothing. "Random stuff."

The look on Megan's face reminded him of their dad, how he'd be when he knew you weren't telling him the whole story, lips kind of pressed together and eyebrows up. "You know," she said, "cousins used to get married all the time. Back in ye olden days."

He'd been taking a sip of water. A little went down his windpipe; he had a coughing fit.

"They say we're attracted to people who look like us,"

Megan said. "It's science." The waiter came over and set the pie down, with two forks. When he was gone, she continued, "Emily is cute. Though I think she's probably gay."

"Okay, this conversation is over. Seriously, dude."

Megan cackled and dug into the pie. "I'm just messing with you. It's one of the few things I miss about home."

"Um, okay, thanks."

She pointed her fork at him. "This pie is actually not the worst. Have some."

He took a few bites. "Also, she's not gay."

"How do *you* know?"

"She told me. She's like . . . I don't know. She's not really into guys or girls."

"Asexual? Aromantic? Gray-asexual-nonromantic? With a thing for cousins?"

"*Oh* my god, please stop."

"But giving you shit is my love language." She took another bite. "Seriously, though, that's cool that Emily shared that with you."

"Yeah, and she's kind of private about it, at least with the family, so."

"Got it."

He ate more of the pie. "I was thinking I should get a job."

"Don't sound so bummed. Working is good. I love

earning my own money, even though it's barely enough. Would it interfere with baseball, though?"

Might as well tell her. Everyone was going to figure it out anyway when they realized he hadn't played a game in weeks. "I'm not doing baseball anymore."

She put down her fork and pointed to her face. "My mouth is literally agape. *While* I'm talking. And eating. It's a skill."

"No one knows," he continued. "I mean, Mom and Dad don't. That's how I ended up here today. I just kind of drive around during practice time. I haven't actually quit, but I'm pretty sure I'm fired. I mean, I *know* I am. I just haven't gone in to talk to Coach Ito."

"But you've always had baseball. That's *you*. That's your thing."

"Not anymore."

"Why? Did something happen?"

"Not really." If he went too far down this path, he might end up peeling back the lid on the whole stinking mess of everything. "I should get home."

"Well, now I'm worried about you," Megan said. "You love baseball."

He did. He had. The smell of the glove, grass. The sound and feel of hitting or catching a ball. He and Coop turning a perfect double play, his body running on instinct instead of thought.

"I guess I miss it." The confession sort of surprised him. That he said it aloud and that he felt it at all. He'd been almost successfully stifling every emotion that tried to rear its head.

"You said you haven't really quit?"

"I'm supposed to talk to Ito. He keeps calling me." He rubbed his face. "I don't know. I don't know what I want. I'm going through a thing. It's hard to explain. Don't tell Mom or Dad I haven't been going. Or Taylor or anyone."

"Don't worry, Taylor's too wrapped up in her own life to pay any attention to me right now."

Kyle rarely talked to Taylor either, unless she was right in front of his face. Not that they didn't get along, but like Megan said, she seemed totally consumed by being at school and trying to be the best college student in the history of ever.

"And I don't talk to Mom," Megan added.

"Are you ever going to again?"

She dragged her fork through the last of the pie. "Someday, probably."

"What about the farm this summer? Are you coming?"

"No."

"But—"

"Most families have a reunion like every ten years, Kyle, not every single summer plus, like, five holidays or family events every year. I can miss some."

"So you'll come in ten years?"

"Sure."

The way she said it—a throwaway, a kind of "Who cares?"—stung. Also she was so sure there'd *be* a family to get together within ten years. "Okay. So, thanks for bailing me out at the gas station. And for dinner."

"I'm glad you called. You don't have to be such a stranger."

"Really, Megan? You're the one who left."

"I know. I just need a break from the whole . . ." She made circles with her hands. "Baker *thing*."

"What is the whole Baker thing?"

"You know," she said with a shrug.

"No?"

"Keeping up appearances, playing it safe, never getting too close to anything uncomfortable. Come on, Kyle."

"Oh." He didn't really know what any of that meant in the context of his family, other than what was happening right now, which Megan didn't even know about. Was he an idiot? Had he been completely misreading his life this whole time?

"I like *you*, though," Megan said brightly.

"Lucky me." He got out of the booth and zipped up his jacket.

She grabbed his wrist. "Don't leave mad, Kyle. I'm super happy I got to see you. I'm sorry you got stranded because of Mom and Dad not dealing with their bills. You have to start making your own life so that their problems don't drag you down, okay?"

Kyle tried to pull his wrist away gently; she squeezed harder.

"Get a job, do your own thing. Baseball or not. Actually, I think you need baseball. Can you talk to Ito? I know he's a hardass, but I bet if you groveled, tell him you need it, he'll give you another chance. Even if it means you're benched for a while."

More like the whole season, knowing Coach and knowing how badly Kyle had screwed up with the team.

"You can be happy, Kyle," she continued. "Even if Mom and Dad aren't."

Did she know something he didn't know she knew? She was swinging his arm like they were holding hands. He thought about blurting out the question, "Do you know Mom is screwing around?" He couldn't.

"Okay," he said. "You can let go now."

She released him.

It didn't look like there was anyone home when he got there, but maybe an hour later, when he was at his desk doing homework, there was a knock on the door.

"Kyle?"

His dad. He came in and sat on the bed. He had on

a Baker & Najarian polo. "Can I talk to you about something real quick?"

"Is 'no' an option?"

"Funny. No."

He seemed nervous. Was this it? The divorce announcement?

"There was bit of a mix-up," he said. "At the bank, with some of our credit cards."

Kyle's face got hot; he had to look away. So embarrassing that this was happening again, the money thing. Only they'd never had their cards cut off before.

"So hold off on using them for a while."

"Okay."

He stretched one leg out, dug into his pocket. "Here's some cash if you need it. Let me know if you need more, but maybe, you know, maybe kind of try to make it last." He got halfway off the bed, tossed a few folded twenties on Kyle's desk. "Until we figure out what the heck is going on at the bank."

"I was thinking about getting a job anyway."

"Hey, it's not that bad. You don't have to do that."

"Why is it so bad to have a job? Megan has two."

His dad looked startled at that. "You talk to Megan?"

"Sometimes. Don't worry. Not about that." *Quality father-and-son time here.* "Anyway, jobs look good on college applications."

"What about ball?"

He shrugged. "I can fit in a day or two a week of working. Other guys do." He didn't actually know if this was true of anyone on the team, but it sounded plausible in theory.

It could have been Kyle's imagination, but his dad seemed relieved. "All right, well, keep me posted." He got up and put his hands in his pockets, rocking on his heels. "Megan has two jobs now? Is she doing okay?"

"Yeah. She's fine." Kyle stared down at his history book, took in a quick breath. Before he could change his mind, he asked, "Who's the guy?"

"What?"

"Who's the guy?" he repeated. "Mom's . . . guy."

His dad stopped rocking. "You don't know him."

How could he be sure about that? "Do you?"

"It's not anything you have to worry about."

"I'm not *worried*. I'm just asking." He forced himself to look his dad in the face. "It's not fair. For her to be living here like it's not happening. For you to have to act like . . ."

Now it was his dad's turn to get red. Kyle could see his hands in his pockets, balled into fists. "It's between me and Mom."

"No, it's not!"

His father took his hands out, held them up. "I'm sorry. Honestly, when I told you, I thought she was close to leaving. Leaving us. I thought you were going to find out anyway."

Kyle nearly flinched at the words, a painful zap to the brain. "*Actually*, when you told me, you said you were waiting it out. You didn't say she was close to leaving."

His dad rubbed his hand over his head, the way he did when he was figuring out how to tell a client about another missed deadline on a project.

"Which is it?" Kyle asked. "Which one is the lie? Or maybe I should ask . . . is anything *not* a lie?"

There it was, the anger that Kyle had only allowed himself to see in himself sideways so far.

"We're not going to talk about this anymore right now. I'm sorry. I'm really, really sorry." His father tapped the money on the desk. "Let me know if this isn't enough."

As soon as the door closed, Kyle said, "You suck, Dad," hoping his dad heard him through the door.

He had unanswered texts from Emily and Nadia and Megan, and he hadn't finished his homework. He turned off his phone, turned off the lights, and crawled into bed with his clothes on.

5

COACH ITO swam laps in the pool every morning, legendary for being there at five thirty a.m., Monday through Friday. The story was that no one in the history of his employment at the school, student or faculty, had ever gotten there before him—not even his wife, who worked there a few days a week. So Kyle knew he would be in his office in the locker room by seven, in his red windbreaker and white shorts, literally the only outfit anyone at school had seen him wear.

Kyle tapped on the office door, but Coach had already seen him through the glass. He waved him in and took off his reading glasses. No hello, no how've you been, just, "Okay, Baker, what's your story? Please make it interesting."

He hadn't exactly thought through what to say. He knew if he obsessed about it too much beforehand, he'd never do it, because of the way Coach was looking at him right now with that skeptical and annoyed thing that was his permanent expression. Ito might have the body of a man half his age from all that swimming, but his face always said, *I'm too old for this shit.*

"Um, I know I've missed—"

"Are you really going to lurk in the doorway for this whole conversation? Sit down."

Kyle stepped into the office and sat in the chair across from Coach, the desk between them. For a guy who kept his workout routine so tidy, his desk was a mess. There were three half-full coffee mugs, a blackening banana peel, stacks of forms, a couple of jerseys. Kyle set his backpack at his feet.

"Well, I mean, I know I'm benched for games, but—"

"Yes. And we're doing fine without you. Ellison stepped up."

Kyle nodded. "Yeah, that's good."

"That's lucky. What if he hadn't, Baker? What if we hadn't had depth?"

He didn't have an answer for that, and Ito knew it. "I was wondering," he said, forging ahead, "if I could come back just to practice and work out?"

"You skipped over the interesting part," Coach said. He picked up one of the mugs, looked into it, grimaced, and set it back down.

"I know I screwed up. I'm really sorry." He tried to think of everything he was supposed to say. "I let you down, I let the team down. I didn't show leadership, and my excuses were flimsy."

"But what *happened*, Baker? In your life? In over twenty years of doing this, I've never had a guy with a starting position just drop out and not have a reason."

Hell if Kyle was going to sit there and tell Coach Ito about his family falling apart. They did not have some father-son *Friday Night Lights* kind of relationship. He shrugged. "It's personal, I guess."

"That's disappointing. And not interesting at all." Coach rolled his chair back and put his feet up on the desk. He was wearing pool slides. His toenails were short and smooth. "I'm probably supposed to teach you a lesson. Make you run laps, be the equipment boy, scrub the locker room toilets with a toothbrush. But I don't care. I'm not into that macho humiliation bullshit. It's high school. Baseball is supposed to be fun. It's a game, okay? I know I've got a reputation for being a son of a bitch, but that's only when it comes to playing the game hard and winning. Because winning is more fun than losing, and I want to have fun."

Parts of this speech were familiar, but now Kyle heard them as promising and started to get excited despite himself.

"But like you said yourself, you know you can't play in the games. Ellison is doing great and that wouldn't be fair to him, and I can't send that message to the rest of the team. Not now, and not in the future and not in the past. That their showing up and my showing up and all the showing up in the history of the team doesn't matter, and commitment is optional."

Even though he'd known this would be the outcome, Kyle couldn't help but be hurt as it sank in what a mess he'd made. This speech, and the shame and guilt it made him feel, was what he'd been avoiding.

He nodded. "I get it."

"And I'm not sure what you hope to get out of working out with us for the rest of the season when no one on the team wants to see your face right now. We can't use you at practice or scrimmage because we need to keep our game-day team warm, and you're not on it."

I said I get it.

"However," Coach continued, "you can try showing up to conditioning workouts in the gym, see how that goes.

And maybe you'll be in a position to reclaim a starting spot again next year if you do me a favor."

"Oh, yeah, anything."

"Don't be so sure. The district wants to implement this mentoring program with the elementary schools next year. Fifth graders." He shuffled through papers on his desk and pulled one out, reading aloud. "They want to make 'the transition to middle school easier.' Not like one-on-one big-brother stuff, but bringing some high schoolers into the mix with their after-school activities. It's all supervised. They want to try it out on a smaller scale before they make it official. I assume they thought, hey, let's pair athletes with athletes. And nerds with nerds, I guess, down the line, but I don't know, they only told me so much. I'm just a dumb coach, and the school district in all its wisdom didn't ask for my advice. But of course they want me to *do* something. Anyway, you could go hang out with the Jackson Elementary team once a week, maybe twice. At their practices."

"Fifth graders? They have a team?"

"Well, no, 'team' is the wrong word. It's just an after-school activity for any kids who want to. My buddy Greg is a history teacher there, and he put it together."

"So, more babysitting than coaching?" This wasn't what Kyle wanted or expected. It sounded like a punishment to Kyle. He'd rather run laps or drag the buckets of balls out for practice every day.

"A little coaching," Ito said. "Mentoring. Helping out. Cheering them on. These aren't exactly elite athletes."

"Does it pay?" Kyle asked.

Coach took his feet off the desk and leaned forward. "No, it doesn't pay, Baker, what the hell do you think being a mentor is? You do it because it's a good thing to do. And as a favor to me to get you off my shit list."

The goal here had been to put something in his life back the way it used to be, not to add a whole new thing.

"I'm taking your silence as a yes," Coach said. "I'll email you the details later."

All Kyle could do was nod and say, "Can I come work out this afternoon? With the team?"

"No. We've been going hard and I called a rest day. Come tomorrow."

"Yep, okay." He got his backpack and ducked out.

"You're welcome, Baker," Coach called after him.

When he came out of the locker room, Nadia was waiting, leaning against the wall.

She looked extra pretty with her dark hair down and wavy, messy instead of ironed out and sleek. Either way, any way, she'd be beautiful. But today it really hit him.

"You can't escape," she said. "I got here early to run around the track with Hailey and saw your car."

The first words out of his mouth were "I'm sorry." He braced himself for what he deserved.

"Don't look so scared, Kyle." She put her hand on his waist, pulled it back. "I just want to know what *happened*. I know it's not something I did. I *know* that. So what is it? What's so awful you couldn't talk to me?"

"It wasn't you," he said, wanting so bad to reach for her hand, but afraid to.

"Like, we talked every day and told each other everything for months? You told me you loved me? Then you weren't there and there wasn't any warning or reason or . . . You could have said, 'Hey, I'm going through something and need some space.' You could have said, 'Let's take a break.' That would have been shitty and selfish, but you didn't even do that." The hallway was getting busier, people were sneaking glances at them. Nadia's eyes remained fixed on his.

"You dodge me in class and around school like a coward. Where do you even go at lunch? Everyone's asking me what's up, and I have no answer. Cooper and Mateo come up to me all 'Why is Kyle bailing on baseball?' and I'm like, 'Kyle bailed on *baseball*?' and you don't even . . ." Her eyes welled up. "You left me. We built this whole you-and-me thing, and then you disappeared."

Hearing her lay out all the things that he knew were true, that he'd avoided thinking about for weeks, was like getting sandblasted. Every little rough edge of denial blew off, and what remained was the clean, smooth reality that he could have and should have turned to her instead of shutting her out.

Maybe it wasn't too late, maybe they could go somewhere and talk and he could fix this.

"Nadia, I—"

"And now I don't trust you."

The bell rang.

Without trust, there was nothing, no chance. The reality of what he was losing, what had already been lost, crashed down in an avalanche of pain that made him hurt everywhere. Limbs, gut, head.

"So this is our breakup," Nadia said.

He leaned agains the lockers, letting his head bang softly against the metal. "Are you sure?"

"Don't do that, Kyle. Don't." She took a step away from him. The traffic in the hall had thinned out. "Don't avoid me for weeks and make me chase you down and say all that and now all of a sudden be back in."

"Sorry, I'm sorry." She was right. And so much braver than him, tougher. He found a scrap of courage in himself and asked, in a whisper, "Can we hug?"

She nodded, wiping a tear away, and reached up to put her arms around his neck and shoulders. He slid his around her waist, found the solid expanse of her back.

He couldn't believe he'd let this happen.

They were both crying. "I'm sorry," he said again, into her hair. "I'm sorry I'm sorry I'm sorry."

He let her go.

After they said goodbye, he knew he was cutting the rest of the day. He wrote himself a note about an appointment and signed his dad's name, dropped it at the office, and headed off to his parking spot under the tree.

6

FOLLOWING HIS mom didn't feel like a decision so much as fate: going early to talk to Ito led to the Nadia reckoning, which led to cutting school, which led to Kyle going to the beach for the morning to cry, then to eating tacos in his car at lunch in the parking lot of the big shopping center near his house because there wasn't really anywhere else to go that wouldn't use too much gas.

He was still beating up his already raw heart for all the wrong steps he'd taken with Nadia when he recognized his mom's car, parked in the next row. The city might be crawling with white Avalons, but only his mom's had the

Baker & Najarian license-plate frame.

In itself, seeing her car wasn't a big deal. This was the Vons where they did their shopping. This was the Starbucks his sisters would go to when they lived at home. These were the food places they'd grab takeout from on busy weeknights. Now, though, every movement of his mom's seemed relevant in a new way.

He slid down in the front seat and waited. It felt like forever before she came into view with a single bag of groceries in one arm and her phone up to her ear. Laughing. Smiling. Two things she hadn't done at home in Kyle's recent memory. She got into her car and backed up, then Kyle started his.

Maybe she was just going home. Going home with some groceries in the middle of the day, no big deal. But from her very first turn out of the lot, in the opposite of the usual direction, he knew she wasn't.

Maybe another errand. Maybe a different grocery store for the special gluten-free bread she liked.

Following another car wasn't as easy in real life as it looked on TV. People constantly changing lanes and turning made it hard to keep at least one car between them, and then he missed a light and got behind for a few blocks. Next, he ran a yellow light to keep it from happening again, sure that his mom would spot him. Except she was on the phone the entire time. Which was illegal.

"Come on, Mom," he muttered. Did she follow *any* rules anymore?

When she turned down a neighborhood street, he stayed farther back.

"What are you even doing?" This time, he was asking himself. With few other cars on the road, she would realize she was being followed, and then what? He pictured her face, defensive, when she'd said, "I'm allowed to have a life."

She made another turn; he let himself lose her, then pulled over to park and turned off the engine.

She existed. His mother existed, outside of their family as well as inside of it. Just like how Kyle kept existing when he was running from Nadia, ditching the team, trying to figure out his own deal.

It seemed obvious, that people existed outside of how you needed them to. But it didn't feel obvious.

A tap on his car window nearly made him jump out of his skin. A woman, probably around his mom's age, smiled at him through the glass. A pretty smile. Her blond hair was pulled back into one of those little knots at her neck. He lowered his window.

"Are you my one thirty?" she asked. "I thought I got here early enough to beat you."

He looked around and saw he'd been parked in front of a small yellow house for sale.

"No, I'm just . . ." Stalking someone? Following my cheating mom around? "I had to pull over to answer my phone."

"Good for you."

"My mom drilled it into me." Ironic. "You're . . . a Realtor? You're showing that house?"

"I am."

He had an urge to see it. He'd always liked tagging along with his dad on reno projects. He liked the actual work—especially when his dad let him sledgehammer walls—but most of it was the pull of stepping into someone else's world, seeing how they lived, from what kind of furniture they sat on to the coats in their closet. All these people, existing, with lives as real as his.

"I'm not, like, in the market for a house or anything, but could I see the inside?"

She bent down to get a better look at him. "Sure. I've got about ten minutes before my appointment." She held up her phone. "Just going to grab a picture of you and your license plate to send to my colleagues, okay?"

"Oh, right."

He got out of the car and stood for the picture, then she led him up the walk. She had on jeans and a long, loose cardigan, low-heeled boots. "The fact that you want to see it means the curb appeal is working, right?" she said as she got the key out of the lockbox.

"Definitely." The house had a front garden that looked overgrown but not out of control—wild pretty, not wild neglected. The door and trim were painted glossy white, cheerful and inviting against the yellow of the rest of the house.

"I'm Dawn, by the way. Coldwell Banker."

"Kyle. Baker. Of Baker and Najarian." He hoped throwing that in would make him seem less like a kid cutting school and more like a junior contractor who had a right and a reason to be scoping out houses.

"Oh, I've seen your trucks around town." She held up the key. "I've only shown this house once. I can practice my spiel on you."

"Go for it."

She smiled, put on her salesperson face. "Okay. This home has had only two owners. The current owners have done a lot of upgrades."

When they went in, the first thing Kyle noticed was the light. Bright but soft, no glare. From the front door you could see straight through to the backyard, which was the same wild pretty as the front, and had a round table and two chairs on a small patio.

"It's not huge," Dawn continued, "compared to some of the newer houses around here. But the space has been well thought out."

He hadn't even noticed the size, though now that

she mentioned it, yeah, it was tiny. A person could feel wrapped up in this house, versus bouncing around like a loose pinball, which was how he felt lately at his.

Dawn jingled the keys in her hand. "I probably shouldn't point out how small it is first thing, right? I just figure people will notice."

"I think they'll notice the light first."

"During the day, yes, that's true."

He took a few more steps in. The front room opened up into the kitchen, with wooden cabinetry painted that same glossy white, and butcher block countertops. The appliances were white, too. So different from the granite and stainless steel most of his dad's clients wanted.

"It's so . . . like, happy," he said.

"I'm glad to hear you say that. I agree. It's a cheerful little house. I'm hoping a young couple or maybe some empty nesters or a single person with maybe a kid or a dog will fall in love with it."

Empty nesters. That would be his parents soon. Or maybe they'd become single people before that even happened. He imagined his dad, a single person with maybe a kid—aka Kyle.

"So are *you* the Baker of Baker and Najarian?" Her smile was so steady.

"It's my dad," Kyle said.

"Ah, I figured."

"Both my parents, actually. And their partner is the Najarian. In summers I work with them on some stuff. Nothing like this, though. More new construction and McMansion remodels." He stood in front of the French doors that led to the back garden. If he had a business like his parents', he'd rather work on this kind of place.

"If you have a card, I'm always looking for contractors to recommend to clients."

"Not on me," he said.

"Well, I'll probably remember."

He turned the lock on the French doors and opened them up. Sun warmed the garden without making it too hot, and he realized he was standing on wooden planks. He turned to Dawn, who was in the doorway, smiling that smile as cheerful as the house. "There's no concrete," he said, "so it won't get scorching out here even in the afternoons. You should tell that to buyers."

"Nine out of ten of them will want to tear out this wood and pour concrete rather than maintain and condition the wood."

"They shouldn't."

"Hey, I wish you could buy this house," she said.

Here in the sun, he could now see the fine lines around her lips that were a tiny bit red from her lipstick, the only makeup she wore that he could tell. He looked at her freckled collarbone, and her hands, and their short, unpainted fingernails. Wild pretty.

If he could look at this person his mom's age and see the attraction, be drawn to her, it shouldn't be that much of a stretch to imagine an actual grown-up guy falling for his mom—seeing her across a room, or bumping into her at a coffee shop, and wanting to be closer to her.

But . . . his mom was his mom. She belonged to *him*, to him and his dad and his sisters. Or, belonged not *to* them, but *with* them. Right? Wasn't that how it worked?

Dawn touched his back, lightly. "Are you okay?"

He swallowed. "I'm only in this neighborhood because I was trying to follow my mom," he said in a rush. "Because I think she was . . . I don't know . . ." *Going to her boyfriend's house.*

The doorbell rang, and Kyle realized what he was saying to a total stranger. Dawn's smile had fallen. He couldn't tell if it was in a kind and concerned way, or a why-are-you-telling-me-this? way. "Hold that thought."

He didn't want to hold that thought. He wanted that thought to go away.

She reached into her back pocket. "Here's my card if you want to send along any information about your parents' company. Like I said, I'm always looking for people to recommend."

"Yeah," he said, taking it.

She was already walking to the door. An older man came in, dark skin, blue cardigan. An empty nester or a single dad or a guy with a dog? This time, Dawn started her pitch by talking about the light. While she showed the bedrooms, Kyle slipped out, closing the cheerful white door behind him.

He got a little lost driving out of the neighborhood and wound up spotting his mom's car a couple of blocks away from the yellow house, parked right in a driveway. If she was trying to hide something, she wasn't doing a great job.

He passed it by, drove a few more blocks, hands tight on the wheel. *Who cares. Who even cares.*

Maybe the person in the house who belonged to the driveway wasn't the guy. Maybe it was a client. Or one of her lady friends. Maybe they were in there drinking coffee and complaining about their families and how all they wanted was to get away from their dumb husbands and annoying kids, shouting, "I'm allowed to have a life!" and clinking mugs.

He pulled over and turned on his phone, tapped on his text thread with Emily.

My mom's car is parked in a driveway and I think it's the guy's driveway. I followed her.

Seconds passed, a minute. More nothing.

He tried Megan. **I obeyed you and talked to Ito. No dice for this season. Maybe next season but now I have to coach kids. hope ur happy**

Another minute. He felt forgotten.

where are you??? he sent to Emily.

Screw it. He drove back to the house where his mom's car was and parked half a block down, behind a Dumpster. He could just barely see the front door. He whisper-sang "Do-Re-Mi," and on the third "That will bring us back to do-oh-oh-oh," the door opened and his mother stepped out. She looked up and down the street. Either he was hidden enough or she wasn't thinking to look for *him*. Probably scoping for a nosy neighbor or something.

Then the door opened wider. A man—tall and thin and bald, a basic-looking white guy—put his hand on Kyle's mother's shoulder. She reached up and touched it with her own. The man seemed to pull her back inside, into the shadowy entryway, and Kyle lost sight of them. When they reemerged, they were laughing. They were playful, pushing and pulling at each other.

He recognized what it was, and the reality of it was a fist to the stomach. It's one thing to know it. Another to see it.

The chime of his phone made him jump.

I'm in school

Oh, right. School. He wanted more from Emily anyway, like an are you okay, or commentary on him following his mom. She didn't give it. When he looked back up, his mom's car was driving down the street in the opposite direction. The front door was closed and now he noticed the number painted next to it: 936. He sat there for the longest time, waiting for Emily or Megan or anyone to release him from this staring contest with a house.

No one came through. He started the car and got out of there, making a note of the street sign when he passed the corner. Snowdrop Lane. Even the name of the dumb street pissed him off. It never snowed here, and never would, and it sounded like something from a kids' fairy tale and not from a nightmare of home wrecking and lies.

7

HE WENT back to the shopping center, thinking he should pick up some job applications. Start making his own gas money. And also maybe get out of this coaching-kids thing. If he said his family needed the money, Ito couldn't do anything about that.

He sat in his car to fill them out but couldn't concentrate.

That look on Nadia's face. *And now I don't trust you.*

Coop flipping him off the other day, telling him he was shit.

Ito being all "You know you can't play in the games."

Text me when you're done with school, he wrote to Emily.

He waited for her reply. Filled out the easy parts of the applications. Walked around the perimeter of the parking lot. When he'd killed as much time as he possibly could and texted Emily twice more, he went home, where the house had that empty, depressing, four-thirty feeling.

Where did his mom go after she left the guy's house? To the Baker & Najarian offices like everything was normal?

Back when Taylor and Megan still lived at home, his parents had kept this calendar in the kitchen and a magnetic notepad on the fridge. Everyone wrote in their plans and left notes about where they were. That had all stopped. Maybe they thought Kyle didn't mind, that he could just take care of himself.

He looked through the refrigerator, hungry again after the small street tacos, but there wasn't anything to eat unless you counted condiments. *Hey, Mom, maybe pick up some food for us while you're buying groceries for your boyfriend?* In the pantry, he found a few bags of pasta with a handful left in each. There was also a jar of nacho cheese sauce. He put a pot of water on the stove and cranked up the heat on the big stainless gas range. Kyle and his dad had done this whole kitchen together last summer, to his mom's exact specs. White granite on the island and countertops, travertine tile, new appliances, including the massive stainless-and-glass range hood that loomed over him now.

What was the point? Why did his mom ask for this specific kitchen if she didn't want to be in it with them?

Still no replies from Megan or Emily. He put his phone on the counter and tried not to look at it. He got a bowl and a spoon and stuck the jar of cheese into the microwave, and then dumped his random assortment of penne, linguine, and shells into the boiling water. He heard the garage door. That meant his mom, because his dad parked his truck on the street. Kyle's heart sped up.

You already knew, he reminded himself. *What you saw today, you already knew.*

She came in through the door that led from the mudroom to the kitchen. Her hair was damp, and she had on leggings and a long T-shirt.

"Hey, sweetie." She kissed him on the cheek. He pulled back. "I was just at the gym."

Go visit the boyfriend for a quickie, then head to the gym to clean up and change out of the adultery clothes. Maybe somewhere in there go to the office. She had a whole system.

"Are you not talking to me?" she asked, leaning against the granite he'd helped install just for her.

"Not really. What am I supposed to say?"

"Say whatever you want. I'm still your mom. I still love you."

"Well I don't love you," he said, stirring the pasta.

He scooped out a piece of penne: undercooked. Then a strand of linguine: perfect, and about to be overcooked. He didn't want to look at her and see that what he said had hurt. Kind of couldn't believe he'd said it.

"I understand that you feel, right now, that you don't love me." She didn't sound hurt at all. She sounded calm and reasonable. Like his mom. "I would still rather you talk to me than not talk to me." She paused. "What are you making?"

"A big ball of gluten and dairy. You wouldn't like it."

"I eat the way I eat because it makes me feel better, not because I don't *like* gluten and dairy."

"I'm only having this because there's nothing else."

She walked behind him and opened the fridge with the obvious intent of proving him wrong. "Oh," she said.

"Yep."

He drained his pasta before it all turned to mush, stirred in the nacho sauce, and scraped it into his bowl.

"I'm making a grocery list," she said, typing into her phone. "Any special requests?"

He imagined her asking the guy the same thing before she went to the store earlier. *Any special requests?* Maybe she had two lists on her phone. One for him, one for home.

"No."

"Kyle, come on."

"Just whatever," he said, and sat at the island. "I don't care."

"Okay, then. Bon appétit," she said, before heading down the hall toward Megan's old room. What was she going to do when Taylor was home from finals in a few weeks?

The kitchen seemed to throb with loneliness. Kyle's dinner now struck him as disgusting enough to take a picture of and send to Emily.

#masterchef

That got her to reply at last.

WHAT IS THAT

He hovered his thumbs, wanting to ask, *Where were you? Are you sick of me and my problems?* Instead, he went with: **dinner obvi**

BTW, she wrote. **Sorry about earlier. I was in class, then study group and then we did a practice SAT and I wanted to wait until I could pay full attention bc . . . YOU SAW YOUR MOM'S BOYFRIEND. are you ok?**

Kyle exhaled. The lonely and forgotten feeling he'd had all day started to dissipate.

I don't know. I think I'm starting to get in touch with my anger.

Nice, she replied, with a devil emoji.

Not sure I like it, he said.

Yet again, Emily's eternal pause.

His shoveled in a few spoonfuls of the mass of orange undercooked-overcooked pasta. Then felt a jolt of pain again when he thought about Nadia saying "Now I don't trust you." Is this how it would be? Her words coming out of nowhere? And now, also visions of her body the first time he'd seen her all the way naked on a green comforter in her room, soft and rounded and golden.

He punched himself lightly on the thigh. *Stop.* Then harder. *You asshole.*

"Okay," he said aloud. "Okay."

He ate more of his neon dinner. Jiggled his leg fast. Scarfed down the pasta and pulled up a video of the barn-raising dance scene from *Seven Brides for Seven Brothers* and propped his phone against the empty fruit bowl on the counter. He needed every available trick for escaping the accusing voice in his head.

The part where the brothers stole the girls away from the uptight dudes in suits used to make him laugh. The dancing style was kind of dumb and there was all this big exaggerated winking, and the whole thing had struck him as funny. Then one time Emily pointed out that the guys were treating the women like property or something and the scene didn't really get good until the women starting getting to choose who they danced with, and the guys were showing off for them and trying to get them to choose rather than just yanking them around the dance floor. "Rape Culture: The Musical," Emily called it once.

He liked was how strong those dancing dudes were, though. The girls, too. Doing cartwheels and jumping on and off tables and hopping around on what was basically a balance beam, all while holding axes. It was pretty badass, and the ridiculous and acrobatic musical number was just what he needed. The sounds and images on his phone pushed the ones in his head out until they seemed far away, something seen through the small end of a telescope.

When it was over, he rinsed out his bowl and the pot and put them in the dishwasher. His phone chimed again. He dove for it.

Did you see the wife and kid? Emily asked.

It took him a second to understand. The wife and kid of his mother's boyfriend. No, he hadn't seen them, and he hadn't even thought about them. Wow, he really was an asshole. Now he wondered what their names were, and if the husband and wife got along and thought everything was fine, or if they'd found out in the time since Kyle's dad had told him what was happening and now they were living like Kyle's family was. Or if it was something in between, if the wife or the kid or both had a sense that something was wrong but didn't know for sure that their lives were in the process of shattering.

Just the guy and the house.

Also I talked to Nadia today. it's definitely over.

He read over his own text, feeling the defeat.

This one time during his sophomore year, when Ito was trying him out on varsity, a game near the end of the season had gone into an eleventh inning. Coach Ito had stuck Kyle out in right field for most of the game, and then they were at bat in the bottom half of the inning and Kyle was at the plate with two outs, their last chance to score with the opposing team one up. He had a headache from being hungry and thirsty and having been outside for four hours in the ninety-degree afternoon. As he stood at the plate, he decided, just decided, he was going to strike out so the eternal, frustrating, hot game could come to an end and he could get into his mom's air-conditioned car and get shakes at the drive-through like they always did after a game.

He'd swung at three terrible pitches in a row, and it was over and his team lost and all he felt was relief.

"You didn't even fight for it, Baker," Ito had said, shaking his head as Kyle made the walk from home plate to the dugout. "You just gave up."

That was exactly what he'd done with Nadia.

He heard the front door open and close, and a few seconds later his dad was in the kitchen and Kyle looked at him and knew the truth. He and his dad, they were both quitters. Cowards. They could do hard things, to a point. Demo and rebuild a kitchen: sure. Load a quarter ton of rocks, one at a time, onto a trailer and unload them, one at a time, at a customer's house for a custom landscape job: no problem.

But when it came to stuff like . . . those moments you really really needed to be understood but were also afraid of it, or you wanted to say what you actually meant without getting laughed at, or you felt like if you didn't grab onto someone, you might fall off the planet and go spinning into space all alone . . . that kind of hard stuff—well, they sucked at it.

"Hey," his dad asked, then did a double take. "You're looking at me funny. Any chance that has something to do with the call I got from school about that note you forged? I said that I signed it to avoid a hassle, but don't do that again."

Avoiding a hassle was his dad's entire approach to life in a nutshell. "You're not even fighting for it."

"What?"

Kyle's frustration surged. "You're giving up. With Mom. You're going to let it all fall apart."

"Kyle." His dad held up his hand, daring him to say one more word. "You're way too young to have the remotest idea how complicated this is."

"Complicated" was a cop-out word Kyle noticed adults using whenever they couldn't rationally explain their dumb opinions or actions.

"Me and Nadia broke up. I let it fall apart. And now—"

"Don't compare a thirty-year marriage to a high school crush." His dad opened the fridge and, guess what, still no food. He closed it again. "It's been a bad day, and I'm not in a frame of mind to talk about this or be accused of giving up. I'm not the one out there screwing around."

"But what are you *doing* about it?" Kyle knew he was pushing.

"I'm trying to keep the goddamn bills paid here, is what. That's *all* I have to give at the moment, and if you want something more out of this conversation, too damn bad." He rubbed his face. He turned in a circle in the kitchen. "I'm starving."

Kyle could have said he'd seen a can of tuna in the back of the pantry. That there were crackers on the high shelf. But why couldn't his dad even face a little obstacle like what to eat without literally spinning in circles?

"I made a contact at Coldwell Banker today," Kyle said. He put Dawn's business card on the counter. His dad stopped looking so lost for a second and picked it up.

"You should email her a brochure and stuff. She said she's always looking."

"You cut school to do Baker and Najarian business? I know you're worried, but school is your number-one priority."

"That's not why I cut."

His dad was still looking at Dawn's card with this puzzled and tired expression. "Thanks for this," he said. "Good looking out."

"Yeah, well." Kyle stopped himself from saying "Someone has to." Instead, he got the tuna and crackers out and set them on the counter for his dad.

8

WHEN KYLE walked into the weight room the next day, the guys barely looked up. It was like they'd collectively decided to freeze him out. Coach Ito gave him a nod of acknowledgment and pointed to the whiteboard where he'd written the workout of the day, but that was it.

Fine. He did his cable rows, his lateral lunges, and his planks, counting under his breath along with his *Hamilton* mix. In his peripheral vision, Coop and Mateo were doing medicine ball slams back and forth, harder and harder as if they wanted Kyle to look. When Kyle went back for a second set of cable rows, Coop said, "No wonder Coach decided you couldn't be on the roster. Your form is shit and you look tired already."

Kyle ignored him.

"Everyone thinks Ito shouldn't have even let you come back for workouts after you went AWOL."

"He did, though, so." Kyle stretched out his shoulder. Some of the other guys were watching. "Sorry for bailing. It won't happen again."

"I knew you could hear me through those things," Coop said.

"Guys," Ito said. "Work your muscles, not your mouths."

Kyle took his earbuds out and stood up; Mateo slammed the medicine ball to him. "Baker, dude," he said. "If you want to go dark and fall off the face of the earth and never play baseball again, you can. But we're supposed to be friends. Being sorry about bailing on the team is only part of it. I'm not only talking about since Arizona. You've hardly talked to us all year."

Kyle slammed the ball back. "I had a girlfriend."

"Had?" Coop asked.

Mateo held on to the ball, watching. "You guys broke up for real?"

"For real."

He felt like the whole room had tuned in to their conversation, even Ito, pretending like he was looking at a bunch of wrinkled papers on his clipboard. He imagined how they'd all be staring if they knew about his mom, too.

Ito caught Kyle's eye, then walked through the room spinning his finger in the air like *Wrap it up*. He called out, "Let's finish the workout and get out of here on schedule."

Both of Kyle's parents were in the kitchen when he got home. It felt like they were waiting for him.

Divorce. They looked like people about to say the word.

"Hey." He dropped his bag on the floor, tossed his keys onto the island.

His dad was leaning on his elbows the way he did whenever his back bothered him, his Baker & Najarian polo stretched tight over his belly. On the other side, his mom was thinner than ever. It was like every pound she had lost had wound up on his dad. There was a plate of cookies between them. Had his mom baked for the divorce announcement?

"We want to talk about something for a sec." His mom filled a glass of water from the tap and handed it to Kyle.

Sometimes two people who love each other very much drift apart . . . Kyle narrated in his head. Shouldn't they wait and do this when his sisters were home? At least Taylor?

"I just got off the phone with Grandma," his dad said.

An image of his grandpa in a hospital room flashed through his mind. *No, no.*

"Everyone is okay," Kyle's mom said. He hated how good she was at knowing what he was thinking. "They *are* old, though," she continued. "That's not news, but maybe you don't realize the farm and the big house are a lot for two people, plus managing the parcels they haven't leased, and at this point—"

"They're selling," his dad said.

"Selling?" Kyle asked. "Like, the farm?"

"And the house. All the land, the whole thing."

Kyle looked from his dad to his mom and back again. A giant chunk of family history and tradition, another piece of his childhood, demolished. And they were all matter-of-fact about it, just like they were with the affair.

"Do Megan and Taylor know?" Kyle asked. What about Emily?

"Not yet," his mom said. "Are you okay?" She reached for him, and he moved his arm away.

"Why? Why didn't they, like . . . pass it down?"

His dad hesitated and then said, "The short answer is money. They've been leasing out parcels, but the property taxes are so high, and the drought and the fires—"

"I don't really understand how they got into such sudden dire straits, financially, so fast," his mom said, "but there it is."

"It wasn't sudden, Karen—it's been a burden for a long time. The only thing that's sudden is having a buyer willing to take on the entire property." He looked at Kyle. "One of the big wineries made an offer on everything."

"I do feel like they're acting a little desperate," his mom said. "They could at least negotiate and maybe try to keep the house. That's just my opinion."

So now they were going to fight. Kyle wanted to laugh. They'd decided to live with cheating, but the farm was a fight. Okay.

"How do *you* know they're acting desperate? How do *you* know they didn't negotiate?"

"Because I know, Jeff, because they aren't like that. They aren't . . . I don't know. Savvy."

"You think they could run a farm as long as they did and manage all those leases and employees without knowing what they were doing? Anyway, I think we all feel Mom and Dad dodged a bullet last year when the fires didn't touch the farm. We might not be lucky next time. None of the kids want to take it on."

"Not even Uncle Mike and Aunt Jenny?" Kyle asked.

"Especially not them. They see it up close day to day."

"You don't want the house you grew up in to stay in the family?" his mother asked. "Explain that to me again, Jeff? Especially after everything we've invested."

Kyle wished the fan over the stove would suck him up and then beam him to a beach somewhere, or even just to his room.

"'We?'"

"Okay, fine. The company. Which technically is 'we,' since I am a partner, but I know you always see it as *you*."

"Can I go tell Taylor and Megan, or are you guys going to?" Kyle asked, mostly hoping to shut them up.

"We're about to call Taylor," his dad said. "This summer will be the last big thing with everyone there. We want to make sure everyone comes, which means—"

His mom took over. "We were thinking that no matter what happens, no matter what's going on between your dad and me, we should go this summer as a family."

No matter what happens. Kyle looked at his dad, who said to the ceiling just above Kyle's head, "We'll put everything on hold until afterward. Go to the farm together and make it a nice memory for everyone. Maybe you can even help us talk Megan into it."

"Yeah, okay." They had no idea how much that was *not* going to happen.

"Really try, okay, Kyle?" his mom said.

"If it matters so much, why don't *you* talk to her?"

"She won't answer my calls."

"Text her." He stacked a few cookies in his palm and started toward his room. He needed to talk to Emily.

"Come on, Kyle," his dad said. "You know you want her there too."

Seriously? His parents were going to be a team *now*,

when it came to coercing him? Yeah, he wanted Megan there. He wanted Megan there and Taylor and his mom and dad like they used to be. He stopped in the hall and looked up, momentarily blinded by the recessed pinspot they'd put in last year. He closed his eyes, seeing sunbursts and floating blobs of black.

"Okay," he said. "I'll try."

Can we FaceTime? he said. **I just heard about the farm.**

Ugh I know. It's terrible. Alex has been crying her eyes out since my mom told us yesterday.

Yesterday? And she hadn't thought to mention it? He swallowed a mouthful of cookie, then hit the video button to call her.

She declined the call. **We're just sitting down to dinner,** she said. **Sorry!**

Oh ok

Sitting down to dinner. Like, what a family does. He imagined them—Aunt Brenda and Uncle Dale, Alex, Emily—at their table, eating a meal that had more than one food group in it. How come Emily got that and he got *this*. His mind went back to his grandma's kitchen and being there with Emily, juicing the limes. How they had this connection and she'd been so *I'm here for you* and been such a good listener and someone to believe in and rely on. To Kyle, that had meant: no matter what. Now she felt as far away as the rest of them.

He texted Megan. **Dude we need to talk.**

Her typing bubbles came right away, and Kyle felt a little hope. But her reply was **Can't, dude. Try me in a few days.**

A few *days*?

He even tried Taylor. **Call me after you talk to Mom and Dad.**

His message to her came back undeliverable with a red exclamation point. He hit "try again" about four times, then gave up. Finished off the cookies. Brushed the crumbs off his shirt. He kicked back on his bed and thought about homework, then instead looked for some good musicals clips to cheer him up. There was Gene Kelly with a cartoon mouse, then Gene Kelly with Leslie Caron dancing by the river in *An American in Paris*. That one was too melancholy and romantic for him to handle. He found the really sexy one of Kelly with Cyd Charisse in *Singin' in the Rain* where Cyd is all legs and fringe and his mind finally stopped spinning on how everyone had left him behind.

He conjured Nadia. Told himself, just this one last time. Imagined her in a dress like Cyd's and high heels to match, the muscles in her thighs flexing and flashing in sparkly cloth. Dancing for him, leaping into his arms— her hips resting on his, her breasts pressing against his chest while she stared into his eyes with total trust that he could hold her and not let go. He pushed his shorts down a little, reached into them, and tried not to think about how using Nadia this way felt wrong, when a message from Emily bannered over the video.

Idk if your "oh ok" is supposed to make me feel bad, but sorry, you're not the only one under stress right now. Do you get that?

He pulled his hand back and covered up with the blanket as if Emily could see him.

Emily continued, **I've had my stupid SAT study group every day and my mom is going through some kind of midlife crisis and now this farm thing and Alex will not calm down. And actually shouldn't you be doing SAT prep too?? How are you not studying all the time? How do you have time to cut class and stalk people lol**

Every word including the lol hurt, and told him he was a selfish dickhead who, by the way, was ruining his life. He wanted to go back to Cyd/Nadia but then he couldn't think of anything but how he'd treated Nadia in real life and now he was sticking her in his jerk-off fantasies like she wasn't even a real person he cared about?

Sorry I'm so selfish, he shot back.

It sounded sarcastic, and he kind of meant it that way, but it was also the truth. He thought about what Mateo had said at the workout. And now that Emily mentioned it, there *was* an unopened email in his school account about test dates.

Don't be like that, Kyle. My dad's a psychologist. Emotional manipulation doesn't work on me.

Sorry, he repeated.

I really am here for you but that doesn't mean I can text 24/7. I shouldn't have to worry that you're pissed at me every time I can't text back within five seconds.

Don't worry, Em. I get it.

Ugh. Kyle. Stop.

Sorry. Sorry. Sorry. He didn't know how else to say it. Emily was right, Nadia was right, Mateo was right. The accusations battered him.

He turned off all his devices and closed his eyes to think about Cyd again, and didn't let her turn into Nadia this time. She became a generic older woman with dark hair and long legs. Straddling a chair, thighs and heels. Then straddling him: curling her hands around his arms and his neck. Then bra off, everything off but her fishnets and heels. Moving her hips and stretching back on his lap until he finally stopped thinking.

9

KYLE TRIED to get himself hyped for the kid-coaching thing, see it as an opportunity for redemption. He was tired of sitting around feeling crushed by the pileup of mistakes—his, others'—and bad news. But he'd been late leaving school because his English teacher wanted to know where the hell his paper was (his exact words), and then he hadn't realized he wouldn't be able to park near the field at the elementary school. When he got there, the kids were already in the middle of a scrimmage, and his lateness was one more screw-up to add to the pile.

He went over to a black dad-aged guy in a green

windbreaker and matching cap, holding the telltale coach clipboard.

"You Kyle Baker?" he asked without turning to actually look at Kyle. "You're late."

"I couldn't find parking. Sorry."

"Park in the teacher lot next time." He gestured with his clipboard behind the field. "There's never any space in visitor parking." He clapped. "There it is! There we go!"

Kyle scanned the field. It was pretty nice for an elementary school, except the playground was right next to it, and a basketball half-court. The kids were so much littler than he'd expected. Scrawny or pudgy or gangly. He saw a flash of a brunette ponytail at first base.

"So it's girls and boys?" Kyle said.

"Anyone who wants to play."

"Oh, okay, so it's not like a serious baseball thing."

Finally the coach turned and gave Kyle a look up and down. "You can't be serious baseball with kids? You can't be serious baseball with girls?"

"No, I just—"

"Some of these kids wish they were at Little League instead, but their parents can't or don't want to commit to that until they're a little older. Some are here because they like it. It may be only an after-school activity, but we are actually teaching baseball." The coach clapped again. "Come on, Ruby!" He turned to Kyle. "That's my daughter. She's one of the ones who want to move up to Little League."

Kyle watched Ruby smack a line drive and the short-stop cut it off. Then Ruby was out and one of the smaller kids was caught in a rundown between first and second. The coach made a note on his piece of paper.

"Keeping your daughter's stats?" Kyle asked.

"Mm-hmm." He looked up. "That kid on the run, that's Jake. After he makes an out here—and he will—you can work with him on his agility. You can do that? Ito said you could do all that."

"Sure. I know some drills."

The coach stuck out his hand. "Greg Malone, by the way." They shook. "I teach history over at the junior high but come here after school for Ruby and this group."

"Cool." Kyle noticed that the kid, Jake, had been tagged out.

"You know how to work with a kid without making him feel bad about himself?"

I guess? "Yeah."

"Be encouraging. I want them to have fun, but also . . ."

"You're also teaching them baseball," Kyle said.

"Right." The kid, Jake, wandered toward the bleachers, where some parents sat watching. Malone cupped his hands around his mouth. "Jake! Jakey!" He waved him over. "I don't know where he thinks he's going."

Jake turned around and jogged toward them. Though it was more like a slow, foot-dragging kind of shuffle that was at least as slow as walking.

"This is Kyle," Coach Malone said. "He's going to help me out here sometimes."

"Hi," Kyle said. Should he shake his hand? He'd always kind of hated when adults shook his hand when he was that age, like everyone was pretending you were a grown-up.

The kid's arms hung there. "Hi."

Malone adjusted his hat. "You two head out to the back of left field. I'd say watch for fly balls, but these kids don't usually hit that far."

"Come on," Kyle said, and started to jog. The kid did the same draggy thing he'd done before, glancing over to the bleachers every few seconds. He didn't exactly have a lot of hustle. Kyle slowed down. "Did you get hurt? In the rundown?"

"No."

Then why are you moving like molasses, little dude? was what he wanted to say. But he was here to redeem himself, not make more people feel bad. "One time I seriously twisted my ankle when I was caught between second and third."

"My name is Jacob. Not Jake."

"Oh, okay." They found a good spot way out. "Do you

know the three-cone drill?"

"We don't have any cones."

"No, yeah, but do you know it?" *Work with me here.*

Jacob shrugged, and Kyle got a more solid impression of him now that they were out there, standing still. He had kind of sand-colored hair sticking out from under his cap, skinny arms and legs, a little belly. Giant feet.

Kyle knelt down and unlaced his shoes. "We'll pretend my shoes are cones. And I guess . . . I'll use a sock for the third one." He dropped his shoes about five yards apart, then put his sock an equal distance from the others, but perpendicular to them. "It's basically an L shape, right?"

Jacob nodded. He was smiling a little, like he wanted to laugh at Kyle.

"I know I look stupid." With his one bare foot. The grass between his toes felt good. "So here's how this goes. . . ."

He demonstrated the drill, which was basically sprinting from cone to cone—or shoe to shoe—and touching it and getting to the next one or back to the first one as fast as you could. Jacob did okay, not great, kind of half-assed.

"Try to get a little faster every time," Kyle said.

Jacob was not a natural athlete. Maybe he was one of those kids who did a sport because his parents expected him to, or because his friends were doing it. Not that there was anything wrong with those reasons, as long as you were having fun. But he didn't seem to be having any fun.

"You want to go one more time? Give it everything. I'll time you on my phone."

"Don't time me," Jacob said, breathing hard and leaning over, hands on his knees.

"How come?" Usually that was a motivator. Kyle had always loved being timed, trying to beat his friends' best times or his own.

"I just don't want to be timed."

"Okay. You don't have to." Kyle thought maybe he'd overworked him, but then Coach Malone called them back in and Jacob sprinted all-out, way ahead of Kyle in a flash. "Damn, kid," he muttered.

He glanced at his phone. Emily had sent him a gif of Fred Astaire saying to Ginger Rogers, "Let's face the music and dance." Was it an apology? Or forgiveness?

what's that from?

Follow the Fleet, 1936

He had to say the right thing. The perfect thing. From now on, he'd be perfect with her.

"Baker!" Coach Malone was calling him. "I'm not paying you to be on your phone."

Kyle put the phone in his pocket and sprinted in to ask, "You're paying me?"

"No. But stay off your phone when you're at practice."

"Sorry."

Malone slapped him on the back. "Go meet some of the parents."

Jacob was walking over to the fence, toward a girl. A very hot girl. Very, very hot and beautiful, wearing big sunglasses and a white button-down shirt tied at her waist. Jacob's older sister? She looked darker than him, hair and skin both. She turned her head like she knew she was being watched and Kyle kept walking toward her, with purpose, as if he had something important to say.

"Hey," he said as he got closer to the fence. Jacob turned around with a look like *Why are you following me?* Kyle said to the girl, "Jacob did a good job today."

"You're the coach now?" she asked.

"Just helping."

"Me too. Gotta give this kiddo a ride home." She tousled Jacob's hair the way you would a five-year-old's. Jacob yanked his head away with a grimace. The girl had short fingernails painted dark red. "Let's go, Jacob. I don't want to hit traffic."

"Are you his sister, or . . . ?"

"No. Just a ride home."

"Um, I'm Kyle."

She smiled politely and nodded like *No one asked, but thanks for sharing.* And they walked away. He wanted to know her name, what to call her in his thoughts. When he stopped staring after them, he realized the crowd of people was pretty much gone. He wandered over to Malone to help organize the equipment. Ruby was there too, sitting in the dugout and writing in a notebook.

"That's Angeline," Malone said as Kyle handed him a couple of bats.

"Who?"

"'Who?' The young lady you were talking to who, when you were supposed to be meeting parents. She's Jake's babysitter, or I don't know what to call her, she helps out his parents when their work schedules are busy."

"Oh." Angeline. Kyle had never known anyone named Angeline. "He doesn't like to be called Jake, he said."

"He should speak up about it, then."

He did, Kyle wanted to say. *To me.* "Are most practices like this? Scrimmage game? Some drills and stuff?"

"Basically. Since we're not part of a league and the elementary schools don't have teams per se, it falls under after-school programs, doesn't run long, and we don't have a uniforms budget or parent volunteers to be driving kids around to all kinda games." He bent down and zipped up the big canvas bag of bats and balls and a few spare gloves. "So I just teach them what I can, and they can move on to Little League and maybe high school teams later on. Speaking of that, when you come next time, I was thinking you could talk to them a little about what it's like to play in high school."

172

Kyle didn't enjoy standing in front of people and talking, but he'd probably annoyed Coach Malone enough for one day. "No problem. You need help with the equipment?"

"Nope." Malone stood and heaved the bag up. He was stronger than he looked. "Okay. I'm off to grade history tests." He gestured to Ruby, and she hopped up to follow her dad. She turned back to wave. "Bye, Kyle!"

Kyle sat in his car, took a deep breath, and texted Emily.

Hey you can say no but I want to video chat soon, when it's a good time for you. No pressure though.

She wrote right back: **sure tonight at like eight would work**

No punctuation, no emojis. But if she was really mad, she wouldn't have sent him that Fred and Ginger gif.

When he got home, he got on his laptop and tried finding out more about this Angeline person. All he had was her first name and her face, and that she probably had a connection to the school's neighborhood. After about fifteen minutes of trying everything and finding nothing, he made himself stop. There was curiosity, and then there was stalking. And he had that English paper to finish.

He made good progress on the homework, did some push-ups and crunches. Didn't go wandering around the house looking for his parents so he could keep score on their screw-ups. When eight o'clock arrived and Emily's call came in, he was ready to show her the best version of Kyle. He thought he'd start by talking about the baseball kids.

"You're pixelated," he said.

"Hang on."

Her face turned into a blur of floor and walls and door-ways, then back again. "Is this better? I'm in my mom's office. The router is in here." She came into focus.

"Hey, you cut your hair off," he said.

Her previously shoulder-length hair was gone, replaced by a short, messy style. It was shocking, almost disap-pointing, to have her not look the way he was used to. But best-version-Kyle would not be disappointed in some-thing as superficial as her hair.

"Oh, yeah. It was making my neck hot and I got tired of ponytails and of random men commenting."

"Sorry. About men." This would be a good time to mention the kids. "I helped out with these little fifth grad-ers today," he said. "Baseball. It was kinda cute. Around Alex's age, I guess."

He kept staring. She wasn't as pretty to him without her hair. With the nose ring and the short hair, she was changing. Could people stop changing for two minutes? Should he even be thinking that his own cousin was pretty?

"Is something wrong?" she asked him.

"No," he said quickly. "Just . . . you know, everything that was wrong before, plus now the farm."

She nodded, and waited. Tilted her head and squinted. "My haircut threw you off."

"No, it looks good."

"You're lying," she said with a slight laugh. "I can tell. I've been getting this all week from friends at school."

Shit. He was messing up, over something so dumb. "I like how I can see your eyes better." That was true.

"I just think it's funny how so many people who aren't me have such strong feelings about *my* hair."

All he wanted with Emily was to be honest. Not weird. Not hiding.

"I don't see you that often," he said carefully. "And I picture you a certain way in my head, and when you just came on and it didn't match up, it surprised me."

"That's fine."

She was mad. He wanted to make her understand how much he needed them to be okay with each other. Not in some and-now-I-don't-trust-you world like with Nadia, or disappointment in him like his friends and teachers, or don't-mind-us-we're-just-burning-everything-you've-ever-known-down like his parents.

"Emily . . ."

"Kyle?"

"Emily."

"Kyle?"

She laughed first, then him. Even though he laughed, his eyes also stung a little with tears. If something like a haircut could throw you off with someone you cared about as much as he did Emily, anything could. It scared him. He didn't know where to step, what words to say to hold on to this thing that suddenly felt fragile.

"I'm sorry I've been up my own ass so much lately," he said.

"Okay. You look super intense. What's up."

He dug deep, so deep that he felt scraped out as he spoke. "I see my parents, you know, and what happened with me and Nadia. How easy it was to lose baseball, too, and friends, and everything that kind of made me *me*." A tear got out; he brushed it away. "And now the farm. I really really really want, like, you and me? You know? To always be good. Where nothing can get in and fuck it up. It matters to me so much right now. Like, it's hard to even express."

Then he truly was glad to be able to see her eyes with no hair falling in the way, because her eyes couldn't lie and he knew she understood what he'd just said, whether or not it was exactly the right thing to say.

"I know," she said.

"I don't like feeling like we're fighting."

"We're not," she said. "And I agree we should always be a good thing for each other. There's enough shitty stuff."

He couldn't let himself be disappointed that it didn't sound as important to her maybe as it was to him. He knew that her reply was one hundred percent honest, that he could trust that she would not say more or less than she felt.

"Tell me . . ." *Tell me we'll always be okay.* ". . . about school and stuff," he said, breathing in, breathing out.

She sighed. "School is a relentless beast that's ruining my life and stealing my joy and hopes for happiness. But only for like five more weeks."

She talked about her AP classes, about her study groups. He heard about Aunt Brenda coming in at two a.m. from a cast party and how upset Uncle Dale was about it. Listening to her talk reminded him of when he and Nadia were good, their lazy bedtime conversations about their days and their families and school stuff.

He missed that. Missed Nadia specifically, but also missed having that person, that special person who wanted to be the one to hear all your random thoughts, and you wanted to be the one to hear theirs.

He watched Emily's face, her newly visible and open face, and realized that she was becoming that person.

10

KYLE KEPT his head down, did his work, fell back into a routine. Got mostly caught up with school and showed up for what he was supposed to show up for. Nothing at home changed and he wanted to not think about it, but that was kind of impossible, given that he saw his parents every day. And he saw Nadia all the time at school and Coop and Mateo and basically daily life was one reminder after another of what had gone wrong. He was learning to live with it. And, if his day really started to sink or his thoughts got too wrapped around themselves, at least there was Emily.

They traded gifs and songs and updates. He battled

himself to not need her too much, no matter how anxious he got. It wasn't easy, though, to resist the quick hit of comfort he got every time she texted him back.

It was too painful to think about Nadia, and Emily lived in a different part of his mind from other girls, so he gave Angeline—the kid Jacob's nanny or whatever—the job of fantasy girl in his imagination. She didn't know anything about him, his life, his family. And he didn't know anything about her. He'd only seen her a couple times since that first day, and only talked to her two sentences at a time. She showed zero interest in hearing or saying more, but it almost didn't matter. Thinking she *might* be there in the bleachers any given day that he was there, and that she *might* be watching him, let him slip into a different skin and perform the role of the extra-patient and extra-fun guy. The kids liked it, and so did Coach Malone. And Emily said this was all going to look good on his college applications.

"Baker," Malone said now. "Take them on laps. I want to shuffle the positions before we scrimmage. Give some of these outfielders a chance to come in and learn not to be scared of the ball."

The kids groaned. Some about laps, some about being asked to actually play infield.

"Aaaand that's extra laps for the attitude," Kyle said, and started to run at an easy pace around the perimeter of the field. He had no idea if Angeline was there or not. Usually she didn't come until toward the end, if she came at all. Sometimes Jacob's mom or dad picked him up, but Kyle had never met them because Jacob would just run off to their waiting car, whereas Angeline parked whenever she got there and watched the rest of practice. "High knees," Kyle said, and turned around to make sure they were doing it.

Ruby and Tatum were in the middle of the pack, laughing while they did their high knees.

"See," Kyle said, "Ruby and Tatum know how to have *fun*!"

A couple of the boys looked, including Jacob, then pretended not to. Kyle remembered how at that age he didn't want to actually be caught looking at a girl—not by the girl, but especially not by one of his friends.

"Kyle, do you have a giiiiirlfriend?" Ruby asked, loud.

"Nope! Okay, now run backward!"

"Do you have a boyyyyyfriend?"

"Nope!" He jogged backward in the opposite direction, until he was at the back of the pack, where a couple of the less athletic kids were dragging. "You got this. You're doing great." They weren't, but in his lifetime on teams he'd seen enough kids put down for being slow or whatever that he knew the only thing it accomplished was making those kids hate sports, school, life.

Jacob was usually in the middle, not the best or the worst. He seemed like the kind of kid who had trouble having fun, his face usually fixed with a grim but determined expression. Kyle jogged next to him. "What's up, buddy?"

"I'm running?"

The way he said it made Kyle laugh, though he didn't think Jacob was trying to be funny. "Yeah, me too. Good day at school?"

"Uh-huh."

"You wanna steal a base today?"

He slowed down, holding his side as if he had a stitch. "I don't know."

Kyle sped up to the front. He found he slipped into this role easily, this coaching-ish thing, and liked it more than he'd thought he would. It was one place in his life that was simple and straightforward.

He had them run normally again, and then sprint, then walk, and it was time to scrimmage. Angeline was there. White jeans, black tank top, her hair wrapped up in some kind of flowered scarf and, like always, the big sunglasses. She had a good view of Kyle in his first-base coaching position. Maybe today he'd say more than two words to her. Just to see how it felt.

When Jacob came up to bat, he nailed a single. Kyle high-fived him at first. "We're stealing, right?"

"I'm too slow."

"It'd be fun, though."

Tatum, who was playing first base, said, "I can hear you."

"That's fine. You should both be ready for it." He said to Jacob, "If an opportunity comes, just go. Don't wait for me to tell you, because then it will be too late. Read the pitcher."

Kyle was about to give Jacob a whole bunch more tips, but then the catcher dropped the ball and it rolled away behind him and Jacob was on the run. He wasn't fast, but he didn't need to be, because the catcher was still looking for the ball. "Oh my god," Kyle said to Tatum, "he's doing it!"

"Go, Jacob!" she screamed.

"Atta boy, atta boy!" Coach Malone was yelling.

Kyle let himself glance over at Angeline. She smiled. At him? Or at Jacob's steal?

Throughout the rest of the practice, it seemed like she was watching him. Giving him signals. Then, at the end— yes, she was waving at him. Like, waving him over. He glanced at Malone, who was showing Ruby something about her swing. Kyle made it to the fence where Angeline stood.

"Hey," she said. Her upper arms in that tank top were *cut*. "Chris, right?"

"Kyle."

"Sorry! Kyle."

"It's fine." He reached up and put his hand on the fence, stretched out as far as it would go, to seem taller. She was going to say something. Maybe about how she thought he was great with the kids, could tell he was a good person.

"You know Jacob?" She pointed across the field.

"Yeah, he's awesome."

"His mom was supposed to get him today but she had an emergency, and his dad's not answering, so she called me. But I have to be at my other job in like five minutes. I could stick him in an Uber, but he hates that."

"Oh . . ."

"Anyway, his mom specifically asked me not to ask one of the other parents unless it's a last resort. She's asked them before." Angeline paused. "She feels judged. But you're not a parent."

He liked her voice. It had a hint of some accent, from another state or even maybe another country. If only she'd take off her sunglasses, he could feel the whole picture.

"So, if you could give him a ride home? It's not too far, but it's in the other direction from where I have to be. I asked his mom, she said it's okay." Angeline held up her phone to show him the screen.

Sometimes asking a favor was a way to flirt. But it seemed like this was just a plain favor.

Jacob had come over to them with his backpack on, cradling his glove in one arm. "Where's my mom?"

"She got called in, sweetie. Kyle's going to give you a ride." She turned to Kyle and said, "Text me your number in case there's an emergency or something."

"Okay, but don't be blowing up my phone in the middle of the night," Kyle teased.

Finally the sunglasses came off. She gazed at him with a squint, and he got a long look at her eyes. Long enough, anyway, to see that Angeline had to be in her twenties. Maybe late twenties. "I won't."

She told him her number, and he repeated it back to her while putting it in his phone. He sent her a text so she'd have his.

"Got it," she said, and put the glasses back on. "Thank you *so* much. See you later, kiddo."

Kyle wasn't sure if by "kiddo" she meant him, or Jacob, or both.

"All right, where are we going?" Kyle asked Jacob once they were in the car.

"You know where the Vons is? It's near there."

"On Hollister? Yep. That's near me, too." He resisted grilling Jacob for all the details on Angeline. They talked about practice, about his awesome steal. "You saw the opportunity and you took it, man. It was perfect."

"Yeah."

"Your mom is pretty busy, I guess?" And was cool with people she's never met driving him home? Maybe the other parents *should* judge.

"She's an on-call surgeon."

"Wow. Legit."

"Mm-hmm."

Okay, maybe a *little* talk about Angeline. "So Angeline is, like . . ."

"She's been my babysitter since I was little. I mean, I'm too old for a babysitter now, but she helps out sometimes. My dad is supposed to be the one who drives me places because he works at home, except he sometimes has meetings and stuff, too."

"When I was your age, my sisters drove me everywhere and they hated it and I hated it." Kyle made a turn. "So when you say you were little, you mean like six or something? And Angeline was your babysitter and she was . . . in junior high? Or high school?" He was trying to do the math on her probable age.

"I don't know. Turn left here."

Kyle signaled, turned.

"Then make a right."

Snowdrop. "This is your street?"

"Yeah. Up there near blue truck."

Electricity ran up Kyle's spine as Jacob instructed him

to pull over at 936 Snowdrop. "Right here? Nine thirty-six? That's your house?"

The house Kyle's mom had come out of. The house with the man. The house with the man with the work-at-home job and the wife and the kid. The wife and the kid who didn't know. The kid who was Jacob.

Face hot, nerves zapping, he asked Jacob if anyone was home.

"No, my dad's car is gone." He opened the door and looked back at Kyle. "Don't worry. We have a dog. He barks at strangers."

A wife and a kid and a dog. Kyle wondered if the dog barked at his mom like it would at a stranger or if it wagged its tail for her by now. "Is your dad coming home soon?"

Jacob shrugged. "I'm allowed to be home alone during the day. Thanks for the ride."

He got out and slammed the door and ran up the walk. Kyle wanted to yell after him, ask more questions, go inside, and . . . what? Ransack the house? Look for evidence? Evidence of what? His mom had already confessed to the whole thing. There was nothing to prove, nothing to confirm or deny. He'd seen his mom walk out of this house with his own eyes, and the guy worked at home and the wife had an important job that kept her busy, and he had a kid. All of which he already knew and could not unknow.

His phone vibrated, startling the hell out of him.

you dropped him off, right?

It was Angeline.

Yes, just now. His hands shook. Every time reality ran up on him like this, it was like finding out all over again. Every time.

Thank you.

He thought about saying *You're welcome* or *No problem* or *Hey, so is Jacob's dad a good guy or are you aware of the adultery situation going on in this house?* or *Weird coincidence, Jacob's dad and my mom are screwing.*

He sent back a thumbs-up and threw his phone into the cup holder.

Fuck.

11

"**KYLE? KYLE.** What happened? Did someone die?"

He'd called Megan. Megan, not Emily, because one, he'd laid enough shit on Emily that wasn't her problem, and two, he remembered Emily's text from when he'd almost told Megan the first time, telling him he should. **She's your sister!!**

As soon as he heard Megan's voice, he started to lose it.

"How come every time I call you, you think someone died? Can't I just call you?"

"Well, you call me *and* I can tell you're crying, I mean."

She paused. "I'm sorry I didn't text you back the other day?"

He managed to say no, no one had died, but he needed to talk to her and he didn't want to go home. "And I'm not fucking crying because you didn't text me back."

"I know, I know. Sorry. Are you okay to drive? Breathe, Kyle."

He did. It helped. "Okay. I'm okay."

"Meet me at my apartment. I'll text you the address so you can GPS it. It might take like forty-five minutes or more at this time of day. Are you okay to do that?"

"Yeah. Sorry." He breathed again.

"Kyle, whatever it is, it'll be all right. Text me when you get here. The doorbell is broken."

He headed toward the 101 with just enough gas in the tank to make it.

The road kept blurring

Why, dude. What's the matter with you.

He kept, like, *crying.* He'd stop, calm down, then think about some moment. Like his dad and his four dumb words. Nadia saying, "And now I don't trust you." His mom laughing and so happy with the guy. Emily, when she called him out for acting like her hair belonged to him. Yeah, they ended that conversation okay, but when he relived it and thought about how ever since he'd been trying harder than she knew not to seem needy, keeping it light and tight when in fact he felt like this bottomless *pit* of need, all he could feel was shame.

He wasn't going to dump more of his garbage on her.

That's what sisters were for.

By the time he got to Megan's, he'd thought through the entire situation a hundred times—what Kyle knew that he shouldn't know but other people *should* know, and how he'd let it all take so much away from him. No matter how he sliced it, it came to shit.

Her building, which he'd never seen before, was one of those old California stucco apartment complexes with just two floors, maybe eight or ten units, a courtyard, a gate.

I'm here.

A few seconds later, the gate buzzed and unlatched. The door to unit five opened on the ground floor and Megan, wearing a tank top and pajama bottoms, let him in. "You cried the whole way here, didn't you."

"No."

"You need a hug," she said.

"You hate hugs."

"I know." She put her arms around him, and it felt simultaneously unnatural and necessary. She was shorter than him, but more substantial. She let go and pulled him to a ratty brown couch. "My roommate, Julie, is here, but she said she'd stay in her room awhile. And you can stay over. if you want. Sleep here." She patted the threadbare couch cushion.

"I have school tomorrow."

"Skip. Or get up super early and go." She stood. "I'm going to have some wine. I know you probably only drink beer at your jock parties or whatever, but you can have some if you want."

"My jock parties? Are you a hundred years old? And do you *know* me?"

"Whatever! I was never invited to those things, so I only know what I see in movies I can stream for free. I assume you wear letterman jackets and chant 'Keg! Keg! Keg!' while bikini babes ride around on inflatable drag-ons in the pool."

He laughed, which he knew was her goal. "Yeah, I'll have some wine."

When she came back, she had a big glass with red wine nearly to the rim for her, and a teacup about one-third full for him. "Just enough to chill you out." She settled into the corner of the couch with her feet up, staring at him.

"You didn't have to work one of your jobs tonight?" he asked.

"I called in."

"Don't you need the money, though? I didn't mean—"

"Don't worry about it, Kyle, okay? You didn't ask to

come here. I invited you. Have a sip of your wine and tell me what's going on."

He took a sip, made a face. But liked the way the burn slipped over his tongue, down his throat, and landed in his stomach like an ember. It was actually his first drink since the night his dad had caught him after the party and put it in the vault.

He stared into the teacup and told Megan everything.

She didn't interrupt or ask any questions. She sat still, one elbow on the back of the couch. When he was done, she grabbed her phone off the upside-down laundry basket she was using as a coffee table.

"What are you doing?" he asked. "Don't tell anyone, don't—"

She held up a finger for him to stop talking. Waited a few seconds. "Dad?"

"Shit, Megan!" he hissed.

She made the zip-your-mouth sign. Kyle could hear his dad's voice. "Mm-hmm," Megan said. "I'm fine. Yeah, I know, whatever, but listen. I wanted to let you know Kyle's with me, he's staying over at my apartment tonight, and don't worry about it." She tapped the phone screen and put it back down.

"What did he say?"

"I don't know. I hung up." She curled her legs underneath her. "Okay. Kyle. So, you never noticed any problems with Mom and Dad before? Before all this?"

He shrugged. "I mean, you know how they are."

"Yeah, I know how they are. But do you? That push-pull game they play?"

"What do you mean?"

"Like . . . one pushes the other away when they feel ignored, by working too much or being really fake and surface-y. Then the other pulls them back, like, to prove they really belong together. You know how I first noticed that? By watching high school couples when I was a sophomore." She pinched her fingers together and punctuated each word with them. "High school couples, Kyle. Games."

He took the last couple sips of his wine. "I don't see any pull happening. Only push."

"And then there's the money thing. What they told you about how Mom is still at home because they can't afford for her to have her own place? I'm sorry, but that's bullshit. Mom and Dad are *not poor*. The have a huge house and two cars and a business and probably too much life insurance. And you have a car. And Taylor has a car. And they're not making her work while she's at school, like not even to pay her own phone bill. And I know you don't pay yours."

"We're on a family plan."

"So not the point, Kyle." She leaned forward. "Yeah,

they're broke, or having a tough time at the moment or whatever. But they're not poor. There's a difference. They could sell it all and pay off their debts, live more simply, tell Taylor to get a job. . . ."

A headache started to tap tap tap under Kyle's left temple. "Maybe, but you don't know how it's been lately," he said. "You're not *there*. I think it really is bad, like they might lose the business?"

"Worst case scenario, the Najarians buy them out." She got up to grab the bottle of wine off the counter that divided the kitchenette from the living room. "Do know how Aunt Gina sends us that goat card every year?" she asked.

"Yeah?" It started a long time ago. Every Christmas, Great-Aunt Gina sent a card saying she'd donated a goat to a family in Zanzibar in their names. They always laughed at it. Making fun of Great-Aunt Gina was kind of a tradition. She was a nun, first of all, in a mostly non-Catholic family. Her order or whatever didn't wear robes and stuff, they just clomped around in sandals with socks and wore no makeup.

"I know we all thought it was a big joke." Megan fell back into her spot on the couch. "One year I looked up the website on the back of the goat card. I clicked through the explanations of how a goat or a few chickens or rabbits or even a llama could make a big difference for some people in the world. There were other parts of the site showing how you could give people and villages irrigation pumps. Stoves. Farm equipment. Kyle, for the price of the phone I was holding in my hand to look up the site, we could have sent a girl to school for a *year*."

Megan was officially on a Megan rant now. Kyle rubbed his temple and closed his eyes. He saw Jacob in the passenger seat, explaining how busy his own father was.

"Then there are the constant upgrades to the house, to the cars, to the gadgets," she continued. "Everything is being replaced all the time whether it needs to be or not, they're just on automatic. They can never just let an appliance or a piece of furniture or a counter surface or a paint color be *fine*. It can always be better. They run a whole company based on the concept that what you have isn't good enough. Think about it. Then there are the extras. Kyle, so many extras!"

He opened his eyes to hear about the extras as Megan ticked them off on her fingers until she ran out of fingers. "Mani-pedis and hair color and blowouts. Baseball camp. Horse camp, surf camp, music camp. *All the camps*, Kyle, we went to all of them. Gym memberships and golf memberships and eating out and vacations and wine collecting. Our family could have educated, fed, and clothed several villages' worth of people by now."

"Okay, yeah, when you list it out it's a lot. But I'm not—"

"No no, my point here is if Mom *wanted* to move out or Dad wanted her gone, she'd be gone. This is their game. Only now they've dragged you into it."

"And Jacob and his mom," Kyle said.

"Who?"

God, she hadn't even been listening. "The *kid*, Megan, the whole reason I'm here right now. The kid of the lady who is the wife of the husband who Mom is seeing." He wanted to close his eyes again. His brain had no juice for processing the money stuff Megan was obsessed with. "Do you have any food? I didn't eat dinner."

"Oh, shit, yeah. Let's forage." She got up and went to the fridge; he followed. "Leftover Thai—it's really good and Julie's parents own the place, so I can always get more. Two pieces of pizza of indeterminate age. Cheddar. We always have cheddar. Um, PB and J." Megan pulled everything she'd listed out of the fridge and put it on the small counter in a pile. "Okay, so the kid, Jacob. He's on your Little League team or something? I was listening."

"No. It's just an after-school fun thing for fifth graders. Coach Ito asked me to when I went to talk to him because *you* told me I should."

She dumped pad thai and curry beef and rice into a bowl and put it all in the microwave. "That's for you. I'm volunteering as tribute to eat the old pizza." She handed him a glass of water. "Chug this."

"Thanks." He looked at her over the rim of the glass while he drank.

"So the goat thing?" she said.

Still on the goat thing. Kyle gave up. "Yeah?"

"I talked to Mom about it back then," Megan said. "And she was all, 'We don't pick where we're born. The way we live is normal for here. The way they live is normal for there.' And I asked why, why is it normal to have so much more than we need? And she said I could feel guilty about it if I wanted, but she wasn't going to, guilt doesn't help anything. So that's Mom. And I bet she doesn't even feel guilty about this kid or the wife." She took the Thai food out of the microwave, stirred it, put it back in. "This is why I cut it all off, Kyle."

"Okay."

"I suggested a *completely* rational plan to do my basics at community college and save that money, and she freaked out like, 'Oh, Megan, you have not worked this hard on your GPA so that you could go to community college!' and I was like, "Why *not*? Who *cares*? You could have three entire schools built in Bolivia for the cost of one year of bonehead gen-ed requirements that I could do online or whatever!'" She took the food out. "Why are you looking at me like that?"

"Because . . . I feel like you're making this all about you and your issues with Mom?"

"And Dad." She took a bite of pizza, cold.

"So, should we tell Taylor? Even though Dad said it's in the vault?"

Megan rolled her eyes. "The vault. I thought Dad only used that with me after he narced on Adam to the police."

"No. I've got like two things in there plus now this, and I've known for over a month and been the only one besides them who does, and I'm telling you it messed up my relationship with Nadia, and baseball, and my grades, and now I'm like . . . *part* of it!" He pointed at himself, stabbed at his own chest. "I'm part of their stupid fucking affair because I know the other people and I know they don't know and now it's like *I'm* cheating on them too."

They stood there staring at each other.

"Well, shit," Megan said.

"Oh my god," Kyle said. "I think I *just* realized that's what I'm feeling."

She nodded. "Contrary to how we were brought up, talking about things and allowing yourself to be upset actually does help. And you know what I'm going to say."

"Something about goats?"

She laughed. "Noooo."

"That I'm not actually cheating on Jacob and his mom?"

"Right. This is not on you, Kyle. Here."

She handed him his bowl of food. The noodles and rice and meat and sauce were all so good, even though they weren't meant to be all mixed up. Kyle ate faster, suddenly starving after weeks of living on protein bars and crackers and cafeteria burritos and cheap fast food.

"The tricky thing is," Megan said, "it's not your secret to keep, but it's also not your secret to tell. Mom and Dad have put you in a super-shitty place."

"Thank you." He glanced at her. "I told Emily."

"Who?" She started laughing almost immediately. "Kidding. Wow, you guys really are close."

"I trust her."

"Taylor is going to figure it out when she comes home," Megan said.

"Do you think I should warn her ahead of time? Just tell her, like, right now?" He finished his food and literally licked the bowl.

"I don't know. She just had a big drama with one of her friends, who treated her really bad, if you believe Taylor's side of it, and I mostly do. . . ."

"Okay, well, no one asked me if *I* could handle it when they dumped this shit on me, so maybe Taylor will just have to eat it."

"Damn, Kyle."

"I'm a little tired of being the water boy for this family's garbage, is all."

She tossed her pizza crusts in the trash and said, "Mixed metaphor."

While he rinsed his dish in the sink, his eyes fell on a picture of him and Megan and Taylor when they were little, at the farm. *The farm.*

"Did Taylor tell you about the farm?" he asked.

"No?"

"Have some more wine."

They went back to the couch and he told her about the farm being sold, what all he knew, what their parents had said about it. She didn't cry, but she did finally stop talking about goats.

"What I want," Kyle said, "is for all of us to be at the farm this summer. You. You have to go." Yeah, it was what his parents wanted, but he wasn't asking her for them. He was asking for himself. "It's the last summer. Forget Mom and Dad. When was the last time me and you and Taylor were all together, with all the cousins?" The fact that she hadn't interrupted him yet meant he was getting to her. "You used to love it as much as everyone else. Come on. Picking pears? Swimming in the pond and trying to convince me it was full of poisonous snakes? Sleeping in the bunkhouse and Uncle Mike scaring us in the middle of the night, pretending to be a ghost from the Gold Rush?"

Her shoulders slumped and she let out a whimper, like she was a kid realizing she was going to have to do something she didn't want to.

"Megan, remember how even when we were little we

barely saw any parents the whole week? You can avoid them. It's a big place. Pretend they aren't there. Do it because it's our place. All the cousins'."

They had a staring contest while she sipped her wine. Kyle didn't flinch, and finally Megan said, "I'll see if I can get time off work."

Not even being exhausted and full of noodles and wine helped Kyle get to sleep on the world's lumpiest couch. After trying and failing to find a comfortable position, he moved onto the floor and decided now that he was past his big emotional crisis, it was okay to text Emily.

I think I talked Megan into coming back to the farm this summer.

It was late and he shouldn't have expected a reply, but that didn't keep him from waiting, adding more.

I'm staying at her apartment right now. It's a dump compared to our house. I guess the independence from my mom and dad is worth it to her. He snapped a picture of the laundry basket/coffee table. **This is her living room furniture.**

Honestly though, he could kind of understand what Megan saw in her situation. The couch was janky and the coffee table doubled as a receptacle for dirty clothes and he could tell that leftovers from her roommate were her main food. Still, she didn't owe anything to anyone. She didn't have to pretend or hide or keep up any illusion of being something she wasn't.

Her life is real, tho, he sent to Emily, wishing she were there with him. It would be like when they were kids, sleeping in the bunkhouse on old metal springs at least as uncomfortable as this couch. They'd talk into the dark and play twenty questions until Alex and Martie were asleep and Taylor and Megan were telling them to shut up. They always outlasted Taylor and Megan, though. The last ones standing.

"Are you still awake?" Kyle would whisper.

"Are you?" Emily would reply.

"Yeah."

Then they'd let themselves drift off, too.

12

HE WOKE up on the floor to the sound of someone in the kitchenette. When he peered around the couch, he saw it was Megan's roommate, Julie, her back to him. She had black hair in a buzz cut, or was growing out a shaved head. Black T-shirt, green basketball shorts. Nice, cut calves.

"Hey," he said, quietly as he could. "Um, I'm here. It's Megan's brother. Kyle. I didn't want to scare you."

She glanced over her shoulder, smiled. "Yeah, I know. Megan told me before she went to bed last night. Want coffee?"

"No thanks." He'd had coffee a couple of times and did

not understand everyone's obsession with something so nasty.

"Did you sleep okay?"

"Sort of . . ." There was a note on the laundry basket and a ten-dollar bill—*If you need gas money,* in Megan's handwriting.

"The bathroom is free right now if you want it, but I have to get in there in like ten minutes to get ready for work. So you know."

"I'm good."

Julie came into the living room and sat on the other end of the couch with her coffee and her phone. She had a tattoo on one of her shoulders, medium sized. He squinted.

"Is that the bear from the California flag?"

"Hell yeah it is. I'm ready for us to secede and run our own country here." She sipped her coffee. "You're the first person from Megan's family I've met."

"I figured. She's not that into us." He pulled his fleece blanket up around him. Julie was just going to sit here on the couch for ten minutes? "Um, that food from your parents' restaurant was amazing, by the way."

"They both grew up in Thailand, so they pretty much know what they're doing."

He searched for a topic. "So, what does Megan say about us?"

"About your family? That you're capitalist pigs who

will die in the coming revolution." She paused. "I'm joking. We don't talk about it that much. Our work schedules don't line up and we have our own lives, but she's never said anything that makes me think she wants to disown you guys or anything."

He was looking again at the bear on her shoulder. Her arms were pretty. Her neck. The way he could see the whole curve of it because her hair was practically nonexistent. "Do you play basketball?" he asked when he realized he was staring at her calves again, tried to pass it off like he was looking at her shorts.

"In high school I did, but only for fun anymore. I'm too short."

She sipped her coffee, did some stuff on her phone.

Kyle said, "I play baseball." Julie glanced up at him, nodded, looked back at her phone. He felt self-conscious and young and wanted to be back in a place where he knew what he was. "I guess I'll go ahead and grab a quick shower."

He was two hours late for school. Mrs. Ito, Coach Ito's wife, worked in the office and told him his dad had called to excuse his lateness.

"Really?" He'd meant to call home but had forgotten to charge his phone at Megan's and now it was dead.

"He said you'd either be late or absent and that you had

a legitimate family-emergency-type excuse. I hope everything is okay."

"Thanks."

He took the hall pass and went straight to geometry, which had already started. Automatically, his eyes found Nadia's when he walked in. After a slight hesitation, she smiled and he felt lifted. After class, they walked together a little bit. The last day of school was still a month away, but that nearly-summer feeling already wafted through the halls, a mix of stress over grades and tests and excited anticipation for being done. It almost felt good. Kyle could almost scoop it up like an easy grounder and feel it in his palm.

Then Nadia touched his arm and said, "I want to tell you something."

She sounded nervous, and Kyle knew this was not going to be good. He stopped walking. "Okay."

"It's not a big deal, but I didn't want you to hear it like a rumor and then not ask me and . . . you know. It's, well, I'm going out with Mateo."

Mateo. He pictured Mateo standing in the gym with the medicine ball, confirming their breakup. Had he just been waiting, all along? "Did he ask you or did you ask him?"

"That's irrelevant," Nadia said in her calming, reasonable voice. "The point is, I respect you and our past, and even though I don't have to tell you, I wanted to."

"But . . . it's only been like two weeks."

She shook her head. "No, Kyle. Two weeks since we actually talked about it, but over a month since you disappeared on me."

Students streamed past them. Kyle felt frozen, but Nadia took his elbow and pulled him to the locker wall. "I know it's probably hard for you that it's Mateo, I know. We were texting a lot about you, actually, when you kind of ghosted us. And we got close."

"You got close? But we were in love." He couldn't believe he said it. Like he had just emptied his pockets, given someone his very last dime.

He checked her face, wanting her to look like he felt: totally broken. But what she looked was infuriated. "Don't, Kyle. Just don't. It's not like that with Mateo—ugh, I don't even know why I'm explaining it after you explained literally nothing about how you treated me."

"It was my parents," he blurted, ready to spill everything, way too late.

Her eyes widened. "Your *parents*? What, they didn't like me?"

"No, they loved you."

The bell rang. Nadia held up her hand before he could say more. "I have to go. I thought I'd be nice and let you know before you heard it anywhere else. If it were me, I wouldn't want to hear it randomly."

He swallowed, tried to salvage what might be the last impression he ever got to make on her. "I'm glad you told me. I'm really sorry. If I could do everything over again, I would do it all so different, Nadia, I'd fix it before it was too late. I want you to have good memories of me," he pleaded. "Don't hate me. Please. I mean you can, you can feel whatever you want, you—"

"I don't hate you, Kyle." Her anger seemed to deflate; now she mostly sounded tired. "I do have good memories and I'll never hate you."

His eyes filled. *Not now. Come on.*

"But the way it ended was awful," she continued.

"I know."

"I'm not over it."

He nodded.

"So just . . ." She closed her eyes. "Just be gone when I open my eyes, okay?"

And he was.

Now he had to go work with the kids and try to treat Jacob exactly the same as he treated the other kids. He'd started to give a few of them nicknames: Ruby-Jean, Tatum-Tot, El Fuego, Bobby One-Sock . . . just dumb stuff to make them laugh. He hadn't come up with anything for Jacob, and now every time he laid eyes on the kid, it reminded him what he'd told Megan last night: that he felt part of it now, part of the lie.

Coach Malone wanted him to set up a drill with half the group to help them with fielding grounders, while Malone took the other half and had them work on pitching and catching. Kyle hoped Jacob would end up in Malone's group, but nope.

He put the fragment of his brain that was still thinking about Nadia on ice and taught grounding skills the way his dad had taught him, step by step, just putting balls on the ground and having the kids practice picking them up with their gloves and coming back to a throwing position. He kept not looking at Jacob, berating himself for it the whole time. Nothing was Jacob's fault, and pretending he didn't exist wasn't going to change the truth.

"Okay, Ruby-Jean-Jean, that's good, but I can see you thinking too much. This is a game of muscle memory."

"What does that mean?" Jacob asked.

Kyle didn't even turn to him then. "It means what it sounds like it means," he said, then, feeling like a piece of garbage, he went over to Bobby to show him how to keep his glove lower. "You want to be able to trap the ball. Good."

He heard Tatum say to Jacob, "Like your muscles remember what to do because they do it so much."

"Less chatter, more fielding," Kyle said, and Tatum

gave him a disapproving, disappointed frown and big eyes. *You're an asshole,* her eyes said.

Oh, I know, he thought back at her.

After practice, while the kids were collecting the equipment, Malone slow walked over to Kyle, arms crossed. "Okay, Baker. What have you got against Jake? Did the hot nanny turn you down or something?"

He'd noticed? Did he have eyes in the back of his head? "No. I mean, I don't have anything against him."

Malone gazed out from the shadow of his cap. "You can't play favorites. Kids notice everything. You can lie to me about it, but never lie to kids. They've got bullshit radar like you wouldn't believe." Malone gestured with his head toward the bleachers and fence. "Go talk to him. Tell him what he did good today and mean it. The point of this is to help *build* their self-esteem, not make them feel worse."

"Yeah, okay."

"And Baker," Malone said. "Don't give the kids rides. Unless there's some major emergency, I mean major like an earthquake or something, we don't do that."

Man, the guy didn't miss a thing. "Sorry. Got it." How many more ways were left for Kyle to fail?

"You didn't know. I should have told you on the first day. That's on me." He gestured to Jacob, who was walking toward the parking lot. "Talk to him."

Kyle shuffle jogged to catch up. "Hey," he said as he got closer. Malone was right. In fact, he should be giving Jacob *extra* attention, not less. Kind of boost him up, so that when the shit of his life eventually hit the fan, he might at least be feeling okay about his ability to field a ball or steal a base.

Jacob glanced over his shoulder.

"Yo. Hey," Kyle said again. Jacob stopped walking. "Um, nice work today. You seemed pretty confident with the grounding stuff."

Jacob shrugged.

"I was kind of distracted from something that happened at school," Kyle continued. "Sorry I didn't answer your question about muscle memory. I think Tatum explained it pretty well, but if you need to know more . . ."

"I gotta go. My mom's waiting." He pointed to a gold Subaru idling in the fire zone.

Kyle's stomach lurched. "Oh. That's your mom?"

Jacob looked at him like, "Yeah, I just said."

"I should meet her." It was impulse, driven by curiosity. Even though he was horrified, he found himself following Jacob to the car.

Through the open window he saw her, a white lady with reddish-blond curly hair, hands on the wheel. When she turned and saw Jacob, she smiled this radiant smile. They got closer, the smile pulling like a magnet.

"Are you Kyle?" she asked, reaching her hand through the window. He shook it. "Jacob told me about you. Thanks for working with the kids. Oh, and for giving him a ride the other day."

"No problem. But I just found out I'm not supposed to."

"I'm sorry. I hope you didn't get in trouble." While Jacob ran around to the passenger side, his mother took off her sunglasses and used them to push her hair off her face. Her eyes were bright, maybe slightly tired. He imagined her with a surgical mask on, saving lives in the ER. "He thinks it's very cool that he gets to practice with an actual high school varsity player. Coach Malone is great, but to someone Jacob's age, he's just another old person."

She was so . . . pretty. She was so warm. She looked younger than Kyle's mom. He'd assumed she'd be, like, ugly or mean or something.

"Anyway," she continued when Kyle didn't say anything, "you're what he wants to be someday."

Ugh, don't be like me.

"Mom." Jacob looked down at his lap.

"I've got to get back to the hospital." She turned to Jacob. "You're with me today, buddy. Dad's got a meeting in L.A. all of a sudden, and Angelina's other job needs her. We'll go home and walk Chase real quick, and then you can do your homework in my office."

Jacob nodded.

"Nice to meet you," Kyle said.

"You too." She put her sunglasses back on and waited. "Can you . . ."

Kyle realized his hands were on the car door. He jerked them back. "Sorry." He leaned down and said to Jacob, "See ya, man."

"Bye."

He watched them drive off.

When he got home, his mother was there. With Jacob's mom fresh in his memory, he found himself comparing them, which felt wrong and strange.

"Hey, sweetie, I'm glad you're back."

She advanced on him. He stepped away, but she persisted and got her arms around him in a hug. He didn't hug back, but he let her do it. "I was only gone one night," he muttered.

There had been probably thousands of hugs between them in his lifetime that he'd barely paid attention to. This one felt more meaningful, like she was trying to tell him something important with it. His guard faltered as her hug soaked in, and it took effort not to at least put one arm around her. When she released him, she asked about Megan. How she was, what her apartment was like.

"She's doing good," he said.

"Did you tell her about the farm? Did you ask her about summer?"

Oh, yeah, he'd almost forgotten. Here he thought she was worried about him or something when actually she had an agenda, a role for him to play in *her* life, this life she wanted to be allowed to have without any consequences.

"She's going to ask about time off," he said.

Her face lit up with this pure mom gladness and it was all so exhausting, not knowing if he should think of her as a bad person or a good person, someone right or someone wrong. And he lashed out with "Only because I told her she could pretend you aren't there," and waited for the pain to cross her face or for her to get mad at him, get defensive, something.

But her face stayed soft. She didn't even flinch. She looked him right in the eye and said, "I love you, Kyle."

It pierced him.

With nothing to say in response, he went to his room, let his backpack slide off his shoulder and fall to the floor. He stripped down, changed into a clean T-shirt and boxers. Got under the covers. He plugged his phone into the charger by his bed.

Megan had started a text thread with him and Taylor about the farm, and they were breaking down the details of a six-screen email from Grandma and a hundred reply-alls from the rest of the family. He skimmed through that, then opened up his Emily thread.

She'd replied to his texts from last night.

I'm excited! I haven't seen Megan in so long. the mysterious older cousin no one talks about.

Then she wrote:

I was at my mom's closing night of the student play she directed.

hello??

anyway I guess text me later!!

oh btw I got a 1390 on the SAT. I want to take it again and see if I can pass 1400. That was my goal. But I'm really happy with this first score. It's close enough.

He read and reread the texts and scrolled through some of their past conversations. He wrote, **Hey. I'm fried from last night and I'll tell you about it later, but I just gotta say . . .** *You're the only person who stays solid for me. Everyone else is lying or mad or moving on. I don't know what I'd do without you. I know sometimes I need you too much, more than you want me to, but I'm so glad you're there.*

You gotta say . . . ???

He smiled but also was pretty sure he was going to start crying again.

Awesome job on the SAT . . . 1390!! You worked hard for it.

She sent back a string of like thirty blushing smiley faces.

Then she added: **when are YOU taking it?**

Uhhhhhhhhhhh.

They messaged a little more. His stomach growled and his eyes were heavy. There was a light knock on the door, and his mom came in with a sandwich on a plate and a glass of milk. "It's peanut butter and jelly." She put the plate on his bedside table; he saw she'd cut the sandwich into four triangles. "Need anything else?"

"No."

"I'm here if you do."

She kept staring at him. Meaningfully.

What, Mom, what?

"Someday," she said, "I think someday you'll understand. Maybe you'll want to hear all about it. Maybe even forgive me. It's not like you think." She reached out to stroke his hair. He let her. He was so tired.

He wanted her to say she was sorry. That she'd do it all different if she could. The words he'd said to Nadia.

He wanted her to say she'd finally figured out how wrong it was, what she was doing, that she couldn't have her family *and* the guy, couldn't ruin their family *and* someone else's and now she was ready to belong to them again and be at home and make sandwich triangles. . . .

"Mom," he said, his eyes closing.

"Mmm?"

"I want this to be over. This thing, this . . . *guy*." It hurt to refer to him directly and aloud.

"I know," she said, almost whispering.

He waited and waited, until he was crushed by her inability to add "I'm sorry" or "I'm trying," because it was obvious: she wasn't sorry and she wasn't trying.

13

HIS MOM went all in on not being sorry, not trying, by going on a trip with the guy. Not that she told Kyle about it, but Jacob's dad having a meeting in L.A. "all of a sudden" and then the next morning his mom leaving a note to say she was going to a home goods trade show to do some buying for Baker & Najarian? He knew what it was.

It was a sign of just how many fastballs of shit had been coming his way that this new one barely affected him. One thing at a time. First, get through the school day knowing he was going to see Nadia and Mateo. Maybe not together, but around. He managed it at first by ducking and dodging the way he had back at the beginning of this whole thing; then, between fifth and sixth period, he passed by Mateo in the hall and couldn't avoid him. They made eye contact and Kyle gave him chin nod that he hoped said *'Sup* and also *I guess you've had your eye on my girl for a while now and so be it but don't expect me to congratulate you.*

After school, he did a conditioning workout with the girls' volleyball team.

"Don't you guys have a game at Cabrillo today?" Alissa Wilkinson asked while she spotted his bench presses.

"The team does." He exhaled, pressed up slowly. At the top of his move, he said, "I'm taking a break."

"Is it your shoulder? It seems fine."

"No. I bailed—I went AWOL," he said, lowering the bar. "Got myself kicked off, basically."

"Why'd you do that?" She stood over him, ready. "You've got two left."

"Honestly," he said, grunting, "I don't even know anymore."

He finished his set and they switched. Alissa put her hands on the bar as he helped her unrack it. "Well," she said, "there's always next season."

At home, Kyle walked through the house.

"There's always next season" was a stale phrase he'd

been hearing most of his life, but maybe now was the time to embrace it, start thinking ahead. Taylor was in finals and then she'd be home soon after that, and then it would be summer. And the farm. He didn't want to let his mom's choices rob him of at least enjoying that, their last time.

He looked at the calendar hanging on the fridge under the *Doctor Strange* magnet he'd gotten one Christmas in his stocking, from Grandpa Baker. That was the movie they'd all gone to over Thanksgiving that year.

He got out his phone, opened Emily's thread.

When did you say the next SAT is?

He was behind in geometry and biology. Doing okay in Spanish and U.S. history. In real trouble as far as American lit. He could write decent papers, but the time and focus it took to do the reading was what was killing him. He had to stop getting sucked into the vortex of all this shit he couldn't control.

Last year his mom had religiously checked on his grades through the school portal and stayed on him. Even as recently as right before the trip to Martie's birthday, she'd taken him out to dinner and helped him strategize how to maintain his good grades and improve his bad ones. Kyle doubted she was even looking now. And did *not* doubt that his dad didn't even know how to look, or that someone was supposed to.

Emily replied.

I don't think I said, but you can look it up online. You have to register ahead of time, though. You know that, right? Like a month ahead?

A vague memory of unopened school emails with subject lines about test registration lurked somewhere in the parts of his brain he had not been paying attention to. He found the College Board website and looked at the dates. The registration deadline for the next test had just passed.

Shit.

I think I missed it???? Did I miss the SAT?

Keep scrolling. You can take it in late summer or even up to late fall senior year. Or the ACT. Either one.

But you already took it.

I'm weird and enjoy tests. She added a shrug emoji and then asked, **Are you okay? Do you want to FaceTime?**

He heard his dad's truck in the driveway, then the garage door opening.

Honestly I don't think I could handle it right now. Three crying-face emojis. He added: **haha ha**

His dad came in through the mudroom, holding two pizza boxes. "Bringing home the bacon," he announced.

It was a joke he'd been telling as long as Kyle could remember, because the family's favorite pizza had Canadian bacon on it. Only the way he said it now was joyless, and three out of five members of the family weren't there to eat it. He put the boxes on the island, then emptied his pockets next to them. Wallet, keys, some coins, a piece of gum, a few business cards, his phone, his Swiss Army knife. He unhooked the tape measure from his belt, then took off his belt and added it to the pile and, finally, peeled off his Baker & Najarian polo and tossed it toward the laundry room.

This was all stuff he never would have done if Kyle's mom was there.

Kyle looked at him there in his undershirt. His dad stared back. "I'm real tired, Kyle."

"Okay."

His dad went over to the sink and tried to pull a paper towel off the roll with one hand; about six unspooled. "Goddamn it." He opened the fridge and got out a half-empty two-liter bottle of cola and a carton of milk. He liked to mix them, which everyone else in the family thought was gross.

He brought the milk and the soda and the six paper towels to the island, got two plastic tumblers out of the cupboard, and sat across from Kyle and opened the top pizza box.

"So we're eating our feelings now?" Kyle asked.

"That's right. You want a brown cow?"

"No. Just . . . cow."

Kyle thought, *Okay, maybe we're finally going to talk.*

Really have it out and make a plan for whatever was going to happen next. But his dad got out his phone and scrolled and tapped and scrolled and tapped while he ate a piece of pizza in about four bites, so Kyle kept working on his homework. Emily had answered his cry-faces with **Seriously though, are you okay.**

I met the mom yesterday, Kyle replied. **The guy's wife. She was picking up the kid and she was really nice and pretty and idek wtf is wrong with adults.**

He slid a piece of pizza out of the box and watched his dad. Something about the way he tapped and swiped was different than whatever his dad normally did on his phone, like read news and sports scores.

Aaaand now I think my dad might be on Tinder or something.

Emily sent a scream face.

"What are you doing?" Kyle asked.

"Nothing." His dad put his phone facedown and got another slice.

There were so many things Kyle wanted to talk about. Like, did they owe it to the wife to tell her what was going on, and how much longer were his parents going to wait to decide if they wanted to separate or divorce, and did either of them even have a conscience or, like, *any* ideas about maybe how to do the right thing in this situation? Like, hello? Anyone?

All of those questions somehow came out as, "Are you on a dating app?"

"No."

"A hookup app?"

He gazed at Kyle in this way Kyle didn't remember his dad ever looking at him before. Like they were in a challenge, caught in what Ito called a hitter's count, advantage batter, and Kyle was the batter.

"Don't worry, Kyle. No one wants me." He shoved the folded piece of pizza into his mouth like someone was about to take it away from him and chugged his brown cow.

"Don't make yourself sick, Jeff," his mom would say if she wasn't on an overnighter with her boyfriend. "Remember your blood sugar," she'd say. "Remember how you feel after too much cheese." And if it were a year ago, she would have kissed Kyle's dad on the top of the head as she moved around the kitchen, putting some salad on the table with the pizza.

Two years ago, Taylor would have been there too, making their dad stay off his phone and teasing him about being addicted to fantasy football.

Five years ago, it would have been Kyle and Megan and Taylor fighting over the biggest slice of pizza, Megan trying to make Kyle laugh so that milk would spurt out of his nose while their mom passed out napkins and made them go around and say something about their day at school.

His dad would have been smiling when he came in and said, "Bringing home the bacon," and his mom would have rolled her eyes or maybe patted his belly or opened a beer for him or said, "My hero," like she used to whenever he came home with dinner and she didn't have to cook.

Ten years ago there would have been bedtime reading and kisses good night.

Where had it all gone? When a family falls apart, where does the old family go?

"Dad," Kyle said. He didn't even know what he was going to say. Only that he wanted to keep talking while he had his dad, had him sitting still and paying attention.

"Go ahead. Tell me what a chicken I am. Tell me how I'm weak and letting you down. Tell me I need to fish or cut bait."

"Yeah, all of that stuff, but—"

"Tell me again what you know about being married for thirty years." His dad stood up, grabbed a pizza box.

"God, Dad, I just want to know, like . . . is this who we are now?"

"I hope not, Kyle, and that's why I'm paralyzed, okay? Because I really really hope not."

Later, he texted Emily.

just kind of had it out with my dad

In a good way? she asked. **Like do you feel better?**

Not really. crazy-face emoji. **but I'm okay,** he added, before she could feel like he wanted her to fix it.

You're really going through a lot this year, Kyle. I'm sorry.

He stared at that. The acknowledgment meant everything. Sometimes that's all he wanted or needed through every little and big shitty thing. For someone to say, "Hey, that's a lot, that must be hard."

But he guessed he couldn't expect people—Nadia, Mateo, Coop—to say it if they didn't know. He didn't want to be like his dad, with this situation or anything else, keeping it all in and putting a bunch of work and pizza on top of it and hoping that things he wanted to change would magically change.

Kyle wanted to be the kind of person who could tell people things, and have the kind of people in his life he could tell them to. Like Emily.

THANK YOU, he wrote back. The words seemed totally inadequate. He wrote them again anyway. **Seriously, thank you.**

14

HIS MOM got back the next day, Saturday, midday. Taylor was coming home for the summer on Monday, and his mom was anxious about it—cleaning the house in ways she hadn't for months, runnings errands, stocking the fridge. Probably realizing how much harder it was going to be to keep her affair from Taylor.

That afternoon, Kyle cleaned the koi-less koi pond in the backyard. No one has asked him to, but it was covered in slime and he was sick of looking at it, sick of all the little things suffering neglect for so long. His mom came out into the yard as he was finishing up.

"Thanks for doing that," she said.

He didn't want to talk to her. Not at all.

"Maybe we can try having actual koi again," she said.

Why bother? he wanted to ask. *Why bother with koi, why bother with small talk?*

"Listen, Kyle—"

He laughed, bent down to move the hose.

"What?" she asked.

"It's just funny how you only talk to me when you want to make sure I'm not spilling the tea on you." When he stood up and saw her face, he knew he'd pitched it right down the middle. That she'd been about to be like *Remember, don't tell Taylor* or some shit like that.

"I mean, do you miss me, Mom? Do you miss talking to me about, like, projects you're working on for the business or about the Rams or about school?"

She was supposed to say, "Yes, yes, Kyle, I miss all of that." But she folded her arms across her body and fixed her eyes somewhere below his. After a few seconds, she said softly, "Do you remember when you first got together with Nadia? She was all you thought about, the only person you wanted to see. Did *you* miss other things while that was happening? Maybe now that it's all over, you do. Maybe you look back and—"

"I'm *seventeen*, Mom. She was my first girlfriend. You're supposed to have this figured out. You dated around and found Dad and married him and you're supposed to just . . ." He didn't know what.

"Just never have feelings again? Just never experience anything new?"

"You're hurting people."

"I don't think anyone can get through life without hurting people, Kyle. We're all fundamentally selfish, when it comes down to it."

"That's so weak," he muttered. "Go ahead and say what you came out here to say in the first place." He crouched down to rearrange some rocks. "I know. Don't tell Taylor."

"With her coming home, I'm moving out of Megan's room and back into the master bedroom with Dad. Taylor will probably know something is off, but she's had a tough first year of college, and I think she really needs home to be what she's used to."

"Yeah, I know the feeling."

"I realize I can't force you to not tell her what you know. Think of it as a strong request. A lot is in the balance, a lot of . . . well, a lot."

"Mom, I know."

I know what's in the balance. I met the wife. I know the kid. I've seen the guy. You and the guy. He stood up and brushed his hands off on his jeans.

"Your judgment is all I can handle, Kyle." Her eyes were pleading now. "Knowing you know and that you judge me is enough. Megan already judges me so much that it hardly matters. But Taylor . . ." Her voice cracked. "Taylor still likes me. She's the last one of us who does."

He felt bad for her. He hated feeling bad for *her*. He wanted to feel bad for himself and for his dad and for Jacob and everyone else.

"I can't promise," he said. "Not to tell her."

She sounded small when she answered, "I understand."

"Okay, Tatum-Tot, come on. Watch the bat hit the ball."

They were working on batting, working on reading pitches. Kind of scrimmaging but not really paying attention to the counts. Kyle clapped his hands, feeling like every cliché of a coach ever as Tatum swung and missed. She'd been swinging at everything and only making weak contact at best, and now it was late and the sun was making a blazing halo around everyone on the field. She probably couldn't see a thing.

Jacob was at catcher. Kyle went over to him, holding his hand up so the pitcher would wait. "Hey," he said, still having trouble actually saying Jacob's name. "You can take a break, I got this." Jacob silently handed Kyle the catcher's mitt. Watching, Kyle felt. Turning his bullshit radar on and having it go wild every time he saw Kyle.

Kyle crouched behind Tatum. "I know the sun's in your eyes, but you gotta pretend it isn't. Pick out your spot and wait for your pitch. If it's not right where you want it to be, just let it go by."

"But what if it's a strike?"

"Unless you have two strikes, it doesn't matter. Another strike and another opportunity to hit is better than a pop-out, right?"

She got into her stance, and he held up the mitt. The next pitch was as sunburned as the last, but low. Tatum let it pass.

"Good eye."

Another pitch came in a little high, but in the strike zone, and she let it go by. That was when a corner of a small cloud moved over the sun, just enough that both Kyle and Tatum could stare right into the next pitch and see it was coming in over the middle of the plate. She connected, and the ball sailed right into the left center field gap, closest to Isaac, a gangly kid who had never once played a ball cleanly as far as Kyle could tell.

"There we go, there we go!" he shouted. "Now we're having fun!"

Isaac scrambled for the ball and underthrew it to second, which Tatum was rounding before the shortstop could even run out and get a solid hand on the ball. She made a spectacular slide into third—even though she didn't need to—and Kyle went running to her for a high five with a euphoria he hadn't felt since way before Arizona.

"That. Was. Awesome!"

"I know," she said, grinning like crazy while she dusted herself off.

Kyle scanned the field. Jacob was back at catcher, waiting for Kyle to return the mitt still on his hand. Coach Malone was staring him down too. "I guess we're holding things up." He bopped her on the shoulder with the mitt. "Great hit, amazing slide."

As he jogged back to home plate, he told himself to say Jacob's name. *Just say it. Act normal. Treat him like everyone else.* "Jake!" he said, "Jake the Quake! Thanks for letting me be pinch catcher." He tossed him the mitt. "How about that slide?"

Jacob eyed him. "It was cool."

"You and me haven't really practiced sliding. We can do that later if you want." Kyle kept his voice up, light.

"Okay." He sounded less suspicious. "I did it once and hurt my butt. So I haven't tried it again."

"It happens. All right, batter up!"

The game got going again, and Kyle stepped back and watched with a strange sensation. It was similar to happiness.

In his head, he described it the way he would if he were talking to Emily:

Do you think we can make a choice to be happy? I had this moment at the kids' practice when I felt like I was choosing it. It was all sunny and this kid Tatum got a triple and slid like a badass and . . . I don't know. Maybe I wasn't choosing it. Maybe it was more like I was letting it.

Malone appeared at his shoulder, arms crossed. "You're good at this sometimes."

"Thanks. It's pretty fun sometimes."

"Would you want to do some work over the summer?" he continued. "I run a baseball camp for girls. It's these two you already know, plus any girls who want to build more confidence and skills. I have some donors, so it doesn't cost parents a dime. A lot of the parents I talk to are scared off by the organized leagues and registration fees and all. That pisses me off, so I started a free camp. It would pay you, though. Not much. Some."

"Yeah," he said. "I'm interested. I do this family trip at the beginning of summer, but after that, yeah."

He sat in his car at the school before driving home and texted Emily.

High five me. Just got a summer job inspiring the youths.

She sent back a gif of dancing orphans from *Annie*.

Wait, she said. **This doesn't affect farm week, right??**

No way. how are you? he asked.

233

**Okay I guess? between Alex and my mom there is a lot
of emotion in my house rn and it's exhausting. they are so
EXPRESSIVE. ugh.**

**IDK what that's like. everyone here is so . . .
REpressive. Taylor is coming home today though so that
might change.**

I gotta go, but tell her I said hi!

Taylor's car was in the driveway next to his mom's. Kyle
hummed "I Have Confidence" from *The Sound of Music*
and leaned over to check himself out in the rearview mirror. He was going to try acting like things at home were
fine and see how that went. If he hated that, he'd decide
what to do next. He hadn't seen Taylor since Presidents'
Day weekend, before everything hit the fan, and thought
maybe he could at least let her first night back be okay.

He bounced into the house. "Yo! Where my sis at?"

"Back here!"

She was in her room, with their mom, unpacking some
plastic bins of clothes. Taylor's first words were "Yes, I've
gained weight, don't say anything and don't give me crap
about it."

"No, you look great," he said. Taylor was almost as tall
as their dad, had his same wispy hair. Now she looked
more grown up and less like a tall child. He gave her a

hug, feeling their mom's eyes on him.

"You too," she said. She scratched his chin. "Trying to grow a beard?"

"Succeeding, you mean." He pushed her hand away playfully. "Nah, I just keep forgetting to shave."

She looked around her room. "I hate unpacking. Maybe I'll finish this later."

"You'll feel better if you get it done now," their mom said. "It will go fast with the two of us."

"Let me take you to Cold Stone when you're done," Kyle said to Taylor. "I think I still have a gift card from Christmas."

"Well," their mom said, "we're all going out to dinner, so maybe you should wait on the ice cream?"

All of them? Out to dinner? He could act normal to an extent, but that would be harder to pull off. "I have a lot of homework," Kyle said. "It's not fair you're done with the semester and I still have weeks of school left." He tried to sound disappointed.

But then Taylor said, "It's Los Hermanos, Kyle, come *on*. I've been thinking about it for two weeks."

"Is Dad going?"

"Uh, *yeah*, Dad's going."

He glanced at his mom. She shrugged and said, "We won't stay out late."

The good thing about dinner at Los Hermanos was that it gave him a chance to practice being with family who didn't know about his mom. He joked with the server about making sure Taylor got a steady stream of root beer, her favorite. His mom asked him about school, and he answered almost as if they'd never not been in normal Mom-Kyle mode, though he did try to pivot the topic away from himself as soon as possible. Taylor complained about her roommate, and their dad ate nearly the whole basket of chips by himself and didn't say much.

The night was pretty smooth at first. Cool how when everyone agrees to pretend, they can basically create a whole new reality.

"Megan better come to the farm," Taylor was saying. "She claims she's going to try, but you know Megan."

"She has your back when it comes to the important stuff, though, right?" Kyle said.

Their mom leaned forward, rested her chin on her fist. "I'm so happy you two are there for each other."

"Eh," Taylor said, holding out her hand and making a so-so motion. "She had some good advice about my roommate one day, and the next day all she said was 'Work it out.' That was her whole text. 'Work it out.' Thanks, Megan."

"I think she's just really busy with her jobs."

"Kyle, I *know*. But how long does it take to answer a text?"

Their dad broke his silence. "Give Megan a break. She's trying to make her own way."

"I'm trying too, Dad," Taylor said.

"Everyone's path is different." Kyle's mom probably meant for that to end the conversation, but then his dad added, "That's for sure."

When they got home, the sun was going down, but it was still warm out. If it had been a year ago, they would all have headed to the patio without even discussing it, maybe had a bowl of ice cream. Now Kyle's dad turned on the TV and his mom worked on a design proposal at the kitchen island. Taylor said she still had a little unpacking left.

But Kyle didn't want to just go to his room like he did every night. Taylor being home reminded him of what it had been like, before. He missed living in the whole house instead of one little corner of it.

Out on the patio, he shook a bunch of leaves and twigs and stuff off a chair, then pulled it over to the pond he'd cleaned up over the weekend and got out his phone.

He told Emily about dinner. Response bubbles appeared then disappeared. Appeared again, disappeared. And again, until he couldn't stop himself from asking:

Okay, what aren't you saying? He added a smiley.

No answer, no bubbles. He closed his eyes out there on the patio, held the phone to his chest. He breathed. Every time he thought he felt the slightest sign that Emily wasn't happy with him, he got scared. Though he'd done a good job not sending super-needy texts lately, he still mostly talked about himself. His life, his problems, his confusion. Probably every time she saw his name on her notifications, she was like, *Great*, now *what?*

Maybe she didn't even like him. Maybe she was just being nice because she had to be, because they were family. It's not like she could drop out of the friendship, because there'd always be the next holiday or get-together and she'd have to see his stupid face yet again. He'd been a bad boyfriend to Nadia, at the end, and a bad teammate and maybe a bad son for being so judgmental of his parents and now a bad . . . whatever he was to his cousin.

It was a physical ache, this worry that the connection between them might be interrupted, and that it would be his fault.

His phone buzzed. He counted to ten before opening his eyes and looking at the phone, steeling himself to find out more ways he'd screwed up.

And in those seconds, he knew he'd gotten entangled in something he hadn't meant or expected to. To need so badly for this one person to understand and care about him. To rely on her words to make him know if he was an okay person or a complete disappointment.

He looked.

IDK, just so ready for school to be over and also some drama bc my mom got a tattoo without telling my dad and he's losing his mind over it.

Kyle exhaled. *Yeah, dummy, it's not about you.*

Really??? he replied. **Everyone has them now. Practically all my teachers.**

Well, it's a BAD tattoo, which I think my dad is more mad about than the basic idea of a tattoo. It's actually kind of funny, but it's like me and my dad are raising our very own teenager and I need a break from being a parent.

Hmmm sounds familiar, he said, still coming down from the adrenaline of getting ready for rejection, but trying to play it light.

Ha. How ARE things over there?

Are you sure you want to know right now? He let his thumbs hover for a second and then added, **It can wait. I mean, I know I depend on you too much. You have stuff going on, too. Like you said that time you got mad at me.**

I wasn't really mad at you, she said.

Yeah you were, he thought. **You know how we said we wanted to always be a good thing for each other . . . I want to make sure it is. A good thing for you.**

It took her a long time to type her next message, and it was disappointingly short after all that waiting. **I think it's okay to depend on people,** she said. **We're family.**

I know, but . . . He couldn't think how to finish that sentence, exactly. After a deep breath, he wrote: **It's different. More like you're my best friend.**

Then added: **Is that okay to say?**

And then: **You probably have a real best friend, I just mean, you know, I tell you more stuff than I tell anyone else right now. It's probably a phase hahaha**

God, he sounded so dumb and pathetic. He was almost certain now that she was just being nice. Being family. Acting as his crisis counselor for the last few months.

You can depend on me, too, you know, he added, now desperate for her to reply. He put his earbuds in and stuck the phone under his leg so he wouldn't be tempted to say more, and so he wasn't staring at her typing bubble feeling like an idiot.

He imagined her in her room, sitting on the floor with her short hair raked back, tossing her phone aside so she could concentrate on her homework without her emotionally fragile cousin bothering her every five minutes.

"We're family," she'd said. Was she saying it like . . . *We're not actually best friends, we're family*? Or like *We're family, which means we'll be best friends forever*?

He brought up *Hamilton*, the only modern musical he

really liked, and tried to relax in his chair, eyes closed again. "Say No to This" started. Kyle immediately skipped it. Too intense, too much like his life. Skip skip skip till he hit "One Last Time," when he leaned his head back and wondered if he could somehow manage never going into the house again.

Someone kicked his foot.

He opened his eyes and stared up at Taylor. She took her hands out of the front pocket of her USC pullover, gestured to her ears, and waited. When he didn't move, she leaned over and yanked his earbuds out.

"You've been sitting here forever."

His phone vibrated under his leg. "Hang on," he told Taylor.

"Who is it?"

"No one. Seriously, just like . . ."

She sighed and went to drag another chair over. While she cleaned it off and got settled, Kyle read:

I remember when we all used to sleep in the bunkhouse at the farm. It was always you and me staying up and talking way after everyone else. You've always been the one I look forward to seeing the most. Maybe because of us being the same age or maybe because Megan scared me and Taylor thought I was annoying or because I didn't feel girlie enough for them or whatever, I don't know. You never treated me like I

was strange or different. So I trust you more than any of the other cousins. It makes me happy that you trust me, too, and that I can be here for you now while you're going through all this. And you shouldn't worry about it so much.

He reread it twice.

I trust you.

Man, he'd needed that. So she didn't actually say, "You're my best friend too," so what. He immediately forgot the sense from mere minutes ago that maybe it was not ideal to depend on *one* person so much for his whole entire sense of well-being.

Then she inserted a gif of James Cagney tap dancing down a staircase in a way that looked physically impossible. Kyle smiled. **How does he not fall??** he asked.

Gravity can't touch him.

Taylor is here now, he wrote. **I'm gonna talk to her, okay?**

TALK talk or taaaalk?

He sent her a shrug and a screaming cat face, then stuck his phone in his pocket.

"Sorry I invaded your privacy," Taylor said. "Usually you hide in your room when you want privacy."

"I'm so tired of my room. And it's nice out."

"So," she said. "What's going on."

It was a question and a statement and a plea and it

sounded like she knew something, but in case his inter-
pretation was off, he asked, "What do you mean?"

She stared at him like *Are you serious*?

"Um, me and Nadia breaking up? Did Megan tell you?"

"Oh, shit, Kyle, no, I didn't know. Are you okay?" She
searched his face. "You're not okay."

"Not really. Not yet."

She put her hand on his arm for a couple seconds, patted it, then said, "But you and Nadia aren't what's making
Mom and Dad weird."

If she'd only been home a few hours and already sensed
it, telling her something would not be this huge reveal.
Still, he hesitated. "The farm stuff, maybe," he offered.

"Yeah, that is terrible and depressing, but . . . it's like
they won't really look at each other?"

Light flooded the yard; their dad had gone into the
kitchen. They watched him move things around in the
refrigerator, his back to the windows.

"Bigfoot," Kyle muttered, and Taylor let out a single
loud laugh and put her hand over her mouth. Megan had
started calling their dad that years ago, because of how
hairy the back of his neck could get. Just straight-up *fur*,
disappearing under his shirt collar.

"Bigfoot hungry," Taylor said.

"Bigfoot need food. Need food now. Enchilada plate
not satisfy."

Their mom was the one who would shave and trim his neck before it could get bushy. Now there was no one tending to him, feeding him, grooming him.

Kyle thought of about six different ways to say it, but ultimately went with the most direct.

"Mom is having an affair."

Taylor laughed.

"I'm not kidding," Kyle said.

"Wait. What? *Mom* is?"

"Yes."

Taylor sat with that long enough for Kyle to experience the crash of anxiety at having told a secret, and then the subsequent wave of relief that now he had both of his sisters in the ring with him.

"How do you know?" Taylor asked. "Did you see something on Mom's phone or something? Maybe it's not what you thought?"

"I know because Dad told me. And Mom admits it. And keeps telling me not to tell. And . . ."

"And?"

"I know who the guy is. His kid is in this group I help coach."

"Oh my *god*. She met him through your baseball team or something?"

"No, I don't know how she met him, but I guess like Dad always says—it's a small town."

Taylor looked toward the window, where their dad finally closed the fridge and, still empty-handed, turned off the light and walked offstage. *Bigfoot sad.*

Kyle filled in more details of what he knew and how he'd found out. The car ride to Martie's birthday, the things they'd said about not wanting to make any decisions yet, the financial issues affecting everything. "*Allegedly* affecting everything," Kyle said. "Megan thinks that's an excuse."

"Megan knows? You told *Megan* and then neither of you told me?"

"I did tell you. I just told you."

"You know what I mean." She started to sniffle, wiped her face with her sleeve.

He glanced at her. "Are you crying because of Mom and Dad or because I told Megan first?"

She laughed a little. "I don't know."

"Emily knows too, so go ahead and yell at me about that, I guess."

"Emily, our cousin?" She wiped her face again. "Okay." She slumped down in her chair and shoved her hands into the pouch of her sweatshirt. "I'm shocked, but I'm not shocked. I knew things here weren't good, even back at Thanksgiving and Christmas. There's a reason I haven't come home much since."

"You noticed stuff at Thanksgiving?"

"Mom was off by herself a lot. On her phone whenever she had a chance. She just seemed kind of . . . disengaged? Even when she was right there. You didn't notice all that?"

He chewed on his knuckle. "No."

"You were busy falling in love, Kyle."

Right as she said that, something rustled behind them, and then a possum shot out of a shrub and darted past their chairs. Taylor shrieked and lifted her legs off the ground. The possum went left, then right, then turned and looked straight at them like it was going to ask for directions.

"Get away!" Taylor shouted, and it did, straight down the walkway between their house and the neighbors'.

"Dude, it listened to you!"

Kyle started laughing and Taylor did her Taylor laugh—covering her mouth with her hand and shaking, her eyes alternately going wide and squinching shut. They couldn't stop. Kyle felt himself losing control and kept his arm over his own mouth so that he couldn't get too loud and wake up the whole neighborhood.

The kitchen light came on again. They looked up. Their dad stood in the window, craning his neck to see what was going on. Kyle pointed. "Bigfoot," he said, almost crying. "Bigfoot curious?"

Their dad tapped on the glass, then pointed at his

wrist. Taylor took her hand off her mouth long enough to barely manage to say, "He's not even wearing a watch," before having to cover her mouth again. She rocked back and forth with tears coming out of her eyes, and Kyle clutched his stomach, finally losing control after all these months of doing a pretty good job keeping it together, finally dissolving into the terrible, ridiculous, unbearable ache of it all.

Part III

SUMMER, NOWHERE FARM

1

ON THE morning of departure for the farm, Kyle overslept. He hadn't set an alarm because in every previous version of his family's existence, his mom or dad would go around and wake up Kyle and Megan and Taylor early and make a whole big deal out of it. In this version, Kyle shuffled down the quiet hall and through the empty kitchen, then found his dad in the driveway, tossing a duffel bag and a small cooler into the truck.

"How come nobody woke me up? Where's the rest of the stuff?"

"Once you load up anything you want to bring, I think we're good to go." His dad leaned into the truck cab and collected some empty soda cans and food wrappers.

"But . . ." Kyle noticed his mom's car was gone. The garage was open and Taylor's was parked inside.

"They already left."

Separate cars? Separate cars and no wake-up and no one had prepared him? It wasn't like he thought it would be the same as ever—stopping in Pacific Grove for a picnic, doing rest-stop jumping jacks with his sisters, playing each other music from their phones.

"This is the *last* summer at the farm," Kyle said, watching his father carry garbage to the can in the garage. "Are we really going out like this, Dad?"

"Looks like it."

The last few weeks of school had been a mix of better and worse than the couple of months leading up to it. Just having Taylor in the house and knowing what was up helped Kyle feel way less alone. They'd talked about telling their parents that she knew too, but then Taylor said, "Let's put it in the vault. For now. Mom and Dad aren't the only ones who can keep secrets."

At first they shared a lot of glances and emails and analyzed stuff with each other and on their text thread with Megan. But then Megan said she didn't want to hear about it anymore, and not long after that, Taylor confessed that she wished she didn't know, too.

"Farm week is going to be ruined," she'd said one night, when they finally did go to Cold Stone to use the gift card. "Maybe it *is* better to pretend."

"We are, Taylor. That's exactly what we're doing."

She looked down at her ice cream, running her plastic spoon around the edge and eating toward the middle, like she'd been doing for as long as Kyle could remember.

"I could try pretending to myself?"

"I tried that," he'd said. "It doesn't work that well, usually."

School sucked, because school. Also he had to keep seeing Nadia and Mateo. They weren't super couple-ish at school, but they were obviously close. And when Kyle heard they were going to junior prom together, he of course thought about how he and Nadia had talked about that. Talked about getting a hotel room, even though they'd already gone from longer and more complicated make-outs with less and less clothing to going all the way on New Year's Eve, in Nadia's room while her parents were out at a party. A hotel room would be different, though. It would mean getting to spend the whole night together. Opening his eyes in the morning and seeing her there, getting to hold her while the sun came up.

Maybe she did all that with Mateo on prom night. Maybe she didn't. He stayed away from social media and any conversations around school about that night.

He'd finished strong with his mentoring gig with Coach Malone's kids, putting the info about Jacob's dad into some kind of vault within a vault in his mind. Pretending to himself, like Taylor said, which he could manage for a few hours a week. As long as he wasn't at home comparing the past to the present. Malone gave Ito a good report, and Ito said Kyle could start next season with a clean slate, if he wanted.

But that would mean more Mateo.

The Mateo and Nadia situation was the one thing he hadn't told Emily.

Every time he thought about it, he'd stop himself, worried he was one of those basic people preoccupied with romantic drama. And worried he'd get into talking about sex. Which he didn't want to do with her, not so much because he was shy about it or she didn't have a lot to say on the topic but, like, it was almost like his and Emily's connection was too pure for that? Maybe that was dumb, or belittling to her in some way, or maybe he was just private and didn't really want to talk about sex with *anybody* he wasn't actually having it with. He wasn't sure.

He'd been telling her everything else, though, and she'd been keeping him updated with Uncle Dale and Aunt Brenda's issues. And last night she'd texted, **Only one more sleep till I get to see my most favorite cousin!**

and it felt like the best thing she'd ever said to him. Or second best, after saying she trusted him.

Now he took a quick shower and finished packing, then jumped in the truck with his dad. When they were a few miles from home, his dad said, "Taylor and your mom just wanted some quality time together. The separate cars thing. And I need to have the pickup in case there's a work emergency or anything I need to get back for."

"Sure, Dad. Makes sense. Also the fact that you and Mom don't want to be trapped in the same vehicle for five or six hours."

"Also that."

Did you leave yet? he asked Emily. **Taylor and Mom will probably get there before us. Separate cars.**

She replied, **On the road now. My parents had a big fight because my mom bought a margarita machine to bring and it was like 200 bucks and took up all this room in the trunk but really they're fighting about her drinking and just not saying it. And my dad has a cold and is being a baby about it. So now we're listening to podcasts and no one is talking.** She punctuated it with a thumbs-up.

Sorry but tbh I feel better not being the only one dealing with parental misconduct.

Also, I can't wait to see you, he added.

She sent back a gif of Maria from *The Sound of Music*

swirling around on a mountaintop.

Then he texted Megan for the fourth time since last night. **ARE YOU COMING YES/NO.** Her last update said she'd gotten the time off one job, but not the other. After that she went MIA. **Don't leave me and Taylor hanging,** he added. **Even if you can only come a couple days. We need you, is all I'm saying.**

During the drive, Kyle endured the sense memories of the last time they'd been on this same drive. How one minute he'd been texting with Nadia, then the next minute his dad had dropped his four-word grenade.

Now his dad was on a call with Al Najarian, his business partner, on speakerphone. Annoying, but it killed some time. They were going through a punch list for a remodel and complaining about the client and then about some subcontractors.

"Just get that completion payment," his dad said. "Do whatever you have to."

When his dad was off the phone, Kyle asked, "Is Baker and Najarian okay?"

"It's fine."

"Really."

"Kyle, don't worry about it."

"Why shouldn't I worry? You keep saying don't worry about money, don't worry about you and Mom, it's fine, you're figuring it out. But it's not fine and you're not figuring it out, and I'm worrying. Worrying isn't something you can just tell someone *not* to do. You do know that, right?"

His dad didn't react.

Kyle scanned through the radio stations and couldn't find anything he liked.

"Just turn it off," his dad said.

"We're going to drive in total silence?"

"Okay, then plug your phone in and put on your show tunes, but I don't want to listen to three seconds of one song and then three seconds of a different song and three seconds—"

"Got it." Kyle turned off the radio. They were only an hour into the trip. He sighed. He didn't want to put on show tunes. Show tunes were private. Something for him and Emily. He sent her a check-in text and she replied with a picture of Uncle Dale asleep in the back seat of their car, clutching a fistful of tissues. **There's drool,** she said.

They joked a little more, when what Kyle was really thinking was how there was this excitement at the pit of his stomach that within hours, they'd be seeing each other. The first time since Martie's birthday. Since everything.

He texted Taylor. **Thx for saying goodbye this morning and telling me wtf is going on**

Taylor: **I was surprised too and you were asleep!**

welp, see you there I guess

They hit some road construction and slowed to a ten-miles-per-hour crawl.

"So," his dad said. "Mom says your grades weren't great this year."

Kyle exhaled a laugh. Now they were going to make conversation. Okay. "They weren't. But I brought them up and I think I did okay on finals."

"Oh, okay. Good."

They inched along. Kyle stared out the window at the road crew in their orange vests, talking on two-way radios.

"Got a girl?" his dad asked. "Since Nadia?"

"Dad. Could we not?"

They'd literally never talked about the breakup before. Or about his grades all year. Or, for that matter, base-ball or his coaching or anything, stuff he and his dad would talk about if this year was normal *at all*. Yet Dad was getting info somehow, through dad osmosis. Indirect communication or no communication at all. Maybe that's what his mom was sick of. Maybe her boyfriend could just come out and say stuff instead of circling and circling thoughts and feelings and opinions like a spooked deer.

The lanes opened back up, and his dad stepped on the gas.

* * *

When they finally made the turn at the first Nowhere Farm sign, Kyle's nervous system zapped again and again. He thought about the last time, when Emily had been waiting for him on the swings. That time didn't feel like this. Was he jittery about the job of hiding his parents' situation from the family or about seeing Emily? It felt like . . . Emily.

Kyle, my dude, find some chill about Emily. He didn't want to, like, burst into tears when he saw her or something.

They went down the long driveway, under a canopy of trees, passing the swing set—no Emily—and the kitchen garden. There were a few cars parked half on the gravel and half on the scrub, including his mom's. Then there was the house and Grandma Baker coming out the front door, waving.

"This is the last time we're gonna see that," Kyle said, but not loud enough, because his dad was distracted by the sight of a little black dog running toward the truck and barking as they parked. "What the hell is that?"

Grandpa Baker came out of the house next, his cap pulled down low. Seeing Grandpa didn't give Kyle quite the same sentimental feeling as seeing Grandma; it hit him in a more melancholy way how he seemed so much older than he had even in March.

They got out of the truck. Grandpa gave Kyle and his

dad handshake-hugs. The dog jumped around. "Who's this?" Kyle's dad asked.

"This little doggo is a gift from Great-Aunt Gina's convent. His name is Pico, and he's been trained to look after old people."

"Did you ask for a service dog, Dad? Everything been all right?"

"No, we didn't ask," Grandma said. She was carrying some bags from the car already, not giving them a chance to do it themselves. "You know Gina. She doesn't wait to be asked. Now what's this about you needing to go back early for work?" Grandma asked Kyle's dad.

"I *might*. Not for sure."

Kyle let the dog sniff his hand and knelt down to scratch his head. When he stood, he saw her.

She was coming down the trail from the olive grove with Taylor and Alex. Alex waved with both arms, but his eyes were on Emily. She had on cutoffs and an orange T-shirt, slow-walking with her fingers in her pockets and elbows out, looking exactly like herself.

Alex ran to Kyle and jumped all over him, and he let her. "Hey, Tigger."

"I'm never going to see you again," she wailed, her arms around his waist.

"Yeah you are. You're gonna see me the same amount, just not here."

He dragged her along and wished for a second he was her age, so he could show his happiness at seeing Emily with that much raw emotion. Just cling and smother and weep. Instead he matched Emily's walking pace and went toward her. Alex finally let go. Kyle *wanted* to get Emily into a huge hug, but not in front of his sister or anyone else. Besides, she might not want that. He held up his hand for a high five. Emily gave him a funny look and slapped it.

"What's up?" he said to her. She laughed, and they just looked at each other for a minute.

"How was it with Dad?" Taylor asked.

"Long and boring and silent. How about with Mom?"

"Not silent. But still boring and long. Did Megan text you?"

"Nope."

"Is Megan coming?" Alex jumped up and down again.

"Maybe," Kyle told her.

Aunt Brenda and Kyle's mom were in the drive now, chatting in a polite way. Kyle went over; Aunt Brenda crushed him in a hug. "Jesus, Kyle, you're more a man every time I see you." She looked at Grandpa. "Sorry. I meant cheese-us." To Kyle: "Uncle Dale would say hello if he weren't in bed day-drinking Nyquil."

"All right," Grandma said, "now that everyone's here, let's sort out the rooms. Gina is on the main floor, as usual. I thought Taylor and Emily could take the attic. It will be hot up there, but there are some fans in the basement you could bring up to get the air moving."

"Oh," Kyle's mom said, interrupting, "I was thinking Taylor and I could share. It was so good to have mother-daughter time in the car, I thought we could keep it going."

Kyle caught Taylor's eye; she put her hands to her cheeks and mouthed, *Noooooo.*

"That's fine," Kyle's dad said.

"Mom," Taylor said. "No."

"It'll be fun!"

"No, it won't. Room with Dad." She shot Kyle a sly look, then pulled Emily's hand. "Let's go get the fans."

They went into the house and Grandpa trailed after them, giving specific instructions about where the fans were, and Kyle watched his dad wander back to his truck.

"Good," Grandma said to Kyle's mom. "So you and Jeff will be in Jeff's old room. There's a box of stuff on the bed I'd like him to go through. Whatever he doesn't take we're going to have to toss."

"Well, tell Jeff," Kyle's mom said, pointing toward his dad.

"I can hear."

Grandma said to Brenda, "And I've got *six* boxes for you."

"I saw."

"I mean it this time. We're renting a Dumpster after camp is over, and it's going to be toss, toss, toss, toss. We're not taking you-all's junk with us when we move."

If she felt sad about the farm sale and leaving it all behind, she sure didn't show it. Grandma never had been sentimental, though. Maybe the inability to express feelings and communicate about anything not superficial was in the Baker blood. Kyle's dad was withdrawn, Aunt Brenda was always performing, and Uncle Mike just wanted to have fun and for everyone to get along.

"Where am I sleeping?" Alex asked. "Are me and Martie in the basement?"

"Martie wants to sleep at her own house, so you'll have it all to yourself!"

Alex's face fell. "I don't want to be alone in the basement."

"Well," Grandma said, "if you and Kyle can get the big bean bag up to the attic, you might be able to squeeze in with Taylor and Emily."

"*Ask* Emily first," Aunt Brenda said.

"I have as much right as her to be in the attic."

"Ask. Maybe *she'd* like to be alone in the basement."

Then Taylor would be stuck alone with Alex, which Kyle knew wouldn't be okay with her. "We could all sleep in the bunkhouse," he said. "Like we used to."

"Except you can't," Grandma said. "It's half demolished,

and Grandpa wants you to finish the job this week."

"Uh, what do you mean, it's half demolished?" Kyle asked.

"I mean it's half demolished. Finishing it is the project. You didn't think there'd be no project this year, did you?" Every summer the cousins had a project, arts and crafts when they were little, turning into real work like sealing the deck or doing fence repair when they were older.

"No, but . . ." The *bunkhouse*?

The place where he and the cousins would play every summer? And Emily would whisper all night? Where he told Nadia he loved her?

"What if I don't *want* to tear down the bunkhouse?" Kyle asked.

"Yeah," Alex added. "What if we don't want to?"

"Too bad," Grandma sad. "Grandpa's the boss."

Aunt Brenda patted Kyle on the back. "Gonna be an *awesome* farm week."

2

KYLE HELPED Alex drag the giant beanbag from the basement to the attic. She didn't ask Emily like she was supposed to, and Kyle promised to back her up. "No one should be alone in the basement this week," he said.

They shoved the bean bag through the small attic door.

"Hello?" Taylor asked. "What are you doing?"

"Grandma said I had to sleep up here," Alex said.

Kyle laughed at her adjustment of the facts, and went over to the attic window where Emily stood looking out. The attic had a view of olive trees, walnut trees, the pear orchard.

He nudged her with his elbow. "Here we are."

"We are here." She put her finger on the glass. "I heard my dad saying the other day that the buyer is eventually going to turn all this to vineyards. Adding to the existing vineyards and letting everything else die off, I guess."

The whole place as they'd always known it would be replaced with something completely different.

"And guess what our project is," Kyle said. "Tearing down the bunkhouse."

Emily turned to him. "I'm going to cry."

He wanted to comfort her, say something good. But then Alex bounced over and stuck her head between them to see out the window. "Uncle Mike and Martie are here!" she said, and sprang away excitedly. Taylor followed Alex out, and Emily and Kyle were alone.

"Grandma said Martie doesn't even want to sleep here," Kyle said.

They watched Martie hop out of Uncle Mike's truck, sunglasses and baseball hat, in a crop top with her phone tucked into the waistband of her leggings.

"I'd probably feel the same if I lived ten minutes away like she does and could be alone in my own room." She turned to him. "So, hi."

Mostly all he wanted was to study her. Notice all the things about her he never had, because she'd just been *Emily*. Like her grayish eyes, and the strong shape of her nose, more noticeable now because of the nose ring. The haircut he'd been so weird about showed her neck, and in the light by the window he could see the halo of fine, light hair on her skin.

She saved the weird moment by stepping toward him to initiate the hug. She felt solid, sturdy. So *there*. Not text on a screen, or a floating face.

They let each other go and Kyle wanted to immediately hug her again. But he didn't. He folded his arms, and they looked down at everyone gathered by Mike and Jenny's truck.

"I talked to your mom for five whole minutes, and it didn't feel too weird knowing everything I know," Emily said. "Maybe it won't be so hard."

"My parents have to share a room and a bed and everything. Mom tried to get out of it, but Taylor put the smackdown on that."

"I've been trying to imagine if it was my parents," Emily said. "They would be so bad at hiding it, though. My mom would probably confess right away and they'd have a big, dramatic separation and my mom would write a play about it."

"And if it was Uncle Mike and Aunt Jenny . . . ," Kyle started. Then they both kind of laughed, and he said, "Yeah, no, it would never be Uncle Mike and Aunt Jenny. They're soul mates."

"If *anyone* is soul mates, and I don't even know if

I believe in that, it's them."

Stay chill, stay chill. Don't say you think Emily might be your soul mate.

"Even though all this stuff is going on," he said, "I'm really happy to be here. You know. To hang with you in person and stuff." He listened to his own words. You didn't have to *say* that to family. It was supposed to go with*out* saying, right?

"Me too," she said in a voice way more casual than his.

At that moment, Taylor looked up at the attic window and waved them down.

"I hope you've all been practicing your Electric Slide," Uncle Mike said to the cousins. "Your dancing at Martie's birthday was a real disappointment."

"Dad," Martie said.

"I'm just saying. This dance party has to be the most epic we've ever had. Last one at the farm."

"My mom brought a margarita machine," Emily said. "That should help with the epicness."

Kyle could tell she was being sarcastic, but Uncle Mike said, "I know. She texted me from the store and I was like, yes, we *absolutely* need that." Mike looked down at them. "Okay, who's gonna help me unload this crap?"

Cousins scattered. Martie and Taylor went off toward the swings, and Alex ran after them. Kyle and Emily stayed to unload the big gas grill, one cooler full of ice and beer and soda and cut limes, and one full of food. Kyle watched Emily's biceps flex as they carried the beer cooler over to the patio. "You're cut, dude. Have you been lifting this year or is that all from swimming?"

"Both. I like being strong."

They set the cooler down under the folding table where Grandpa usually set up the bar. Emily folded her hands behind her head and gave Kyle this look, a look so direct and open and beaming out this pure Emily spirit that he almost wanted to hide. That feeling was overridden by how much he wanted to soak it in.

Uncle Mike rolled the grill over. "I'm still perfecting the playlist for Saturday night. So if you guys have songs you want, submit them to me for approval."

"Not 'Rock Lobster,'" Kyle said.

"But that's your aunt Brenda's favorite," Mike said with a wink.

Emily rolled her eyes. "We're aware."

"Gather 'round, all ye Bakers and former Bakers!" It was Grandma, stepping out onto the patio with a cardboard box. The phone box. He always forgot.

Kyle's parents followed, along with Aunt Brenda and Aunt Jenny. "Now that all's ashore who's coming ashore, phones go in the box. Send your last messages in a bottle now."

269

For a second he thought with a start, *But how am I going to talk to Emily?* Then he remembered she was standing right next to him. He glanced at her with a smile and was the first to go to Grandma and toss his phone in.

Emily went next. Taylor said, "Let me check something real quick. . . ." and Martie looked at Uncle Mike to ask, "But . . . I'm not really staying here, so I'm getting it back at the end of every day, right?"

Grandma said, "I don't see why. No one else will have theirs at night."

"Mom," Uncle Mike said, "come on. That's not reasonable. You know I have to check in with work. We all do."

"I will distribute phones to the adults twice per day, before breakfast and after dinner." She rattled the box and said to Martie, "Once a day for everyone under thirty."

"You can't make up new, random rules every time, Mom," Kyle's dad said. "Mike's right about work."

"I *can* make up new, random rules. I'm your mother."

Kyle's dad tossed his phone in but muttered, "When I need it back, I'm going to take it back."

Martie threw hers in and stalked off toward the pear orchard. "I'm going to find Grandpa Navarro," she said over her shoulder. "Yeah, remember him?"

Kyle wondered what *that* was about, then noticed his mom literally clutching her phone to her chest with this expression on her face.

Of course she'd panic. The phone was her portal to her other life. She turned away from the group and sent a text, then powered her phone off and set it in the box.

While the rest of the adults argued about the rules, Great-Aunt Gina came around from behind the house with her walking stick, still moving slowly from her hip operation. Kyle hadn't seen her in a year. She looked exactly like Grandpa Baker. Nearly the same height, same long arms and craggy face and basically the same haircut.

"I have an announcement," she said.

"I'm sure you do," Aunt Jenny said quietly. "Why bother saying hello when you have an announcement?"

"The dog, Pico, is supposed to be learning to respond only to your grandfather. He's not a pet to play with. Please don't undo the months of training we undertook at the convent, and don't give him table scraps." She waved her hand. "That's it, that's all I have. Carry on saying goodbye to the ball and chain you all seem to enjoy carrying around in your pockets. I'll be on my walk."

They watched her disappear around the side of the house.

"You gotta love her," Aunt Brenda said.

After everyone had turned over their phones, Kyle asked Uncle Mike what Martie was mad about.

"Haven't you been reading the emails?" He explained that Grandma and Grandpa had agreed to the farm sale without even mentioning it to Grandpa Navarro. He'd heard about it when someone in town asked him what he was planning to do now that he was retiring.

Uncle Mike looked from Emily to Kyle. "This part wasn't in the emails, but the real deal is that Jenny thinks Eliseo should get some proceeds from the sale, and I don't disagree, but no one is talking about it. Don't be surprised if you don't see a lot of Aunt Jenny and Grandpa Navarro around this week or if you feel like there's an elephant in the room."

Two elephants, Kyle thought.

"Well that sucks," Emily said.

"Is that why Martie doesn't want to sleep over?" Kyle asked.

"I think that's part of it. Though also she's pretty into her own dramas right now. Fifteen, you know." He said it as if Kyle and Emily were way, way past that.

"I'm going to go check on my dad," Emily said. "I think everyone forgot he exists."

Kyle took a step to go with her, then stopped, then started again, stopped. She hadn't invited him and was already ten feet away and not looking back.

"You okay?" Uncle Mike asked.

"Yeah."

"Then help me with the propane tank." Kyle walked with him back to the truck. Then Uncle Mike asked, all casual, "Hey, how's Nadia? We sure enjoyed having her over at Thanksgiving. I know Martie was disappointed she couldn't come out for the quinceañera."

"She's . . . she's good. She's fine," Kyle said. "But we broke up."

Uncle Mike turned to him. "You broke *up*?"

"Yep."

"Wow. Jenny and me were saying at Thanksgiving how you guys reminded us of how we were in high school."

Kyle grabbed the handles of the propane tank. "Thanksgiving was a long time ago."

"Sounds like you don't want to talk about it."

"Not really. Not right now."

Uncle Mike showed him where to put the tank and tried to say some meaningful stuff about love and letting go, but Kyle couldn't engage with it. He finished helping and then wandered around the grounds. Not exactly looking for Emily, but not *not* looking. He passed the old climbing tree that seemed so small now and thought, *Never seeing it again after this week*. He circled the pond and wondered if the new owners would keep it or drain it. He walked along the fence that the cousins had repaired a couple of summers ago. The new owners would have no idea a bunch of kids had done that.

Every familiar path and fencepost and tree and branch and twig, all lost.

Nadia. His friends. His parents as he'd known them. The farm. The person he was.

Gone.

Emily would still be there, he assured himself. Emily wouldn't change.

He headed toward the swing set. Maybe she'd be there, waiting.

She wasn't, but his mother was.

Kyle watched her from a distance before she noticed him. There was something lonely about it. Her on a swing, holding on to the chains and pushing off with her toes every few seconds. She didn't seem like a mom.

Then she saw him there, and he was stuck. He had to keep walking toward her. As he did, she wiped her face.

"Hey there," she said when he got to her.

"Hey." He sat on the swing next to her.

"Your drive with Dad go all right?" she asked.

"We got here."

"So did we."

He pushed his feet into the dirt and got as big a push off as he could, then tried pumping his legs like he had when he was a kid, but now his legs were too long and kept hitting the ground.

"It's sad, isn't it," she said. "About the farm."

"I thought you never super loved it here."

She shrugged and dabbed at her eyes with the corner of a tissue. "Oh, you know. It's hard for me with all the Bakers together. I know I don't fit in as well as Dale, or Jenny. But it's not like I can see my own family. What's left of them."

Her parents were dead. She had a sister she hadn't talked to as long as Kyle had been alive, and he'd heard some other extended family existed, but they'd never been a part of their lives and he didn't know the story there. He wondered what that was like—not being a part of your own family, then also not totally being a part of your in-law family.

He fought against his sympathy. If family life was already so hard, why would you screw it up and make it even harder?

"Your dad is already saying I should go home. He'd rather tell everyone than have to share a room with me."

"What happened to united front? One last great summer for everyone? Anyway, you were sharing at our house. Ever since Taylor got back."

She smiled and sniffled. "No, we weren't. We'd stay up until we were sure you two weren't coming back out of your rooms, and then Dad made his bed on the couch."

He almost told her right then that Taylor knew, so she could at least stop that part of the act. But he felt like he couldn't do that without consulting with Taylor.

"Why are you even here?" Kyle asked.

She leaned back in her swing, gripping the chains, and stared up at the sky.

Then she said, "I don't think you've been hearing me, Kyle. This is my family. This is the only family I've known since I was about twenty, when I met Dad. This place . . . these people. They all mean something to me, even though our relationships aren't perfect. Even though it can all be so difficult. No, I don't totally fit in, but they're what I have." She let out something between a huge sigh and a bellow. "Maybe if I could go back in time a year, six months, three months, I wouldn't have made the same choices. I don't know. None of us gets to have a time machine."

A seed of tenderness sprouted in Kyle. Here she was, finally saying the words he'd wanted her to for so long, words he understood in his own way because of his own regrets with Nadia.

But he didn't want that seed to take root, because then would that mean he'd have to forgive her? That he couldn't be angry anymore?

"Nope," he said, "we don't." He jumped off the swing and headed back to the house.

3

ALL THE cousins except Martie were sitting at the patio table while Aunt Brenda, holding a tumbler of wine, showed them a couple of scrapbooks from one of the boxes of stuff Grandma was making her go through. Emily somehow sensed him there, glanced over her shoulder, and scooted over to make room for him on the bench.

"This is the front page of the paper the day after the men's gymnastics team won gold in 1984," Aunt Brenda was saying. "Yes, children, in the olden days we cut things out of actual newspapers and put them into photo albums."

Alex climbed halfway across the table to look. "Did

you have a crush on one of them or something?"

"No, honey. Well, maybe Mitch Gaylord. We were just really proud, as a country." She turned the page. "Oh," Aunt Brenda said to Kyle and Taylor, "here's all of us sending your dad off to college."

It was a Polaroid of young Grandpa Baker with massive sideburns, and Grandma, and Uncle Mike and Aunt Brenda in high school or maybe junior high, standing around in an airport.

"Cool outfit," Taylor said with a laugh, pointing at teen Brenda in a paisley shirt two sizes too big, which she wore over long johns.

Kyle studied his eighteen-year-old dad, skinnier than Kyle had ever known him to be, with a bushy head of blond hair and an uncomfortable expression on his face that Kyle recognized.

"Looks like you," Emily said to him quietly.

"If I never cut my hair."

Aunt Brenda pulled the album closer. "That was when you could go right to the gate to meet people or send them off. You went through a metal detector, but it was fast and easy and you could *be* there when someone you loved stepped off a plane." She shook her head and took another sip of wine. "So much for those days, I guess."

Her mood had changed; Kyle could feel Emily tense up next to him. Aunt Brenda flipped through a dozen more pages, mostly of her with her theater friends in high school and college, in plays and working on the stage crew. All she said about each of them was the name of the play; then she'd turn the page.

"*Twelve Angry Men* . . . well, *Twelve Angry Jurors.*

"*Sweeney Todd.*

"*Anything Goes.*

"*Glass Menagerie.*

"*Arsenic and Old Lace.*"

Emily said, "*The Glass Menagerie* was the first one you directed, right?"

"Yep. I hated that play, but it's a small cast, so my teacher thought I could probably handle it."

"Did you ever do *West Side Story*?" Kyle asked.

"Twice! Once in college as a member of the chorus, and then I codirected it for the San Jose Light Opera a few years ago."

"You did?" Emily asked.

Brenda turned some more pages in the book. "You had the flu. I guess it was more than a few years ago. I probably have a program or a clipping in here somewhere. . . ."

There were a few blank pages, and then one with a picture of a young woman, maybe high school age, black, with bell-bottoms and an embroidered blouse, smiling at the camera. Aunt Brenda stared at it, expressionless.

"Who's that?" Kyle asked.

"Loreen."

Taylor pulled the album closer. "Who?"

"Your dad never told you about Loreen?" Aunt Brenda asked, looking from Taylor to Kyle.

"No."

She drained her glass of wine. "Loreen used to baby-sit for us. I barely remember her, but Jeff was older, he should remember." She touched Loreen's face. "She died at Jonestown."

"What's that?" Alex asked.

"There was this cult that got big right around here," Aunt Brenda said. "For a while they were in Santa Rosa. That's when Loreen's parents got involved. Anyway, later on, a bunch of them went to this place in South America to start, like, a commune, and Loreen went too. And . . ." She closed the photo album. "A lot of people died. Way before you were born, Al."

"How did they die?" Alex asked.

"Brenda, don't." It was Uncle Dale. He'd come out of the house and stood behind Kyle and Emily.

"She's old enough. She hears about the *news* every day."

"Mom . . . ," Emily said.

"Okay, fine." She looked the table. "The world is very shitty sometimes. And this is why I need each of you to swear to me you will vote in the next election. That you will always vote. Local, national, special elections, everything. Not all shitty things are preventable, but some are. Such as electing a criminal president." She slapped her hand on the table. "Promise!"

Taylor said, "We promise."

"Okay, Brenda," Uncle Dale said. "Save up some of your righteous anger for the rest of the week?"

Emily stood up and put her hand on Kyle's shoulder. "Let's go for a walk."

"I don't like it when she gets like that," Emily said.

They were walking to the pond. "She's passionate."

"Oh, *that's* fine and I agree with her and she's right. But watch. The whole rest of the night she's going to sit in a corner drinking, and if anyone tries to talk to her, she'll do that the-world-is-shitty speech again and not be able to get out of her bleak mood until after a pot of coffee in the morning."

"I can't believe that thing about their babysitter," Kyle said, in a little bit of a mood himself. "Loreen. Like, why has it never come up before here?"

"Bakers don't like to kill the party vibe. I know. It's depressing."

They'd reached the gazebo, far enough from the pond to avoid the clouds of gnats and mosquitos that hovered over the layer of green scum on the water. Emily jumped up onto one of the gazebo benches and leaped from it to another bench, then back again, her arms open.

"Who am I?" she asked.

"Liesl, obviously." From *The Sound of Music*. Except in cutoffs and a T-shirt instead of a floaty dress.

"That makes you Rolf."

"I don't want to be Rolf. He was a Nazi and a traitor!"

"But for a minute he was cute and they were in love."

She jumped to another bench, seeming oblivious to the awkwardness of what she'd just said, and Kyle tried to think of a joke or a line from "Sixteen Going on Seventeen" to sing that wasn't too weird. Then one end of the bench sort of collapsed under Emily. She squealed and leaped out of the way, landing in a squat.

"Oh my god," she said, laughing.

"Are you okay? The wood is rotting." He reached out his hand; she took it and he hoisted her up. Her hand was warm and strong. She pulled it out of his so she could brush off the back of her shorts. They stood close.

"I feel happy when I'm with you," he said. That was okay to say, right?

"You'd better," she joked. "It would kind of suck if we did all that texting and everything and then we *didn't* feel happy while we're actually here." She grabbed his arm. "Look."

The sun had dipped part of the way behind the hills in the distance. Kyle felt Emily's fingers on his forearm, her breath calming down after jumping around the benches.

The gazebo would be gone soon too, added to the inventory of losses.

But this moment, this moment he didn't have to lose.

He tried to stay in it, inside every micro moment within the moment, and not think about how it would feel at the end of the week, when they'd have to say goodbye.

4

KYLE AWOKE way too early, could see around the edges of the curtain in his tiny room that it was just getting light. Disoriented, he thought about Nadia. Like that it was Thanksgiving again and she was in the house, and he had to go down and see her.

"Rise and shine, buddy."

What the—

Grandpa Baker stood over his bed, talking in the loudest possible whisper with a cup of coffee in each hand, his cane hanging on the crook of his elbow. He held one out as Kyle sat up.

"Oh. I don't drink coffee."

"You might want to start."

No, he didn't want to start, but Grandpa had brought him a mug and he had to take it. He took a sip, for show. It was hot, really freaking hot and terrible. He grimaced.

"Coffee starts as a necessity, then grows into a pleasure."

"Um, okay," Kyle said, and blew on the surface of his coffee before he sipped again. It was only slightly less terrible. "Why are you . . . why are we awake?" He noticed Pico the dog sitting calmly by the door, ears up.

"I want to go over the bunkhouse plans with you." Grandpa tugged the blanket off Kyle. "You're in charge."

Kyle groaned and pulled the blankets back over him. "I don't want to be in charge."

"You're the oldest."

"Megan's the oldest."

Grandpa looked around the room. "Do you see Megan here?"

"Taylor is older than me, Grandpa. Literally I'm the *youngest* in my family." He tried another sip of coffee. Yep, still awful. "Anyway, there should be no one in charge. It makes the girls hate me. Make us all equally in charge."

"Oh, boy. Sure. Great idea, everyone equally in charge, no matter their skills and experience." He had a way of talking that turned everything into a speech. It dawned on Kyle that Grandpa and Aunt Brenda were kind of alike even though they had such different opinions about the world. "Answer me this: Am I wrong in thinking you're the only one of your cousins who's worked for a contractor?"

"I mean, I help my dad."

"Who is a contractor." Grandpa sucked his teeth. "Kyle, you're my only male grandchild. You're the only one carrying on the Baker name when the rest of us are all gone. I'm probably not supposed to say this in this day and age, but I think of you differently than I think of the rest of them. Oh, get that expression off your face."

"What?"

Grandpa leaned in close enough for Kyle to get a strong whiff of coffee breath, which smelled way worse than coffee. "Like you feel guilty."

"I mean . . ."

"Don't worry," he said, drawing back. "I'm not saying you're my favorite. Just different. I think you're a good man, Kyle. Or on your way there."

His voice shook. He made a fist against his leg.

"Really?" Kyle asked quietly. "You think that?"

"Yes." His voice had gone back to steely. "Now get dressed and meet me downstairs."

Grandpa leaned over the numerous sheets of yellow legal paper laid out on the big kitchen table. There were also blueprints.

"What's this?" Kyle asked. "I thought it was a demo project only."

"Well. I wanted you to see the endgame here." Grandpa tapped the papers. "Know what you're working toward." He walked Kyle through the plans. It was a total upgrade and redesign and expansion of the bunkhouse. It would have six separate living quarters—super small but each with its own mini-kitchenette and private, tiny bathroom with a toilet and shower just big enough to turn around in. They were going to add more windows so that all six units had natural light. "I'll hire some guys to finish it after you all leave," he said.

"But why?" Kyle asked. "I mean, if you're selling, why do all this work? Maybe the buyers won't even want the bunkhouse. Maybe they're going to end up tearing it all down anyway."

Grandpa smoothed out the blueprints. His big hands were splattered with reddish-brown age spots. His face wasn't all that wrinkled, considering he was like eighty-three or whatever. Not as wrinkled as Grandma's, with the deep lines that ran the width of her forehead, and around her mouth, and all down her neck. With Grandpa, where you saw it was his eyes—red rimmed, a little cloudy, sometimes confused. Not now, though.

"You can help me out, here," he said, holding up a few of the yellow sheets, "or you can not help me."

"I'm gonna help you! I was just curious."

"Well." Grandpa's voice softened. "Curiosity is over-rated."

Kyle put his mug down, still more than half full. "So's coffee."

They went down the orchard path with Pico to look at the bunkhouse. The sun had come up while they were in the kitchen. It wasn't full light yet; the pink-tinged sky was soft and the air was cool. Birds sang like crazy, though Kyle couldn't see any. When they got to the two picnic tables by the bunkhouse, he thought back to the night in the spring when he and Emily had talked out here, the starry night.

"We keeping the tables?" he asked Grandpa.

"I forgot about them." Pico walked in a circle around the clearing.

"It's nice to have a place to sit, eat outside, whatever."

Grandpa put his hands in his pockets and rocked back on his heels, studying the tables. "This wood is going rotten. I guess if the buyers want furniture out here, they can get some of their own."

Grandpa showed Kyle how he wanted the demo material piled clear of the walking path, sorted by type of material and salvageable and unsalvageable. "I don't want a mess out here."

"I know." Kyle looked at the tables again and had an idea. "I bet I could use some of the salvage to build a couple of new picnic tables. I mean, that would be cool, having tables made out of the old structure as part of the new structure."

Grandpa was quiet, then said, "No one would know the history. They wouldn't appreciate it." He sounded tired, like his enthusiasm for the day had already been drained.

"We would."

"You'll never see it again after this summer."

"But we'll know it's here."

Maybe they couldn't keep anyone from coming along and tearing down what they'd built. Maybe it was wrong to try to preserve something that had served its purpose. But it still seemed worth caring about.

He followed Grandpa into the bunkhouse. It smelled like something had died in there.

"It's a dump," Grandpa said.

"It's old."

"Even when it was new it was a dump."

Pico had come in and was sniffing under one particular bunk.

"And the reason," Grandpa continued, "the reason I want it torn down and replaced with something new is that the new owners are putting in grapes. On every inch of the tract. It's going to be a huge operation, and there *are* going to be workers. And if I leave this like it is, they might be tempted to actually make people live here."

Kyle laughed. "Like it is *now*? No one would do that. You wouldn't."

Grandpa raised his wiry eyebrows. "Oh no? You think not? People are greedy, Kyle. And cheap. I am. I ran this place greedy and cheap back in the early days. Your think I haven't been listening to your aunt Jenny about worker exploitation and whatnot, but I have."

He talked like Kyle had been in on some conversation he hadn't been, but with Grandpa sometimes it was better not to say much.

"So," Grandpa went on, "I guess I'm trying to repent by building some living quarters that are halfway decent, for anyone who works here in the future."

Pico started barking and growling. Kyle went over and got down on his knees so he could see under the bunk. A decomposing ground squirrel lay on its side. He pulled Pico away by the collar and told Grandpa, "I'll get everyone started on this after breakfast."

"Which will be ready soon. Let's not keep Grandma waiting."

Kyle got the desiccated squirrel out with a stick, pushing it along the floor, then outside, flinging it as far as he could into the surrounding trees.

Grandma Baker got very extra with summer farm-week breakfasts.

Biscuits. Eggs, with cheese and without. Bacon and veggie bacon. Home fries, cubed melon with mint from the garden, sliced apples, and fresh pear juice from their own trees. Pinto beans, too, almost always pinto beans with breakfast, a tradition straight from Grandpa Navarro and Aunt Jenny. And coffee cake, because breakfast was followed by breakfast dessert.

Kyle didn't see Emily. He wanted to tell her about the plans for the bunkhouse, his idea about making new tables from the old materials, what Grandpa had said about being greedy.

Or just see her, because he wanted to hold this image in his head of farm-week breakfast and Grandma's kitchen, and she should be in that picture.

His dad sat on a stool in the corner of the kitchen with his phone and pocket notebook, doing some work with his pre-breakfast phone privileges. Kyle wondered how the night had gone for his parents, if they'd really slept in the same bed or if one of them had snuck down to the basement. How would it feel to lie there, arms and legs touching, with someone you'd sort of broken up with?

Kyle grabbed a plate from the counter and got in line.

"Eliseo first," Grandma said, waving Grandpa Navarro over.

He looked the same as always: Wranglers and boots and a long-sleeved collared shirt. He rarely came out of his truck to join in at meals or stay long. He'd do his rounds on the access roads, making sure all the systems were working and that the people leasing land were doing everything right. "I'm giving Martie cuts," he said now.

Martie spun around and sashayed to the buffet. "Navarro privileges!"

Taylor came in and stood behind Kyle. "When we get our phones, I want to call Megan," she said in a low voice.

"Where's Mom?" Kyle asked.

"Still getting ready in their room. I don't think they even change clothes in front of each other anymore. Alex and Emily went to give Larry an apple."

Oh, shit. Larry. The last living horse from when they were kids. What was going to happen to him? He was too old to ride now or pull anything. He just kind of hung out.

They got to the food. Kyle tucked bacon into a biscuit and starting eating that while he loaded the rest of his plate. Someone put bluegrass music on the outdoor speakers, and Grandma came in and out, weaving through everyone while holding her spatula and telling them not to make a mess.

Kyle wanted to remember this. How Grandma ruled the kitchen, made every meal a feast, and how the cousins and aunts and uncles crowded in. Some cranky before they'd had their coffee and food, some using their cheerfulness as a weapon against the cranky ones. How the sun came in through the glass doors and left patches of light on the cabinetry.

Grandma interrupted his Instagram moment by sidling up to Kyle to say, "Too bad about Nadia."

So Uncle Mike had spread the word. Which was fine. Better than Kyle having to tell every single person who asked over and over again. Ugh, where was Emily?

Then, as if he'd made her appear by force of will, there she was, coming through the patio slider with Alex. She had on leggings and a long-sleeved T-shirt and knit cap.

Her eyes her eyes her eyes.

He needed her to see him, see what he was feeling about this moment in the kitchen and the family and all of the years, the loss of it all, the loss of how the sunlight hit and how the biscuits smelled and of everyone together, right here.

He needed her to see it all exactly like he did, and he'd know he wasn't alone.

She smiled at him.

She put a hand on her chest and held one arm out, and sang to him across the kitchen, from *Oklahoma!* "Oh, what a beautiful mornin'! Oh, what a beautiful day!"

Aunt Brenda put up her hand. "No singing yet. Please."

"You two," Uncle Mike said. "I'm gonna miss this."

"We're not breaking up the family," Kyle's dad said. "Just selling some land. Okay?"

"He speaks!"

"Yeah, Bren, I do. And I say, don't be sentimental about property. You learn that in real estate and construction. We had a fine childhood here, but that was a long time ago. It's over. We'll have holidays somewhere else and . . ." He looked around the kitchen. "What?"

"God, Jeff," Aunt Brenda said. "Read the room."

After breakfast, a bunch of them loitered on the patio. Kyle and Emily were at the table eating coffee cake, and it felt completely normal and not loaded with all that stuff he felt in the kitchen. The intensity in his mind around Emily was this bright sun that sometimes burned and sometimes, like now, was simply and gently warm.

Taylor sat with Martie on the wicker love seat in the shade of the patio roof. They were playing with Pico, trying to get him to dance on his hind legs and shake hands.

Great-Aunt Gina called to them from the other side of the patio, where she and Uncle Mike sat. "That's a *service* dog, girls. He should be inside with your grandfather."

"He's out here, though," Martie muttered to Taylor, and took Pico's front paws in her hands. "Dance, doggie, dance!"

"He's like, 'I don't want to be a service dog—I want to be a ballroom dancer!'" Taylor said.

"You can see in his eyes that's his true dream."

"If I had my phone, we could be making the most popular video the internet has ever seen."

Martie laughed. "Like you can't get your phone." Then she glanced at Taylor and said, "What, you don't know where they are?"

"Uh, no?"

"Me neither," said Emily.

"Nope," added Kyle.

"Guys." Martie sighed. She whispered, "They're in an old pickling crock in the big pantry. Behind one of those ten-pound bags of beans." She looked at Kyle. "Your mom was in there for like half an hour last night. I can't believe you didn't notice."

"Yeah, well, she's pretty skilled at sneaking," Kyle said. Taylor glanced at him with a raised eyebrow.

"It's easy to get to the phones," Martie said. "The only problem is that Grandma is in the kitchen so much."

"Except for right now," Taylor said, nodding over to where Grandma had dozed off in a chaise.

Taylor bent down and picked up Pico. "I'll take him in," she called to Great-Aunt Gina.

"Just point him in the direction of Grandpa's room. He'll know what to do."

"Wait," Kyle said. "We need to start on the bunkhouse. Who even cares about phones?"

"I just want to see what's up with Megan. I have no

patience." Taylor whispered to Martie, "Do you want yours?"

"Nah. I just checked it like an hour ago."

Taylor tucked Pico under her arm like a football and went inside. Kyle said to Emily, "Be right back." He followed Taylor in.

She set Pico down. "Go to Grandpa," she whispered. The dog looked up at them, panting. "Go see Grandpa." She pointed toward the front of the house, where Grandma and Grandpa's bedroom was, then gave him a nudge with her foot. He finally got the hint and trotted off, his nails clicking on the kitchen tile.

There was a small pantry right in the kitchen, but the one Martie had been talking about was a narrow but deep room you entered from the laundry area. Grandma kept all the bulk and backup food there, like the produce she canned herself, as well as big bags of flour and dried beans and potatoes and onions and stuff. The knee-high crock was right where Martie had said it would be.

The phones were in a pile, with kitchen towels underneath and around them. Taylor found hers near the top, but it wouldn't power on. "Dead battery. Which is something that happens when your phone is in a jar for twenty-four hours, abandoned and unloved. Maybe yours has life."

Kyle didn't want his. He liked how things were. Being *there*, being with Emily. Forget everything else. Pictures of Nadia lived in the phone. Texts with her. The workout tracker app he was still on with the team. All the evidence of his former life.

"Hurry up," Taylor whispered. "Do you *want* to get caught?"

Fine. He did actually want Megan there. But when Kyle found his phone near the bottom of the pile and it still had life and there was nothing from Megan, no replies to his texts from yesterday morning, he was pissed. Literally the least she could do was say she wasn't coming.

Taylor grabbed at his phone. "I'm calling her."

Kyle held his arm up and out of reach. "She's not coming, Taylor. She doesn't want to be here. Trust me, I laid on all the think-of-the-cousins shit I could. It's not happening. She doesn't care."

Just then, another one of the phones buzzed and lit up.

Taylor reached in to retrieve it. It had a green polka-dot case. Their mom's.

The screen lit up again with a string of messages from a number with no name.

Just touching base about the thing.

Is the thing still on? LMK.

If we need to resched, call my office. ;)

Kyle felt sick.

"That has to be him, right?" Taylor whispered, pressing the button on the phone to try to unlock it.

297

Jacob's dad.

They heard the kitchen screen door slide open. Taylor grabbed Kyle's arm and dragged him into the powder room off the kitchen.

"I bet I can guess her code," she said

"Don't."

"She's used the same one forever. ATM, gym padlock, home security system—"

"You think it's that code?" Kyle said, incredulous. One seven seven seven. It had no significance other than being easy to remember.

She tried it. Strike one. Relieved, Kyle said, "Let's just put it back."

"Hang on."

"You've got one more shot at this. Three times, and she'll know someone was messing with it."

"Actually, you get six tries. I'm not saying I broke into my roommate's phone, but I'm not saying I didn't."

"The thing," the message said. What was the *thing*?

"Try seven seven seven one," Kyle said.

"So you *do* want me to do it."

He did. He didn't. It wasn't going to help anything. Also it was, like, wrong.

"Curiosity is overrated," Kyle said, repeating Grandpa from that morning.

"No, it isn't. I'm doing it."

Mom's home screen icons filled the phone face.

"Oh my god," Taylor muttered.

She clicked on the messaging app and scrolled through screens and screens of texts while Kyle read over her shoulder.

Their mom and Jacob's dad seemed to think they were speaking in code, disguising their conversation as some business thing, but it was all so obvious. After reading a bunch, it became clear that "the office" was his house and "the boss" was his wife and "my assistant" was Jacob. Like, **Have to resched; my assistant came home early from school.**

"'From school.' What a fucking idiot," Kyle muttered.

So "the thing" was that they were planning to meet up this week. *This* week. Farm week. As in, he was or was going to be in Santa Rosa, about a half hour from the farm. Like they'd planned it all so that Mom could sneak off and visit him while being here.

After all that bullshit about one more farm week, make it good, don't ruin it. His mom saying on the swings that she might make different choices, knowing what she knew now.

Tell him not to come, then, Mom. Call off THE THING.

"This is so disturbing," Taylor said.

"Try looking his wife in the eye."

"Jeez. Get your shit together, Mom."

From the texts, they saw his name was Troy. Kyle wanted details beyond "Troy, Jacob's dad." He took the phone and copied the number the texts were coming from, then pasted it into the search engine for a reverse phone lookup. The first few hits just said, "Verizon customer in Santa Barbara, CA." But then one came up on a directory of app designers looking for gigs. There was a name, and there he was.

Troy Partel. Goofy grin and wire-rim glasses and big teeth.

"You should really close your mouth when you smile, Troy Partel," Taylor muttered.

His bio read:

Troy Partel has eighteen years' design experience with employers and clients such as Oracle, Yahoo!, and Royal Semiconductor, as well as numerous smaller companies, start-ups, and individuals. End-to-end design services starting with your app idea to final delivery. Flexible rates based on your needs and company size. Troy lives in beautiful Santa Barbara, California, with his wife, son, and golden retriever.

Ugh.

He did more searching and found Troy Partel's Facebook page, and through that found his wife's, and there was Jacob's smiling mom from the parking lot that day. Anna Partel in her profile pic with Troy on one side and Jake the Quake on the other and the dog in front of them, on some hiking trail somewhere, all smiling and happy and—

The bathroom doorknob rattled. Taylor, startled, grabbed the phone and put it in her pocket.

"Just a sec!"

Kyle flushed the toilet and Taylor looked at him. "What was the point of flushing? We still have to walk out together and now it looks like we were having brother-sister toilet time."

"I have to go!" It was just Alex, calling through the door.

Kyle exhaled and opened the door.

"What are you guys doing?" she asked

"Family conference."

"I beat Emily at backgammon! I never beat her!"

"That's great, congratulations." Taylor gave Alex a high five.

When they heard Alex lock the door behind her, Taylor darted back into the pantry, lifted the lid of the crock, and threw their mom's phone back in.

5

KYLE TRIED to concentrate on organizing
the bunkhouse teardown without being a bossy asshole
about it. The texts between his mom and Troy Partel
scrolled through his mind. They shouldn't have looked at
her phone. The more stuff he knew, the more he worried
that he was supposed to do something about it. What was
the tipping point between not doing something about a
situation and doing something?

He watched Emily pulling nails out of boards. He
wanted what she had—her kind of calm, her steadiness.
Like no one could knock her off her feet. For a moment,

watching her, he felt if he could just, like, soak her up so completely that he could be him *and* be her and always be able to access those Emily things he needed so much. . . .

Well, that's creepy AF, he imagined Megan saying.

He threw himself into the job. His instincts about how to approach the job felt right—getting the roof off and the materials sorted into reusable stuff and then stuff to take to the dump. After a couple solid hours of work, Taylor said, "It's too hot to be doing this."

"We should have started earlier," Martie said. She threw a piece of one of the rotting roof beams onto the pile of stuff for the dump. "No dicking around after breakfast tomorrow like we did today."

Alex came over and showed Kyle her hands. "I have blisters. I'm going back to the house." He said fine and she ran off.

"That's not fair. If she's done, I'm done." Martie took off the work gloves she'd borrowed from her dad.

Taylor gave Kyle a look. "It's almost time for our phones. I'm calling Megan once I get mine plugged in."

"Okay, well, bye, all you quitters," Kyle said.

When Taylor was gone, he asked Emily if she was leaving too.

"Are you?" she asked.

"Not yet. I want to do some more sorting."

Emily wandered around the site, collecting nails and adding them to the pile of hardware. Kyle snuck glances at her, wondered what she was thinking. "We got a lot done today," he said when he couldn't stand another second of waiting for her to talk. "Considering the late start and all."

"I guess it doesn't take *that* long to completely destroy childhood."

"Nope," he said. "It's pretty fast."

"What your dad said in the kitchen earlier was like . . . whoa. Do you think he really doesn't care about the farm? I mean, 'Don't get sentimental about property'? What *was* that?"

"He cares. Just like he cares about my mom and stuff. But he doesn't like *feelings*. Which I've been realizing might be a Baker family trait."

She bent down to pick up a nail. "That's funny, because after my mom got her tattoo, my dad said maybe she should take a break from drinking and working and having all these big dramatic *experiences* so that she can see how she actually *feels* about her life."

"What did she say?"

"Nothing, because she was on her way out to a rehearsal."

"Then there's Uncle Mike, who's awesome, but he never seems sad or angry or cranky or anything. That's not possible, right?" Kyle asked. "To never have a bad feeling?"

"No, not possible." She crawled along in a squat, collecting more hardware.

"So, I found out a new thing about my mom this morning, but if you are totally and completely sick of hearing about it, I'll keep it to myself."

"You can't say that and think I'm not going to want to know."

"First, like, don't think I'm the worst . . . but Taylor and I broke into our mom's phone."

Emily stood up, tilted her head a little; and he detected the slightest judgment in her eyes. "Go on."

"I know. It's a violation of privacy. And I wish I hadn't let Taylor talk me into it."

"The woman hath made me eat of the fruit!" she said in a deep voice.

He laughed. "What?"

"Adam and Eve? In which the downfall of humanity is blamed on the wife? Anyway, continue."

"My mom is planning to meet up with her boyfriend *this week*. Right in town."

Emily clutched her head. "*Seriously*, Aunt Karen?"

"I'm so tired of it all, Emily. Especially of not knowing what to do, if I'm even supposed to do anything. I feel like I let this whole thing just . . . steal my life."

She stepped closer. "I know," she said. Then she grabbed his hand. "Come on."

They stepped into the bunkhouse and stood in the middle of the now-roofless structure. The trees almost made a canopy over them.

"I loved sleeping out here when we were kids," Kyle said. "I can't believe we're never going to do it again. Man, it sucks so much."

"You know what you were saying about Bakers and feelings? You're pretty good at having them. I don't think you have the same problem as your dad or anyone else."

"Yeah, *having* them is no problem."

The afternoon light washed her in soft yellow. She had bedhead, and dirt under her nails, and there was a small streak of blood on her white shirt from where she'd brushed her hand after pulling out a splinter. Kyle felt like his heart was being crushed by the realness of her, but in a good way.

"Yeah," he continued. "I definitely have feelings." He touched his chest. "I just don't know how to get rid of them."

"You say that like they're termites or something."

He laughed. "Kind of."

"My point is, I know you pretty well, Kyle."

He listened so hard, desperate for her verdict on him.

"And I've witnessed a lot of your feelings," she continued, "and how you deal with them. And if you're worried you'll turn out like your dad or Grandpa or whoever, you're not. Also, whatever happens with your parents, I know you're going to be okay."

He brought his knuckle up to his mouth, chewed on the skin where his index finger bent.

"I mean, *you* know you're going to be okay too," she said. "But I guess I mean . . . whatever it feels like, you'll be able to handle it. All these feelings, they hurt, but they're not going to kill you."

"You sound so sure."

"My dad is always saying that to Alex, who has the biggest feelings around, and she's not dead yet."

She smiled at him and he wanted to say something as good as what she had. All he could do was hold her eyes with his and be glad for the moment.

A bluebird flew overhead, over the roofless roof. "We could sleep out here tonight," Kyle said. "Before we tear out the bunks."

"Yes!" She bounced on her toes. "That's perfect. Yes."

There were footsteps outside, and in a second Martie appeared in the doorway. "There you are. My dad is about to put chicken and carne asada on the grill and Grandma sent me to get you because we're supposed to set up the rest of the stuff for tacos." She stepped farther in, her arms crossed, looking around the bunkhouse. "History."

"We want to sleep here tonight," Emily said. "Like we used to."

"With no roof? Or mattresses?"

"I bet there are some camping mattresses in the basement."

"I have a very comfortable bed at home only twelve minutes away," Martie said. "I'll think about it."

They started on the path up to the house to chop onions and tomatoes and cilantro, and grate cheese and slice avocados, like they had for every taco night since always.

"Did your mom make tortillas?" Emily asked Martie.

"No. We got store-bought."

"Aw, man," Kyle said.

Martie shook a rock out of her flip-flop. "I guess she didn't feel like being the tortilleria for you guys. She already has a job."

Kyle stopped walking for a few steps, then started again. "Just saying . . . I like her tortillas."

Martie lifted her arms in an exaggerated shrug. Then she turned around and walked backward. "Did you guys hear Megan is coming?"

"Are you serious?" Kyle said. "Taylor talked to her?"

"I guess. I saw her on the phone walking through the orchard, like it was all private. Megan's getting here late tonight or maybe in the morning."

If he'd gotten that news at the start of today, he'd have been so happy. She was the last missing piece of this week. But now, knowing that Taylor must have told her about all the texts from Troy Partel, he didn't know if she was coming to be part of the family, or coming to confront their mom and blow it all up.

6

WHILE THE cousins had been working on the bunkhouse, the aunts and uncles had been cleaning out more of their stuff. Uncle Mike had on a Van Halen concert T-shirt from 1985 that stretched tight across his chest. Kyle's dad had a Sunday school participation ribbon pinned to his collar. During dinner, Aunt Jenny and Uncle Dale sat at the corner of the smaller table, like they were already tired of their Baker in-laws.

Kyle's mom sat with them. She looked pretty. And sad, even when she was talking or smiling. Kyle was so mad at her, but also, like, part of him *got* it. How you could want and intend to be a certain kind of person but also keep getting deeper and deeper into the hole you had dug for yourself. It was hard to climb out. At least when he'd messed up with Nadia, she'd eventually drawn the line, and in a weird way, that had helped him start to get unstuck. Whereas with his mom, it seemed like they were all letting her just stay down there.

But whose job, exactly, was it to get her out?

The cousins and Great-Aunt Gina were all around the big table. Kyle sat with them and listened to Alex tearfully try to talk Gina into taking Larry the horse back to the convent with her.

"We don't have a fenced area, honey. Or anyone who knows one thing about horses."

Kyle tuned out, imagined Megan pulling up in a cloud of dust and stomping out of her car straight to Mom and being like, "What's this shit about you using farm week as an opportunity to do some more cheating?" Flipping tables, some big scene.

When his mom stood up, he tuned back in.

"I didn't bring my migraine medication with me," she said, "and I feel a bad one coming. I'm going to run into town and get my prescription transferred to the pharmacy here." She smiled a tense, fake smile, which did sort of look like the smile of someone who was about to get a migraine.

"I'll go with you," Taylor said. "You shouldn't drive if

you're about to get one of your bad ones."

Maybe Taylor really was worried about her driving, or maybe she wanted to be the one to give Mom the assist and tell her to stop. Maybe Kyle should say he'd go to the store with them and they could do an intervention. Maybe his dad should wake the hell up and *act* instead of stuffing tortilla chips in his face.

"Get ice," Aunt Brenda said.

"We just *got* ice," Grandma said.

Uncle Dale laughed. "Two words, Helen: margarita machine."

Meanwhile, Kyle's mom stood there, her smile frozen. "I'm fine on my own, and I really . . . I need to make just the one stop and get the meds so I can knock this thing out."

Kyle's dad reached for more chips and guac.

"Okay then," their mom said. "Be back shortly."

In the kitchen, Taylor made massive amounts of noise rattling plates and cups and silverware while she rinsed.

"You're going to break something," Kyle said.

"I *want* to break something."

"What did you think was gonna happen if you went with Mom? It's not like you need to catch her in a lie to know the truth."

Taylor handed him a couple of glasses. "For one thing,

I thought she might really be getting a migraine and might need me to drive. For another, what she's doing is wrong and it makes me crazy how she can be so wrong and not care, and *I* care and I thought maybe I could say something and stop it."

"I know," Kyle said. "I felt exactly like that when I first found out."

"Kyle, don't do that. Don't be all, 'When I was your age,' especially when I'm older, okay? *You're* the baby."

He put a row of plates in the dishwasher. "I'm trying to help you because I know it sucks."

"Sorry," she said quietly. "Now we're going to look back on our final farm week and it's going to have this extra garbage on top."

"You told Megan about the texts, didn't you."

"Of course I told her. I told her the guy was here and Mom is seeing him and we needed her. Anyway, I thought you wanted us all here? Nothing motivates Megan like anger."

"Yeah," he said, "but I didn't want angry Megan here. I just wanted Megan. Our sister Megan."

He could picture Megan at ten, eleven, her two dark braids and how she wasn't afraid of anything and would step on the spiders in the attic with her bare feet. How she'd turn off the flashlight when they were walking around the farm at night and let everything be pitch-black until Taylor or Kyle or Emily begged her to turn the light back on.

"Ugh, I'm so mad. Migraine medication. Using a real thing she has that way. It's trash."

"I guess I think it's probably kind of complicated," he said, then hated himself for using that cop-out word. "Anyway, what about Dad? Why isn't he doing anything? Maybe there's a reason Mom went looking."

"Are you seriously defending her?"

"No. I'm just saying."

There was a tap on the sliding door; Martie stood outside with her arms full of dishes. Kyle opened the door. "I think this is everything," she said, and put them on the counter. "I decided I do want to sleep out with you guys tonight," she told Kyle.

"Me and Emily thought we should sleep in the bunkhouse tonight," Kyle explained to Taylor. "Before it's gone."

"There's no roof."

"So?"

"I like being indoors. Anyway, I want to wait here for Megan."

"I'll go get Alex to help me dig out the camping mattresses and stuff," Martie said.

Kyle and Taylor finished with the dishes, and Kyle went out onto the patio while Taylor snuck another look at her phone. Emily and Great-Aunt Gina were walking up from the lake, Pico trailing behind them.

When he saw Emily, he felt both better and worse than he had in the previous moment of not seeing her. Better because she kept saying amazing things to him and he felt so understood. Worse because in a few days he would go back to hardly seeing her at all, and then what?

The aunts and uncles were hanging out around the big patio table, playing poker. They'd lit citronella candles, and the table was covered with beer bottles and a bottle of tequila and a bag of quartered limes.

Emily came over to Kyle and draped her arm around his neck. "I guess they don't need the margarita machine if they're just drinking straight tequila."

"Saves on ice."

"Em!" Aunt Brenda called out. "Come over here, I've barely seen you all day, I miss you."

Emily dropped her arm and went over to the table and perched on the edge of her mom's chair. "Are you winning?"

"Not yet."

Kyle stood behind his dad, who had pocket tens. Uncle Mike was dealing, and a ten came on the flop. Finally, some tiny amount of good luck for his dad.

Aunt Brenda touched the back of Emily's neck. "I wish you hadn't cut your hair."

"So you've mentioned."

"I wish you'd done, like, an intermediate step. Long to bob before pixie."

Emily leaned away from her mom's grip. "My body, my choice. Like with your tattoo."

Kyle's dad looked up from his cards. "Uh, what?"

"Her tattoo," Emily said. "Didn't you show them?"

Aunt Brenda folded her cards. "Wow, Emily. Way to throw me under the bus."

"Mom!" Kyle's dad called, meaning Grandma, who sat in a patio recliner with a book. Great-Aunt Gina sat in the chair next to her, her face lit by the glow of her e-reader.

"Jeff!" Aunt Brenda reached across the table to hit his shoulder. Aunt Jenny and Uncle Mike looked like they were going to burst out laughing.

Grandma set her book down. "It's getting loud, kids."

"There's no one around here for ten miles, Mom," Mike said.

"There's your father, who's resting, and I'm sure he'd like to be able to hear himself think."

"One of your kids got a tattoo," Dad said. "Guess which one?"

Grandma's eyes immediately went to Aunt Brenda. "You didn't." After a pause, she asked, "Where?"

"A place near campus," she answered.

Aunt Jenny and Uncle Mike lost it. "She means where on your *body*, Bren," Jenny said, and then everyone else laughed too. Everyone but Grandma.

Emily took her mom's arm, about to help her roll up her sleeve, but her mom grabbed it away and stood. "Now I'm not showing it. It's personal."

"Oh, come on," Dad said, holding out his hands and accidentally showing his cards. "You have to!"

"Nope, I actually don't. Trip tens, Jeff? Nice."

Kyle's dad threw his cards in. "You're going to wear long sleeves all week? In this weather?"

Emily's mom shoved Emily off the chair—kind of joking but kind of not. Kyle watched Emily's face. She retained her usual chill except for one twitch of her eyebrow that told Kyle she didn't like being shoved by her mother.

"We're sleeping in the bunkhouse," Kyle announced.

"Oh, I don't know, honey," Grandma said.

Great-Aunt Gina set down her book. "They'll be fine, Helen."

"You'll have to round up all the gear yourselves. Oh, *there's* Karen. . . . I hope she was able to get her pills."

Kyle's mom's car crunched on the gravel drive. She'd been pretty fast. Maybe she'd gone to town just to tell Troy goodbye forever, or maybe she really was getting pills. Maybe she'd only wanted to be alone, away from this chaos of all the Bakers all at once.

He wondered if he'd ever be able to trust a simple explanation again.

"This was a dumb idea." Martie sat on a top bunk, swinging her legs.

"This was a *great* idea," Emily said.

They'd inflated mattresses, laid out sleeping bags and pillows, put up a few battery-operated lights. Emily was already in one of the bottom bunks with a book. Kyle was amazed at how she could do that—serenely read with people moving and talking around her. No wonder she got such good grades.

"We need snacks," Alex said. She slapped at her thigh. "And bug spray."

"Yeah, why don't you guys go get some food and stuff?"

"By 'you guys' you mean me and Alex because you think you can boss us around? Just because you're oldest?" Martie said, lightly kicking Kyle's shoulder.

"I don't mind!" Alex headed to the door.

"You don't know enough about life yet to mind," Martie said to Alex.

"You do?" Kyle asked, laughing.

"Don't treat me like a baby."

"Don't act like one."

Emily put her book down. "Kyle."

"Sorry," he said.

"It's fine. Hey, get the Mexican to do it." Martie climbed down the ladder from the top bunk. "That is the whole history of this bunkhouse, after all.

"Sorry," she continued, "but I found out that when Grandma and Grandpa Baker sent out an email to *your* parents and *Kyle's* parents about selling the farm, my mom and grandpa weren't on it."

"That's messed up," Emily said.

"My *dad* was on it, and Grandma is trying to play it off like she just assumed he'd tell my mom, but literally everyone but the kids got the email."

"I'm sorry, dude." Kyle tried to remember if Grandpa Navarro had participated in any of the family email chains Kyle had been on. "Is your grandpa even on email?"

"Yes, Kyle, he's on email! He's not some ancient Mexican riding around on a burro, wondering how email works! How do you think he runs this whole farm? Oh my *god*."

Alex was by the door, listening, eyes big.

"Yeah that was a stupid question," Kyle said. "I'm sorry."

"Super dumb." Martie looked around the bunkhouse. "You know what, I don't want to sleep out here. It's a fun yay cousin camp thing for you, but . . . I think I don't ever want to come out here again."

"Staayyy, Martie," Kyle said, jostling her shoulders.

She shook her head. "I don't want to." Her face crumpled, like the adrenaline of her anger had morphed into something more sad, and she turned and left. Alex watched her go, looked at Kyle and Emily, then ran after her.

"Wow, I really said all the right things." He imitated himself in a dumb-guy voice: "'Is your grandpa even on email?' Idiot."

"She'll forgive you," Emily said. "Really she's mad at Grandma and Grandpa."

"She should be." Kyle sat on the bunk opposite Emily. "When I went to see Megan that time, and told her about my parents, she said all this stuff about our family I've never thought about. Our house and cars and the fact that we could be buying like a herd of goats for a whole village instead."

Emily laughed gently. "What are you talking about?"

"I don't even know. I'm talking about our family, I guess." He lay back so he could look up into the trees. A robin seemed to stare down at him and then fly away. "My mom's affair isn't, like, the *one thing* that's messed up. I mean, I know we have our issues, but when I brought Nadia here for Thanksgiving, I felt like we were a pretty good family to meet."

"We are. 'Pretty good' is . . . pretty accurate."

"But I thought we were better."

She was quiet, then said, "It's hard to let go of the idea of something. Especially when the idea is important to you. But if you don't let go of the idea, you can't actually live in reality."

He propped himself on his elbow so he could watch her face. "How are you so smart at this stuff, while I'm so far behind?"

"My dad being a psychologist helps." She kept staring into the sky, which was getting more and more darkly blue, more and more quiet. "But also, like, I grew up the way we all do, with people talking all the time about crushes and romance and who you like, and you're supposed to want that. To be part of some romantic couple or whatever. Every song and every movie and TV show and book . . . every old musical that me and you love watching." She turned her head to him. "I had this idea that I should want that too. And I know I seem like a confident, badass aro ace now—and I *am*—but it was hard to let go of the idea of what I was supposed to be. So that I could just be who I am."

Kyle kept his mouth shut, in hopes she'd keep talking and talking. She didn't, so he said what he felt. "Who you are is awesome, Emily."

She smiled, then propped herself up on her elbow too, a mirror image of him.

"And maybe you need to do that with your mom, your dad, the whole family," she said. "Let go. Let go of what you thought it should be. And see what it is."

"What is it?" he asked, only half joking.

"A bunch of flawed people trying to love each other?"

"A bunch of flawed people trying to love each other and also just survive life," he said.

"A bunch of flawed people trying to love each other, survive life, and maybe be happy sometimes." Emily continued, "Anyway, I think letting go of what you thought things should be happens whether you want it to or not."

Like it had with Nadia, how avoiding her when he didn't know the right thing to say didn't make anything better. At all. How skipping baseball when he could have been relying on a group of friends only left him lonely. How wishing as hard as he could that his mom wouldn't do what she was doing hadn't made her stop. Him or his mom or anyone else trying to make a perfect last farm week wasn't going to change the fact they were losing that too.

All this loss, all this change. Hiding and avoiding and resisting it had been like twisting against a knife that was going to cut him no matter what.

And face-to-face in real time with Emily like this, he felt he was actually *seeing* her. Seeing *her*. And he understood he'd had an idea of Emily, too, that he needed to let go of so that he could keep seeing her like he was right now. He wanted to be in reality with her, not in a fantasy in his head of her always being there for him the second he needed her and never being mad and never disagreeing, him wanting her to swear to be best friends forever no matter what and trying to get her to promise nothing would ever change.

He knew, in that moment, he could survive the reality of being flawed people trying to love each other. With Emily, with his parents, with himself.

"Emily," he said, "I'm glad you're my cousin. I'm glad you're my friend. I think you're smart and nice and inter-esting and a good person."

She reached her hand across the gap between their bunks; he grasped her fingers.

When she let go, she turned over on her back again. "I kind of like having no roof."

"Me too." The light above them had turned deepest blue. Once in a while there was a final goodnight song from a robin. The chirp of crickets. And the hum of a mos-quito nearby. "We actually are going to need bug spray."

"I know." She cupped her hands around her mouth and shouted, "Alex!"

He laughed. "I . . . don't think she'll be back. Are we still going to sleep out here?"

"Yes!" She sang a line from *West Side Story*. "Tonight, tonight, the world is full of light, with suns and moons all over the place!"

He continued it in his head: *Tonight, tonight, the world is wild and bright . . .*

"I might actually be drowsy," she said.

"Not me."

"You can keep talking if you want. I'm going to close my eyes."

He kept his open until the crickets and the sound of Emily finally soothed him to sleep.

7

APPARENTLY BIRDS thought four a.m. counted as dawn, and Kyle woke up to the song of a robin. Pretty, but loud.

"I think that bird only got like three hours of sleep," Emily muttered. "I have to pee."

"Me too."

"I don't really want to pee in the woods. Let's go down to the house."

"I didn't bring a flashlight," Kyle said.

"I did."

They walked on the path, surrounded by the rustling of birds and squirrels waking up. "Is that Megan's car?"

Emily shone her flashlight at the mass of vehicles parked wherever they could fit.

Kyle's stomach clutched slightly. "I hope she's not here to stir shit up," he said. It was one thing to talk under the stars about letting go and living in reality and accepting that they were a flawed bunch of people, and another to actually be in that reality.

"Well, it *is* Megan. . . ."

He sighed. "Yeah."

They paused at the outer edge of the patio. The house looked so peaceful. The glow of hall lights, everything quiet. The margarita machine and a bunch of glasses from last night still on the big picnic table, Grandma's book on the patio chair.

"Okay," Emily said. "I really gotta pee. And then probably sleep a few hours."

"Good idea."

He headed to his room to get a little more sleep too, then woke to the smells of cooking. Four breakfasts left at the farm, including today. When he got up and headed down for food, he ran into his mom in the hallway, holding a pillow.

"Kyle," she said. "Hi."

"Been sleeping in the basement?" Kyle could hear that his voice had lost the edge of judgment that had been in his conversations with her for months.

"No, actually. On the second-floor balcony."

"Really?"

"It's not bad. A little damp in the mornings." She smiled nervously. "Why are you looking at me like that?"

"I didn't know I was looking at you any kind of way."

"Like you want to say something."

Maybe he did. Tired of secrets, tired of withholding, tired of being enemies. "Mom . . ." He brought his voice as low as it would go. "We looked at your phone."

"Excuse me?"

"Me and Taylor saw your phone. We saw the messages and stuff. With Troy." He meant it as a confession and maybe a warning, not an accusation.

She closed her eyes and clenched her jaw. "Shit." She opened her eyes. "Taylor knows?"

"I told her the night she came home. Um, also Megan knows."

A loaded pause. "I see."

"Do you think maybe . . ." He stopped, because they heard footsteps on the stairs above. Then Uncle Dale appeared.

"Is this the line for the bathroom?"

"Yup," Kyle said.

His mom waved her hand. "Go ahead." And she turned and went to her room.

He wondered what she thought he was going to say.

Something harsh, probably, like "Do you think maybe you could get your shit together? Do you think maybe you should just leave?" What he'd planned to say was: "Maybe don't see Troy while you're here, for your own sake, so you can enjoy the last few days here after so many years of the farm? Leave feeling strong, leave maybe even feeling loved by *this* family?"

Downstairs, there was a crowd around the food, but he didn't see Megan. Taylor sat outside in a lawn chair, eating a slab of sausage-and-egg casserole. Kyle's stomach growled.

"Where's Megan?"

"Sleeping in the basement. She got in at like two."

"I'm going to wake her up."

"You sure you want to do that?"

"She can't miss breakfast," Kyle said. "That will only make her madder."

He went in and down the basement stairs. Megan lay on the sectional, still dressed and sleeping with one arm over her face like she always had.

"Megan," he said. No movement. Then, louder, "Megan?"

"Hmph."

"Get up or you'll miss farm breakfast."

She bolted up. "What time is it? Why didn't you guys wake me sooner?"

"Don't worry, there's still plenty of food. I should have let you miss it, though, since you never responded to any of my texts. Thanks for that."

She ran her fingers through her hair, stretched her arms overhead. "Sorry. I was still deciding."

"You could have said that, I mean—" He stopped himself. Silence with no explanation was exactly what he'd done to Nadia. He laughed a little.

"What's funny?"

"Nothing."

"Let's go eat."

"Wait, I just saw Mom," he said. "I told her me and Taylor saw her phone. And you know everything. So I mean, she knows you know, you don't need to ambush her or anything."

"I wasn't going to do that, Kyle. What did she say?"

"Not a lot. Uncle Dale interrupted us." He watched her face. "So, what *are* you going to do?"

She let out a big sigh. "I don't even know. I was all mad when I got in the car, but it's a long drive and I got to think a lot and I don't know what the point of any of it is. She's fucking up and part of me wants to put her on blast. I still might. But I came here for you and Taylor. And the farm and I guess everyone."

"Realllly?"

"I'm not dead inside, Kyle."

"I love you," he said.

"Shut up. I haven't had coffee yet."

When they went up to the kitchen, their dad was in there getting seconds, it looked like. He put down his plate when he saw Megan and said, "If I hug you, are you going to bolt?"

"Probably not." She actually went to him, and Kyle watched as he gave her a bear hug, lifting her slightly off her feet. "Okay, Dad. That's . . ." He put her down and turned his head away, cleared his throat a couple of times. "Bigfoot cry?" Megan said.

Kyle laughed. God, he missed his family. Even right now, when it was in front of his face, he missed it.

"I hope everyone doesn't make a big deal about me being here." Megan peered over their dad's shoulder to the patio. "Where's Mom?"

"Haven't seen her this morning."

Kyle handed Megan a plate. "Let's eat."

They got their plates of food and went out, and Megan waved her hands around and said, "Yes, I'm here, it's very exciting, let's move on."

Aunt Brenda raised her mimosa. "To Megan, still being Megan!"

Everyone else lifted their classes and mugs, laughing.

Kyle and Megan sat with Emily and Martie and Taylor at the smaller table. Alex was over on her dad's lap at the big table.

Martie hugged Megan, then extended her fist to Kyle. He bumped it with his; she nodded. Then she said, "I used to imagine how *we'd* be over at the big table some-day and all our kids would be at this one."

"We can still do this," Taylor said. "Like, even though it won't be *here* we can get together, all of us. I mean, our house is almost big enough for everyone. We could fit a couple of tables in the backyard."

"If our house is still a thing at this time next year," Kyle said.

"What do you mean?" Martie asked. "Are you guys selling or something?"

Taylor said no at the exact same time that Megan said, "Probably."

"We don't actually know," Kyle said.

"Okay, everyone stop talking like this is the last time we're going to be together," Emily said. "We have options!"

Voices at the adult table got louder, and the cousins leaned in to listen.

"This isn't one of those farms that's been in the family for generations," Grandpa was saying. "It was our dream and our project and we did it, and now it's over."

Aunt Jenny said, "You're going to shrug it off like that? 'It was our dream and it's over'? As if it didn't affect anyone else?"

Grandpa Navarro clucked, waved his hand. "Jenny. I am ready to retire. I was ready ten years ago."

"I know, but—"

"Ahora no, Jenny."

"Hablemos de esto más tarde," she muttered.

"Ya veremos."

Martie cupped her hands and shouted over to Grandpa Navarro, "¡Usted siempre dice eso!"

"None of you kids wants to run a farm," Grandma said. "Correct me if I'm wrong?"

"Not I," Aunt Brenda said, and Kyle noticed she and Uncle Dale were holding hands under the table.

Kyle's dad said, "But Mom, you guys didn't *raise* us to run it. We weren't in on the business and you didn't teach us how to do it." He pointed in Kyle's direction. "Kyle's been working summers with me since he was about ten. He could build a house if he had to. I wouldn't know *what* to do with the farm, because Dad treated us like we were in the way."

"That's not true," Grandpa said.

"Yeah, it is, Dad," Uncle Mike said.

"Um, I could not build a house," Kyle said to the cousin table.

Taylor laughed. "If you *had* to, though." Then her eyes shifted. "There's Mom."

The patio slider opened, and Kyle's mom came out with a cup of coffee. She seemed to scan the patio until she saw what she was looking for: Megan.

Megan put her fork down. "I'm just gonna go say hi real quick to get it over with."

Kyle watched Megan go to their mom, and it was so weird knowing this big drama was going on—right here, right now—while at the other table they were still arguing about the past.

"Now," Grandpa said, "if we'd lived farther south and gotten into almonds. Well." He shook his head. "Who knew? Almond milk, almond flour, almond butter, almond cheese . . ."

"Notice how Grandpa just kind of mowed over whatever my dad and Uncle Jeff were trying to say about their childhood," Martie said.

Taylor's eyes were on Megan and their mom, too, sitting in a couple of lawn chairs off to the side of the patio. "I can't handle this," she said. "I'm going to start clean-up."

Emily stood too, and she and Taylor collected empty glasses, plates, handfuls of silverware.

"What's going on?" Martie asked Kyle.

"This is the first time Megan and my mom have talked in a long time." *Also: everything.*

He didn't feel nervous watching them, though, like Taylor had. It didn't look like Megan was ripping into her. More like they were making awkward small talk.

"Well now, who's that?" Grandma asked, looking toward the sound of tires on gravel.

Kyle turned to see.

A gold Subaru came into view.

His whole body clenched.

There were a lot of Subarus in California. There were even a fair number of gold ones. But only one that belonged to the wife of his mom's boyfriend.

Kyle heard a faint "Oh, Jesus," from his mom, and he looked at her and saw pure terror in her eyes. Kyle's dad saw it too, and asked, "Who is it?"

His mom wasn't moving, and neither was his dad. All the aunts and uncles were looking at his parents, and exchanging glances, but also not moving or speaking. Taylor stood holding the stack of plates. Emily looked at Kyle, a question in her face, and he looked back with the answer: *Yep.*

The only one *doing* anything was Pico, who ran barking toward the car.

"I'll go," said Kyle.

It felt like his moment. He knew all the players, every domino that was about to fall.

He met the car where it stopped along the side of the

house. Anna Partel rolled down her window and took off her sunglasses. There were those bright eyes. "Why do I know you?" she asked.

Kyle saw Jacob was with her. "You *brought* him?" he asked Anna, incredulous.

"It's Kyle," Jacob said, sounding equally confused. "From baseball."

In the back, a golden retriever bounced around, trying to get a look at Pico, who wouldn't shut up.

"Baseball?"

"We met one time when you were picking Jacob up," Kyle said.

"I'm sorry. I'm . . . what are you doing here?"

He looked past her at Jacob, then back to Anna. "Maybe we could talk alone?" he said, and hoped she heard the do-you-really-want-to-do-this-in-front-of-your-kid? question.

She turned off the engine. Unhooked her seat belt. "Stay here," she said to Jacob.

"I think Chase has to go to the bathroom."

Anna swore under her breath. Kyle looked behind him, where the whole family was watching. For all most of them knew, he was giving directions to someone who'd gotten lost or thought the farm was open for fruit picking. He really did not want Anna getting out of the car. It looked like Jacob and the dog were going to have to.

He made a come-over-here waving motion toward Emily and Taylor, hoping one of them would get it. They both did, putting down their dirty dishes and coming over. Then Taylor said something to Emily and stayed behind, moving to be by their dad while Emily came to the car.

"This is my cousin Emily," he said to Jacob. "If you want to come out with the dog, she'll hang with you a minute."

Jacob looked at Emily, at Kyle, at his mom. "Can we just go?" he said quietly. His grip around Chase's neck tightened.

"Take Chase out to pee, sweetie," Anna said. "I'll be right here. Two minutes."

Two minutes. Plenty of time to solve months' worth of lies and deception.

Jacob got out, and Kyle slid into the passenger seat.

"My childcare fell through," Anna said. "I told him we were going to go to Great America. I *planned* to go to Great America and just forget this whole thing, but then I kept driving. Just kept heading for Troy's dot on the phone. He's a software developer, you know. And he left his 'find my phone' on. He's not very good at adultery."

"Neither is my mom."

Anna stared at him.

"It's my mom," Kyle continued. "My mom is the girl-friend."

He gave her time to catch up. Then she said, "You knew? When I met you that time? Did you know?"

"Yeah."

Anna put her hands to her temples. "Is that why you started working with the team? Were you trying to get close to my family? Why is your family trying to hurt us? I'm sorry . . . I'm so confused."

"I know. I'm—"

"I followed the dot. I woke up at four and drove six hours to get to the dot, and now the dot is way up here with someone else from Santa Barbara? They couldn't stay *there* and screw around so I didn't have to drive my child six hours for this?"

Everything he'd imagined about how it would feel for her to realize all these people knew, but not her, was even worse than Kyle had imagined it. Maybe because he hadn't imagined it happening at the farm, with the kid and the dog.

"Did you tell Jacob?" he asked.

"I may have said some stuff. In a vague way." She craned her neck to get a better view of the patio. "Which one is she?"

Kyle checked over his shoulder. "My mom is the one in the blue skirt."

She paused, studying Kyle's mom, then asked in a pained voice, "Why are they all looking? Do they all know? Does literally everyone know but me?" She leaned out the window and waved Jacob back to the car. "Let's go, hon."

Chase and Pico tumbled around and played in front of Emily and Jacob like this was the most fun day they'd ever had.

"They don't all know. Me and my sisters and my dad." No need to mention Emily.

"Your *father*? Your father knows and I didn't?" She put her sunglasses back on. "Jacob! In the car, now." She looked at Kyle. "I have to get us out of here. Pretend this didn't happen."

Kyle got out of the car. The dogs were going crazy. Jacob opened the back door of the car and *both* dogs jumped in, and Kyle tried to get Pico out and then a smaller blue car appeared at the top of the drive.

"I think . . . Dad's here," Jacob said.

"Shit," Anna said. "What are you *doing*, Troy?" She looked at Kyle, frantic. "What's happening?"

The blue car came to a stop. The Bakers and Navarros all watched as Troy got out.

Pico jumped back into the Subaru, in and out, like it was a game.

"Everything," Kyle said to Anna. "Everything is happening. What do you want me to do?"

"I don't know! If you could get that goddamn dog out of my car . . ."

Kyle got hold of Pico's collar, but it was all too late. None of them were going to be able to escape this.

"Jacob," he said, "lemme show you this cool demolition we're doing on a building down that path?" He pointed, made eye contact with Anna, hoping she'd get the hint. *Down that path. Far away from the shit show about to go down.* "We'll take the dogs."

"Yeah," she said, nodding. "Yeah. Jacob, go with Kyle."

8

IF THIS had happened two months ago, Kyle might have relished it, might have thought his mom was getting what she deserved and that she had brought this on herself. Now, all he felt was sad. Now, he wished she didn't have to go through it. But she did, and everything was out of his hands, except that Anna had trusted him with Jacob and he wanted to come through.

Kyle walked with Jacob toward the bunkhouse, the dogs up ahead of them.

"How does your mom know my dad again?" Jacob asked, looking back over his shoulder.

"Um, I don't actually know how they met." He pointed

ahead. "The bunkhouse is down here."

"My mom told me we were going to Great America."

How much do you tell a fifth grader? Almost sixth?

"Yeah, I think she intended to take you there. She said she talked to you some in the car? About why she was coming up here?"

"She told me my dad was supposed to be in Portland for a conference, but he wasn't. And that he lied to her and she was trying to find out the truth because he kept lying."

"Uh-huh." Kyle thought he probably shouldn't fish. He pointed out the orchard, named all the things that grew on the farm. "We come here every summer. The whole family. Well, we *did*. This is the last time."

"Because of my dad?"

Kyle looked at him. "No no no. My grandparents are selling it so they can retire."

"I hate my dad."

Aw, man. Had he hated him before, or only now, after seeing him scramble out of a car in Northern California when he was supposed to be in Portland?

They made it to the clearing and then the bunkhouse. "Check it out. Me and my cousins used to sleep out here in summers. We actually slept out here last night, some of us."

"There's no roof." Jacob sat on one of the bunks that

still had an air mattress on it. "This is cool."

The dogs came in, panting and circling all around and wagging, and then went out again.

"So, my dad's girlfriend is your mom?" Jacob asked.

Welp, so much for beating around the bush. "Yeah."

"Are my parents getting divorced?"

"I don't know."

Jacob stood up and looked out the glassless window. "I've been practicing my slide. I don't like baseball that much, though."

"Really?" Kyle tried to sound surprised. "What happened to wanting to be just like Kyle, man?"

"I didn't mean I wanted to play *baseball* like you."

"Oh."

Jacob turned to him. "It would be awesome to have cousins." He looked out the window again. "Mine are all in Illinois. I don't really see them because my mom usually has to be at the hospital and we can't travel too much."

"That sucks. I'm sorry."

There was a lot else he could say, but Kyle wasn't about to give a pep talk to someone who'd had the rug yanked out from under his feet. He knew the feeling. All the feelings. Sometimes what you really needed was someone to listen and then say, "That sucks, I'm sorry," and then shut up. That's what Emily had done for him, essentially, and he knew how much it could mean.

"I'm kind of really hungry," Jacob said. "We didn't stop for food or anything."

"Oh, you are in the *right* place for being hungry. Come on."

When they got back down to the house, the cousins were on the patio, sitting around and talking. Alex jumped up when she saw Kyle and Jacob, and he introduced them, and then everyone went around and said their names. Then they took Jacob into the kitchen and Martie listed off every single food and beverage option available, and ended up making Jacob a sausage biscuit and warming up hash browns. He had a deer-in-the-headlights look on his face, but honestly it wasn't that different from his usual expression at baseball practice.

Alex and Martie entertained him while Kyle and his sisters and Emily went to the laundry room.

"What's happening now?" he asked. "Where is everyone?"

"I think Jacob's mom and dad went up to the swings," Taylor whispered. "Aunt Gina lectured Grandma and Grandpa about minding their own business and forced them to walk around the pond with her."

"My mom and Uncle Mike went with your dad," Emily said to Kyle. "I don't know where, somewhere in Uncle Mike's truck."

"Where's Mom?" Kyle asked Megan. "Is she okay? I hope you guys didn't leave her all alone out there."

"Uncle Dale stayed with her," Megan said. "I offered, but she asked for him." She shook her head. "This is so awful."

They went back into the kitchen, and Jacob asked, "Is my mom coming back?"

"Yeah," Kyle said. "We're going to wait here for her to be done talking to your dad."

"That could be a while," Taylor said. "What do we do now?"

"Work on the bunkhouse?"

Martie groaned.

Emily caught Kyle's eye. "We should watch movies."

They hauled the big beanbag back from the attic to the basement, bringing along every pillow they could find. Martie stood at the top of the basement stairs and threw down bags of chips and popcorn, which Emily caught while Chase and Pico jumped at them. Kyle was pretty sure Pico's training had been entirely forgotten. Martie also found homemade cookie dough in the fridge and brought enough spoons for everyone.

"What happens when Grandma goes to make cookies later and there's no dough?" Alex asked, because she'd gotten in trouble before for eating Grandma's cookie dough.

"It's an emergency," Martie said.

Emily and Kyle found the box of VHS tapes, discussed the programming, and popped in *Singin' in the Rain*. Jacob had never seen it, which made Alex extra happy and also extra annoying because she kept saying, "This is my favorite part!" and had about a hundred favorite parts.

When Donald O'Connor and Gene Kelly and Debbie Reynolds did their big dance scene, Kyle watched Jacob to see if he liked it. Maybe he'd think it was corny and dumb or get tired of Alex going, "Watch, watch." He seemed okay, though. Quiet and kind of serious.

Kyle's favorite thing was that Megan was lying on the floor, on her stomach, with her chin in her hands. Light from the TV flickered across her face, and she lazily ate popcorn from a little pile in front of her.

Taylor sat next to him on the sectional with Emily on her other side. He nudged Taylor, like, "Look at Megan," but her eyes were on the movie and her fingers were pressed to her mouth, concentrating. He turned back to the TV just in time to see Gene Kelly, a huge smile on his face, stand with arms open and face up to the pouring rain.

"This is my favorite part," Alex said again.

Toward the end of the movie, Aunt Jenny came down the stairs.

"Hey, guys. Can you pause that a minute?" She clicked on a lamp and looked around. "Are you eating cookie dough?"

"Yeah?" Martie said.

"Hey, Jacob, your mom is in the kitchen and wants to talk to you for a minute, okay?"

He put his popcorn aside and ran up the stairs, Chase following after.

"Okay, guys," Aunt Jenny said. "So, here's what's happening right now. Uncle Jeff and Aunt Karen need some time alone. They're going to head over to our place for tonight." Aunt Jenny looked at Martie. "And we'll stay here. Just tonight."

"I don't have any of my stuff."

"It'll be fine. We'll camp out down here. We offered Jacob's parents some time alone, too. They have a room in town, but Jacob is probably going to sleep over here tonight, if he's okay with it." Aunt Jenny looked at Kyle. "We'll put a cot in your room."

"Did you organize all that, Aunt Jenny?" Megan asked, sounding impressed.

"Pretty much." She collapsed onto the end of the sectional next to Martie. "Me and Grandma. This family comes together pretty well in a crisis, but this is a new one." She said to Megan, "I guess you guys knew?"

"We knew," Taylor said. "Kyle knew since Martie's birthday."

"You're kidding. Oh!" She put a palm to her head. "I was supposed to say that your parents want to talk to you before they head over to our place. When Jacob comes back down, give it like five minutes and then you guys go up. It's all coordinated."

Their parents were in the kitchen, waiting. Their dad looked exhausted and puffy. But it was the mortified and broken look on his mom's face that made her the one Kyle wanted to hug. He went and did it, even though it felt like they should all be on Dad's side. When he let go and stepped back, his mom seemed like she wanted to say something but couldn't.

Megan was shaking her head. "This is some real messed-up bananas shit."

"Yeah," their dad said. "It is. We messed it up."

Taylor reached for his arm. "*You* didn't do anything, Dad."

"It takes two to torpedo a relationship, Taylor," Megan said.

"Your sister is right. I've been passive, I've been in denial. . . ."

"Are you saying you deserve this, Dad?" Kyle asked. He really wanted to know if his dad thought that.

Taylor said, "No one deserves to be cheated on."

"My point," Megan said, "is—"

"Okay." Their mom raised her hands. "We want you to be able to vent. We want to answer all your questions. We want you to feel free to talk about anything with us. That's all going to happen, but not right now, not here. We'll do it when we're home. *Our* home."

Kyle saw his mom and his dad exchange the kind of look that parents do, a kind of we're-a-team look. *Now*, in the job of trying to explain how everything had gotten so profoundly devastated, they were a team. Finally.

"Are you going to say you're sorry?" Taylor asked.

"Yes, Taylor. Of course." She looked at Kyle, though. Not at Megan and Taylor, but straight at Kyle, like she actually at last understood that these months had been the worst of his life. "I'll be saying it a lot."

After his parents had left for Uncle Mike and Aunt Jenny's house, Kyle went out in search of Emily. He went up toward the swings and saw Alex and Jacob and the dogs there, playing. Alex seemed thrilled to have someone her age there, never mind the reason.

Kyle had a flash of nostalgia about the lifetime of summers. Especially the years when they all played together and weren't yet separated into high school and non–high school factions. All of them, playing red rover under the trees, playing soccer, playing a version of freeze tag that Grandpa Navarro called encantados. Enchantment. Kyle loved that word, and the way he said it, and also desencanta—unenchantment, when you got tagged and unfrozen.

He went down to the bunkhouse, in case Emily had gone there. It was deserted. The piece of wood over the door with the burned-in words, Grandma's House: Where Cousins Go to Become Best Friends, was still there. Kyle found a hammer and knocked it loose of the frame to carry to the house and put with his stuff.

The sun was getting low. It would be time to gather for dinner in a minute. With his parents not there, he figured they would be the main topic of conversation. Maybe not at dinner, not in front of Jacob. But later, when Aunt Brenda fired up the margarita machine and Great-Aunt Gina and the grandparents went to bed, the aunts and uncles would definitely sit around the table and discuss. Who had known, who had guessed, would this be a divorce—the first in the family—why that bald guy, how could they be so dumb as to try to meet up right down the road . . . who what when where why how.

He and Emily and the rest of them would sit around talking, too, when they were grown-ups. *Remember that summer Aunt Karen's boyfriend showed up?* They'd talk shit about this and about everything that was going to happen in the next five, ten, twenty years. Like they'd said that morning, they'd find a place to go year after year. They'd have some fights. They'd have some stories.

There were footsteps in the brush, and when Kyle turned around, Emily stood, hands in her shorts pockets.

She smiled. "There you are."

"I wanted to get this." He held up Uncle Mike's sign. "Before it got lost in the scrap heap."

"Gonna hang it in your room back at home?"

"Maybe."

"So, what a day," she said, breathing out a laugh. "How are you doing?"

"I . . . have no idea." He looked at the sign in his hand. "But I'm glad I'm here."

She flung her arm around his shoulder. "Me too."

They walked back down to the house like that, toward the lights, toward the flawed bunch of people who would be waiting.

9

BY LUNCH the next day, they'd demolished the bunkhouse all the way to its concrete foundation. Martie had decided to keep working on it after all, finding some satisfaction in tearing it down, and Jacob's and Megan's help made it go faster. So did the fact that Alex and Jacob talked to each other practically nonstop. Well, mostly Alex talked and Jacob listened.

Kyle went to Emily, where she was double-checking that nothing salvageable had wound up in the pile for the dump. They sorted through the hardware and the lumber. "I'm having feelings," he said.

"Me too." She gestured to the pile. "Behold, our childhood, may it rest in peace."

Alex shrieked about something. It turned out she was excited to see Uncle Mike, who walked into the clearing with Aunt Brenda, both carrying open bottles of beer.

"Hole-eeeeee shit," Aunt Brenda said. "You guys really tore it down!"

"Yeah, that was the point," Emily said.

Uncle Mike patted Kyle on the back. "Nice work."

"Hello, Dad, we helped, too," Martie said.

"This is unsettling." Aunt Brenda stood in the middle of the bare foundation. "This is . . . okay, I have managed not to cry all week, but I'm going to now."

Alex ran over and put her arms around Aunt Brenda's waist. "It's okay, Mom."

"We weren't even allowed here when we were kids," Uncle Mike said. "Workers lived here and we were supposed to stay away. I always wanted kind of a clubhouse so bad. You guys were lucky."

"Good riddance to it," Martie said.

Aunt Brenda stepped off the foundation. "I know. I'm just thinking about you all when you were little. You were so freakin' cute, every last one of you."

"And you're still lucky," Uncle Mike added. "You all have way cooler parents than we did."

"Maybe not all of us," Megan said.

"Yes, you too, Megan."

"I don't know, man. What my mom did? And my dad is so passive and boring and materialistic."

"Hang on," Uncle Mike said. "You're talking about my big brother."

"Okay," Aunt Benda said. "Everyone but Kyle and Taylor and Megan go . . . help Grandma or whatever."

"Why?" Alex asked.

"Come on." Emily pulled her down the path. Jacob and Martie followed.

Kyle sat on the concrete of the foundation, suddenly slammed with exhaustion. He was going to sleep for a hundred years when this was all over. Taylor sat next to him and tilted her head to rest on his shoulder.

Uncle Mike said to Megan, "You may think your dad is boring and passive. You may think a lot of things. Based on knowing your dad my whole life—"

"What you see as materialistic," Aunt Brenda said, jumping in, "is him wanting to give you guys everything you need and make sure you're secure."

"But—"

"It's okay." Aunt Brenda put her arm around Megan, jostled her a little. "Megan. I know you think you're like thirty years old and know everything, but you're not and you don't. I know because I was like you."

"Megan, you're gonna be the Aunt Brenda when we're old," Taylor said.

"Probably not a Stanford professor, though," Kyle added.

"Thanks, Kyle."

"All we're saying, what we came up here to tell you," Uncle Mike said, "is that your mom and dad are back from our place, and they both feel like shit, and maybe we could all just try not to be assholes to either of them." He pointed at Brenda with his beer. "Including you."

"Yeah, including me."

"Also, we love you guys, okay?" Uncle Mike looked at each of them. "And we hope next time something big goes down, you know you can count on us." He paused just long enough for everyone to feel embarrassed. "Aaaaand, the other very important piece of info we came to deliver is that the dance is *tonight*, instead of on the last night. Well, we could dance on Saturday, too. But we definitely need it now."

"The cathartic power of getting down," Aunt Brenda said.

"The healing balm of the beat," Uncle Mike said.

"The life-changing magic of the boogie."

"The seven habits of highly effective busting a move."

"The—"

"Stop," Megan said, finally cracking a smile. "I think we get it."

Aunt Brenda put her hands on her hips and nodded at Uncle Mike. "Our work here is done."

In the early afternoon, Kyle and Emily played catch with Alex and Jacob. The mood on the farm was low-key, quiet. That calm after a drama, or plain exhaustion.

Emily grimaced after having to reach up high to make a catch. "Every muscle between every rib is sore from pulling hardware."

"I'm not sore," Alex said.

"Your mouth is probably sore from talking so much, though, huh?" Emily threw the ball way over Alex's head so she had to go run for it. "I've had about enough family togetherness," Emily said to Kyle.

"I feel like no one actually wants to dance tonight. I feel like we want to sleep."

"Right?"

"There's my mom," Jacob said.

The gold Subaru came down the driveway. Anna Partel waved.

"She said we could go to Great America on the way home."

Kyle stood by Jacob. Coach Malone's voice boomed in

his head: *Never lie to a kid.* He tried to think of what to say, something that would be honest but not depressing.

"You're probably not going to have the best summer," he said. "Like, it's not going to be the absolute best summer of your life, I think we can say that. Right?"

Jacob eyed him, suspicious. "Yeah."

"But it doesn't mean everything is shit. I promise." He glanced toward Anna, sitting in the car. She'd better really be taking him to Great America. "Remember, it's okay to still feel good if you want. Like, if you're having fun, don't stop and go, 'Oh yeah, my parents' and think you shouldn't have fun. But . . .'" Dang, it was hard to give a pep talk about this and still be honest. "But like, if you're *not* having fun and you *are* sad and it *does* feel like everything is shit? It's okay to feel that, too."

Anna called out the window. "We gotta go, sweetheart. Get Chase."

Kyle leaned down and said quietly to Jacob, "Just remember, sometimes adults are kinda . . . dumb."

Jacob nodded and called Chase. The way he called, "Here boy, here, Chase," all cheerful while patting his leg, made Kyle's heart hurt.

Alex and Emily walked over, and Alex gave Jacob a hug, and it was super awkward, especially when Alex started to cry. Emily pulled Alex to her side. When Jacob had gotten in the car, Emily said to Alex, "You did a good job being really nice to him when he got dumped with a bunch of strangers. It really helped."

"He's not even looking back!" She kept crying as the car went up the drive. Emily rubbed her back and mouthed, "The drama!" to Kyle over Alex's shoulder.

He laughed a little, but honestly Alex was breaking his heart too. Her scrawny body and giant tears and the way she still kept looking up the drive, like the Subaru was going to come back, were the total embodiment of the pain of saying goodbye. And he knew his turn was coming.

10

TAYLOR AND Megan were on the patio with Uncle Mike, each holding a big red cup.

"We're reviewing the playlist," Uncle Mike said.

"Well, no one needs to hear 'Mony Mony' again, ever," Megan said, scrolling through Uncle Mike's phone, which apparently he'd gotten back from the phone box. "Also FYI, I am deleting 'Bizarre Love Triangle' for obvious reasons."

Kyle peered over Megan's shoulder. "It's so much eighties stuff."

"If it's not clear by now," Uncle Mike said, "the dances are not for you. You guys have a dance every other week at school or at parties or whatever kids do. Opportunities for dancing go down like ninety-five percent once you pass college so, yeah, I admit it. The playlist is for us."

"My dad won't dance," Kyle said.

"He *can't* dance," Taylor said. "Some of these aren't even that danceable."

Uncle Mike took the phone back. "Those are the cool-down songs. We're old, guys. We can't do more than three good dancing songs in a row." He put his arm around Kyle. "And your dad *can* dance and he *needs* to dance and he *will* dance. I planted a bomb on this playlist, and when it detonates, I guarantee he will get on the dance floor."

The rest of the afternoon, Aunt Brenda churned out adult slushies on the margarita machine while Grandma and Grandpa napped, and Kyle helped his dad and Uncle Mike set up the sound system. At one point he had to go out to Uncle Mike's truck to look for an extension cord and noticed his mom's car was gone.

He brought the cord back. His dad was up on a ladder; Kyle went over to steady it. "Where's Mom?"

His dad came down one rung. "She left. For home. She wanted to slip away and not have it be a big thing."

Kyle looked up at him.

"For real," his dad said. "I'm not trying to hide anything from you—she specifically asked me not to tell until people noticed she was gone, and that is the whole truth. She wants a little time at home alone. To nest, she said."

"Oh. Cool, I guess. I just thought . . . I don't know."

"Imagine if she stayed. Having to deal with everyone avoiding her or the topic or pitying or judging." He came down another rung. "Kyle, I'm so sorry I put this on you back in March. If I could go back in time and handle it all differently, you know I would."

Kyle nodded. "I know, Dad."

Meanwhile, Megan, who would be twenty-one in a week, had gotten in on the booze. Taylor, who was still two years off from legal, kept sneaking it too. They were supposed to be clearing the patio but were actually kicking back in lawn chairs next to Emily and Great-Aunt Gina, talking in semi-hushed tones.

Kyle headed in that direction, to see if Megan and Taylor knew about their mom leaving and also to do a little chilling himself, when there was a giant crash, then Brenda swearing. Apparently his dad had come off the ladder to help Brenda reposition the drinks table for the tenth time, and now the margarita machine was in pieces on the concrete patio.

"Jeff!" she shouted.

"What? That wasn't me!" Kyle's dad protested. "The cord wasn't long enough!"

"I just paid two hundred bucks for that thing! It was brand-new!"

Uncle Mike called over, "I guess you'll have to suffer through the horror of unblended margaritas tonight, Bren."

"Why me, God?" Aunt Brenda yelled, shaking her fist at the sky.

They heard Grandma from inside the house: "People are trying to nap!"

"Help me up," Great-Aunt Gina said to Emily. "I left my stick inside and I need to go in for a rest myself." Emily got her up and they went into the house.

Rest. The word alone was enough to pull Kyle down onto one of the chaises. He took Taylor's big red cup of whatever and helped himself to a few sips, passed it back, and closed his eyes.

"Mom's gone," he mumbled.

"We know," Taylor said.

"Okay." The cup was in his hand again. He sipped, eyes still closed, then held it out until someone took it away. His breathing slowed down. "I think she really loved that guy. Or loves."

Megan scoffed. "For some reason."

Kyle was drifting off.

"I don't know," Taylor said. "Do you think Jacob will be okay?"

"Will we?" Kyle mumbled, and that's all he remembered until he woke up at dusk, sore from falling asleep, and hard, on strips of vinyl. Uncle Mike had started playing some low, chill countryish music to set the mood. Emily was playing backgammon with Uncle Dale while Alex watched. Kyle headed into the kitchen to grab a couple bites of leftovers, and when he came back out, Aunt Brenda was downing her unblended margarita and harassing Uncle Mike until he declared it, officially, time to dance.

The playlist started with classic Stevie Wonder. Easy enough to get everyone onto the floor. Even Kyle's dad, who'd been drinking a bottle of beer, let Taylor coax him out of his camp chair, though halfway through the song he faded back and chatted with Great-Aunt Gina and Grandpa Navarro, who both watched from the corner.

"I'm glad Uncle Mike finally admitted this is pretty much all for him and my mom," Emily said. She and Kyle were on the very edges, where they could sort of look like they were participating but not actually *dance* per se.

"I know," Kyle said. "This is his happy place."

"How did Megan and Taylor learn to dance?"

"Not from my dad. He can barely clap to 'Happy Birthday.'"

His sisters seemed to naturally know what to do, whereas Kyle took more after his dad with not quite being able to find the rhythm. Aunt Brenda danced up to Taylor and Megan while the Gap Band played, and then Martie and Alex jumped over, too.

"There she goes," Emily said. Alex's entire dancing style was based on jumping.

When the Gap Band faded down and Prince faded up, Aunt Brenda chugged the rest of whatever drink she was on and threw the cup to the side so she could give her full attention to dancing. She spun right into Uncle Mike and they both almost fell. Emily groaned.

During the first slower-song break, Uncle Mike swept Aunt Jenny into his arms and swayed with her, clasping her hand to his chest. She buried her face in his neck. It made Kyle think about him and Nadia enough that he had to look away.

Martie and Alex came over to sit on the ground next to Kyle and Emily, drinking cups of ice water. "How are we going to have a dance party next year?"

"Our house," Martie said. "I'm already thinking where we could put the sound system."

"You know what we should do, Emily?" Kyle asked.

"What should we do, Kyle?"

"Someday, *some*day. What if we took, like . . . tap lessons. And learned a Fred and Ginger routine or something."

"Together? Like we do all the lessons together? Even

though we live four hours apart?"

"Yes, and then perform it. At farm week. Or whatever we call farm week when the farm is gone."

Uncle Mike cupped his hands around his mouth and shouted, "Break about to be over! Everybody up!"

When the song started, Kyle's dad jumped to his feet and said, "Dude!" to Uncle Mike.

"Oh, no," Kyle said to Emily. "This is like my dad's favorite song."

Emily got up, suddenly energetic. "I'm going out there." If she'd taken his hand, he'd have gone too. But she just skipped away. He heard Alex's voice: *He's not even looking back.*

His father hit the floor in his golf shirt and knee-length jean shorts. He bobbed his head and bit his lower lip like a bad parody of a white dad dancing, except Kyle knew it was totally authentic. Then he made eye contact with Kyle, mouthing lyrics, coming toward him.

"Shit," Kyle said under his breath.

In a second, his dad's hands were clasped on Kyle's, dragging him out. He flashed back to Martie's birthday and Aunt Brenda. What was with this family? It was like you weren't allowed to not dance.

"Okay, okay," he said, and did his own pathetic two-step.

His dad kept holding Kyle's hands. It was weird, and then it wasn't. They didn't let go.

Emily was next to them now, and when the chorus started, she and everyone else sang, "Lido! Whoa-oh-oh-ohhhh!" and then in the next verse, his dad dropped Kyle's hands so he could point to the sky and shout, "Toe the line or don't, and that was all she wrote!"

During the snapping part of the song, Kyle stepped back to watch his dad along with the little crowd of family that had circled him. Jeff Baker snapped off the beat. He spun on one foot. He closed his eyes. He kept shouting lyrics, missing half of them but still moving his mouth.

If Kyle's mom could see him now.

Boz Scaggs faded out, and Aunt Brenda was trying to push into the circle formed around his dad. It felt like if they'd been strong and sober, they would have lifted his dad up on their shoulders like a winning soccer team. Kyle laughed at how sweaty his father was and then did a double take and thought, *No, he's crying—well, yeah, he's also super sweaty, but those are tears on his cheeks.* And his first instinct was to look away before his dad caught him seeing, but why?

He wanted to see. He wanted to be seen. He wanted to be seen seeing.

Then he did what he *really* wanted to do, which was

get his dad in a bear hug, or get himself into one from his dad.

They embraced. Over his dad's shoulder, he saw Emily dance a little jig, sort of to the music, and Kyle laughed and his dad thought he was laughing at him, at them, and they goofed around pretending to dance like an awkward junior high couple, and it made everyone laugh, and they acted like they were stretching out the joke but really they were holding on and holding on and holding on.

At the end of the night, some of the kids were lying on the patio, some sitting on the ground. The adults were in lawn chairs and camp chairs. Only Great-Aunt Gina had given up and gone to bed. Pico lay at Grandpa's feet, eyes closed. Big citronella candles at the perimeter made the shadows jump. Uncle Mike had switched to a dreamy, mellow playlist full of guitars and singing in Spanish.

"How do you know about Carlos Lico?" Grandpa Navarro asked Mike, clenching an unlit pipe in his teeth.

"How do you think?" Aunt Jenny asked her father.

Grandpa Navarro hummed along, then got up and walked into the shadows to smoke.

Aunt Brenda and Uncle Dale held hands. Emily said they practically hadn't let go of each other ever since finding out about Kyle's parents, like marriage problems might be contagious and they already had enough of their own.

Grandma Baker started talking about how much she was looking forward to having less stuff, being in a smaller space. She had an idea for a mystery novel she wanted to write.

It was like everyone had agreed to not get sad tonight. Even though there were so many sad things, and they were so tired. Uncle Mike had been right. They'd needed to dance.

Part IV
COACH KYLE

These kids kill me.

He'd snapped a pic of Ruby and Tatum posing with their ball caps pulled low, elbows out. It was supposed to be for the team Facebook page but he sent it to Emily too.

"Guys," he told them. "You gotta be nicer to the new girls."

"We're nice!"

"No, I know. You're not mean. But you played together all year and they just started, you know? Try to include them."

They look like a pain in the ass haha, Emily said.

That too.

He put his phone in his pocket before Coach Malone caught him texting. Later on, he'd tell Emily about his 960 on the SAT. It was garbage compared to her score, or his sisters', but considering how the year had gone, it was a start.

"Cone drill, let's go!" he shouted, clapping his hands. Every time he clapped his hands like Ito or Malone, he felt fifty years old and vowed to never do it again, and always did it again. The girls sprinted and pivoted cone to cone to cone. He timed them and tried to spark a little competition without being a dick about it.

It was three weeks since the farm. His mom was still living at home, but in Megan's old room and not trying to pretend like she wasn't. They'd had a few family dinners. His parents were going to start therapy next week.

He'd seen Jacob once, taken him for ice cream, and then Anna Partel said it was all too weird and she'd rather make a clean break from the Bakers. Which seemed kind of shitty for Jacob, because they'd started to bond, but there wasn't a whole lot Kyle could do about it.

He'd seen Megan a few times and Emily none, except on video. Last time they talked, she'd shaved her head completely. Not bald bald, but like a buzz cut. Now Aunt Brenda wanted to try it.

Saying goodbye to Emily at the farm had been as bad as he'd thought it was going to be but almost in a good-pain sort of way. The kind of pain that was there to remind you something special was happening and it wouldn't always be like that.

They'd walked to the gazebo the morning they were leaving and listed off their favorite farm memories of all time: the first year they were old enough to sleep in the bunkhouse, the year Megan was fifteen and "borrowed" Uncle Mike's truck without asking and drove all the kids into town for ice cream in violation of every driver's license regulation in existence, the summer Aunt Brenda was finishing her dissertation and made the kids act out some experimental play she'd written about the afterlife.

Last Thanksgiving when Nadia was there was on Kyle's list. "That's on my list too," Emily had said.

"Really?"

"Yeah. This sounds dumb, but it was like, 'Oh, yeah, Kyle exists outside my phone and has this life with all these people in it. . . .' You know what I mean? Like when you see your teacher in the grocery store and you're like, 'Oh, they're real, too. Other people are real.'"

He'd looked at her, a little stunned. "Yeah. Exactly. I know exactly what you mean."

"Coach Kyle?" It was Flore, one of the new girls. "It's *hot.*"

It was ninety degrees in the sun. He jogged over to Coach Malone and asked, "Water break?"

"Yep, good call." He blew his whistle. "Ten minutes in the shade, sippin' that water. Come on come on come on. Mrs. Coach will set you up." He waved them in, and they went over to his wife, aka Mrs. Coach, who organized the schedule and did conditioning with the team at a rec center a couple times a week.

Kyle helped her pass out water, made sure the kids got out of the sun. He had some water, too, before strolling to the pitcher's mound for a break from their chatter.

At the farm, he and Emily had walked back from the gazebo, slow. "This summer," Kyle said. "This summer is on my list too, I think."

"Oh, definitely this summer."

He stopped walking. "Let's say goodbye now. Before we get to the cars and stuff."

"Bye!"

"Okay then, bye!"

They pretended to walk off from each other, and laughed. Kyle didn't know what to say even though he'd had days to think about it. He was making it too serious.

"It's not like it's goodbye forever or anything," he said.

"No, but it's goodbye forever from *here*."

Here. It was more than just Nowhere Farm, the place. Here was his parents' marriage like it was. Here was Jacob seeing for the first time how profoundly adults failed. Here was a particular Emily. A particular Emily and Kyle.

"Goodbye forever, here," he said.

"Adios, here!"

They'd hugged goodbye for real, and Kyle tried to let it sit gently, lightly. Not put every feeling he'd ever had into the one hug.

A few nights before that, after the dance, when they were sprawled out on the patio agreeing to not be sad, Emily had lain down on the cement next to Kyle. "I'm dead," she said. Pretty soon she was breathing quietly next to him, maybe asleep. Her hand, resting on her stomach, rose and fell with each breath. Kyle tuned in to it, slowing his own breath down.

Megan and Taylor were drinking cups of water to dilute the alcohol they'd had. Martie had snuck her phone out of the pickle crock and was texting with a boy under the cover of the sweatshirt in her lap. Alex, on a chaise, had her arms folded behind her head and was looking up at the night sky through the slats of the patio roof trellis.

"Are you awake?" he'd whispered to Emily, the question he'd asked into the dark on so many summer nights, waiting for her answer.

This time, she'd answered by taking her hand off her stomach and finding his. Kyle closed his eyes. Emily squeezed his hand and let it go, and for a second he wanted to grasp hers again, not be disconnected, cut off.

He'd kept his eyes closed, breathed.

He'd thought about night at the farm. He'd gazed up so many times, like Alex was doing. And without looking he knew: The stars made bright pinholes in the dark blanket of the sky. Some were clustered, some were scattered. A fat slice of moon shone.

Now, his phone buzzed, and after a glance at Malone, Kyle checked it.

I picture you like this when you're coaching

It was a gif of Gene Kelly goofing with kids, singing "I Got Rhythm" from *An American in Paris*.

(Only without the rhythm), she added.

That's no way to talk to your future tap partner.

Haha. We're not doing that!

"Baker!" Malone shouted. "How'm I supposed to expect these kids to follow the rules if you don't?"

"Sorry!" He put his phone away and clapped his hands yet again. "Okay, break's over."

He called the team back onto the field and watched them run toward him in the summer light.

ACKNOWLEDGMENTS

With special thanks to Paula Huston, Kevin Emerson, and Jorge Robles. I'm grateful to the Hultberg family for helping to keep a roof over my head and to writing comrades near and far who work alongside me in the day-to-day. The whole team at Balzer+Bray has been wonderful, and I'm especially thankful for my editor, Jordan Brown. As ever, thank you to Michael Bourret for being in it for the long haul, and to my husband for three decades and counting of loving support.